PRAISE FOR CATHERINE BYBEE

WIFE BY WEDNESDAY

"A fun and sizzling romance, great characters that trade verbal spars like fist punches, and the dream of your own royal wedding!"
—Sizzling Hot Book Reviews, 5 Stars

"A good holiday, fireside or bedtime story."
—Manic Reviews, 4½ Stars

"A great story that I hope is the start of a new series."
—The Romance Studio, 4½ Hearts

MARRIED BY MONDAY

"If I hadn't already added Ms. Catherine Bybee to my list of favorite authors, after reading this book I would have been compelled to. This is a book *nobody* should miss, because the magic it contains is awesome."
—Booked Up Reviews, 5 Stars

"Ms. Bybee writes authentic situations and expresses the good and the bad in such an equal way . . . Keeps the reader on the edge of her seat."
—Reading Between the Wines, 5 Stars

"*Married by Monday* was a refreshing read and one I couldn't possibly put down."
—The Romance Studio, 4½ Hearts

FIANCÉ BY FRIDAY

"Bybee knows exactly how to keep readers happy . . . A thrilling pursuit and enough passion to stuff in your back pocket to last for the next few lifetimes . . . The hero and heroine come to life with each flip of the page and will linger long after readers cross the finish line."
—*RT Book Reviews,* 4½ Stars, Top Pick (Hot)

"A tale full of danger and sexual tension . . . the intriguing characters add emotional depth, ensuring readers will race to the perfectly fitting finish."
—*Publishers Weekly*

"Suspense, survival, and chemistry mix in this scintillating read."
—*Booklist*

"Hot romance, a mystery assassin, British royalty, and an alpha Marine . . . this story has it all!"
—Harlequin Junkie

SINGLE BY SATURDAY

"Captures readers' hearts and keeps them glued to the pages until the fascinating finish . . . romance lovers will feel the sparks fly . . . almost instantaneously."
—*RT Book Reviews,* 4½ Stars, Top Pick

"[A] wonderfully exciting plot, lots of desire, and some sassy attitude thrown in for good measure!"
—Harlequin Junkie

TAKEN BY TUESDAY

"[Bybee] knows exactly how to get bookworms sucked into the perfect storyline; then she casts her spell upon them so they don't escape until they reach the 'Holy Cow!' ending."

—*RT Book Reviews*, 4½ Stars, Top Pick

SEDUCED BY SUNDAY

"You simply can't miss [this novel]. It contains everything a romance reader loves—clever dialogue, three-dimensional characters, and just the right amount of steam to go with that heartwarming love story."

—Brenda Novak, *New York Times* bestselling author

"Bybee hits the mark . . . providing readers with a smart, sophisticated romance between a spirited heroine and a prim hero . . . Passionate and intelligent characters [are] at the heart of this entertaining read."

—*Publishers Weekly*

TREASURED BY THURSDAY

"The Weekday Brides never disappoint and this final installment is by far Bybee's best work to date."

—*RT Book Reviews*, 4½ Stars, Top Pick

"An exquisitely written and complex story brimming with pride, passion, and pulse-pounding danger . . . Readers will gladly make time to savor this winning finale to a wonderful series."

—*Publishers Weekly*, Starred Review

"Bybee concludes her popular Weekday Brides series in a gratifying way with a passionate, troubled couple who may find a happy future if they can just survive and then learn to trust each other. A compelling and entertaining mix of sexy, complicated romance and menacing suspense."

—*Kirkus Reviews*

NOT QUITE DATING

"It's refreshing to read about a man who isn't afraid to fall in love . . . [Jack and Jessie] fit together as a couple and as a family."

—*RT Book Reviews,* 3 Stars (Hot)

"*Not Quite Dating* offers a sweet and satisfying Cinderella fantasy that will keep you smiling long after you've finished reading."

—Kathy Altman, *USA Today,* "Happy Ever After"

"The perfect rags to riches romance . . . The dialogue is inventive and witty, the characters are well drawn out. The storyline is superb and really shines . . . I highly recommend this stand out romance! Catherine Bybee is an automatic buy for me."

—Harlequin Junkie, 4½ Hearts

NOT QUITE ENOUGH

"Bybee's gift for creating unforgettable romances cannot be ignored. The third book in the Not Quite series will sweep readers away to a paradise, and they will be intrigued by the thrilling story that accompanies their literary vacation."

—*RT Book Reviews,* 4½ Stars, Top Pick

NOT QUITE FOREVER

"Full of classic Bybee humor, steamy romance, and enough plot twists and turns to keep readers entertained all the way to the very last page."
—Tracy Brogan, bestselling author of the Bell Harbor series

"Magnetic . . . The love scenes are sizzling and the multi-dimensional characters make this a page-turner. Readers will look for earlier installments and eagerly anticipate new ones."
—*Publishers Weekly*

NOT QUITE PERFECT

"This novel flows extremely well and readers will find themselves consuming the witty dialogue and strong imagery in one sitting."
—*RT Book Reviews*

"Don't let the title fool you. *Not Quite Perfect* was actually the perfect story to sweep you away and take you on a pleasant adventure. So sit back, relax, maybe pour a glass of wine, and let Catherine Bybee entertain you with Glen and Mary's playful East Coast–West Coast romance. You won't regret it for a moment."
—Harlequin Junkie, 4½ Stars

NOT QUITE CRAZY

"This fast-paced story features credible characters whose appealing relationship is built upon friendship, mutual respect, and sizzling chemistry."
—*Publishers Weekly*

"The plot is filled with twists and turns, but instead of feeling like a never-ending roller coaster, the story maintains a quiet flow. The slow buildup of a romance allows readers to get to know the main characters as individuals and makes the romantic element more organic."

—*RT Book Reviews*

DOING IT OVER

"The romance between fiercely independent Melanie and charming Wyatt heats up even as outsiders threaten to derail their newfound happiness. This novel will hook readers with its warm, inviting characters and the promise for similar future installments."

—*Publishers Weekly*

"This brand-new trilogy, Most Likely To, based on yearbook superlatives, kicks off with a novel that will encourage you to root for the incredibly likable Melanie. Her friends are hilarious and readers will swoon over Wyatt, who is charming and strong. Even Melanie's daughter, Hope, is a hoot! This romance is jam-packed with animated characters, and Bybee displays her creative writing talent wonderfully."

—*RT Book Reviews*, 4 Stars

"With a dialogue full of energy and depth, and a twisting storyline that captured my attention, I would say that *Doing It Over* was a great way to start off a new series. (And look at that gorgeous book cover!) I can't wait to visit River Bend again and see who else gets to find their HEA."

—Harlequin Junkie, 4½ Stars

STAYING FOR GOOD

"Bybee's skillfully crafted second Most Likely To contemporary (after *Doing It Over*) brings together former sweethearts who have not forgotten each other in the eleven years since high school. A cast of multidimensional characters brings the story to life and promises enticing future installments."

—*Publishers Weekly*

"Romance fans will be sure to cheer on former high school sweethearts Zoe and Luke right away in *Staying For Good*. Just wait until you see what passion, laughter, reconciliations, and mischief (can you say Vegas?) awaits readers this time around. Highly recommended."

—Harlequin Junkie, 4½ Stars

MAKING IT RIGHT

"Intense suspense heightens the scorching romance at the heart of Bybee's outstanding third Most Likely To contemporary (after *Staying For Good*). Sizzling sensual scenes are coupled with scary suspense in this winning novel."

—*Publishers Weekly*, Starred Review

FOOL ME ONCE

"A marvelous portrait of friendship among women who have been bonded by fire."

—*Library Journal*, Best of the Year 2017

"Bybee still delivers a story that her die-hard readers will enjoy."

—*Publishers Weekly*

Half Empty

"Wade and Trina here in *Half Empty* just might be one of my favorite couples Catherine Bybee has gifted us fans with so far. Captivating, engaging, lively and dreamy, I simply could not get enough of this book."

—Harlequin Junkie, 5 stars

"Part rock star romance, part romantic thriller, I really enjoyed this book."

—Romance Reader

Faking Forever

"A charming contemporary with surprising depth . . . Bybee perfectly portrays a woman trying to hold out for Mr. Right despite the pressures of time. A pitch-perfect plot and a cast of sympathetic and lovable supporting characters make this book one to add to the keeper shelf."

—*Publishers Weekly*

"Catherine Bybee can do no wrong as far as I'm concerned . . . Passionate, sultry, and filled with genuine emotions that ran the gamut, *Faking Forever* was a journey of self-discovery and of a love that was truly meant to be. Highly recommended."

—Harlequin Junkie

Say It Again

"Steamy, fast-paced, and consistently surprising, with a large cast of feisty supporting characters, this suspenseful roller-coaster ride will keep both series fans and new readers on the edge of their seats."

—*Publishers Weekly*

Everything Changes

Everything Changes

Creek Canyon, Book Three

CATHERINE
BYBEE

 Montlake

Published by Montlake, Seattle

www.apub.com

Amazon, the Amazon logo, and Montlake are trademarks of Amazon.com, Inc., or its affiliates.

ISBN-13: 9781542009898
ISBN-10: 1542009898

Cover design by Caroline Teagle Johnson

Printed in the United States of America

For Whiskey.
I hope you're chasing rabbits on the other side of the
rainbow bridge.

CHAPTER ONE

If one more person asked Grace when she was going to find Mr. Right and settle down, she was going to deck 'em. Why did weddings and baby showers bring on the incessant questions regarding her nonexistent love life?

On the dance floor, Colin wrapped around his newly minted wife, Parker, in a slow dance. Her brother was all smiles, and her sister-in-law had shed actual tears while reciting her wedding vows. It really had been the perfect ceremony.

Colin was the first of them to get married. Grace was fairly certain her other brother, Matt, wasn't far behind. He danced with his live-in girlfriend and her fellow bridesmaid, Erin. Yeah, they were just as lovey-dovey as the ones who'd tied the knot.

Truth was, Grace was insanely happy for both her brothers.

Only now that they were paired up, all family eyes were on her. Even Grandma Rose, whose dementia often resulted in Grace being called Nora, her mother's name, followed by a question about coming home late from school . . . asked if Grace was ever going to find a man.

Grace leaned back in a chair, legs crossed, with her toe swinging in the air to the slow music. The lights were dim, and all eyes and cameras were focused on Colin and Parker.

Behind her, the sound of a chair scooting out from under the table had Grace glancing out of the corner of her eye. Aunt Bethany.

Grace lifted the hand holding her champagne in the air before her aunt had the chance to speak.

"Don't."

"What?"

"Not one word."

Her aunt was Grandma Rose with a full-watt memory.

Grace heard the woman sigh over the music.

Three bars of music passed . . .

The chorus . . .

"Weddings always make me nostalgic," Aunt Beth started.

Grace felt her easy grin turn into something painful.

"Nostalgic?" Grace found herself responding.

"Oh, yes . . . for those early days of romance and possibilities."

"Yup." God, this was painful. It was like watching a train barreling down the track toward a crossing with dysfunctional arms and wondering if the oncoming traffic would get caught in its path.

Okay, maybe not that bad . . . but still.

"So, what is it about all your relationships that keeps you from having someone at your side at these events?"

And there it was.

Grace felt her hand tighten around the caterer's cheap flute.

Option one: toss champagne at her aunt and cause a scene at her brother's wedding.

Nope.

Option two: drink the champagne and grit her teeth to the point of pain.

Check.

"Grace?"

She swallowed half the glass in one gulp and proceeded to cough as some of the liquid went down the wrong pipe.

She grabbed for a napkin to keep from spitting wine all over her dress and then fled the room.

Eyes followed her retreat.

Outside the ballroom, the hotel lighting and decrease in noise stopped her forward motion.

Air . . . she needed air. Across the hall were double doors that led out to the hotel's garden. Colin and Parker had taken copious numbers of pictures there only a couple of hours before.

Grace cleared her throat and marched toward the doors leading outside.

The second she passed the threshold, brisk December air rushed down her back.

"Holy moly." She considered turning around.

Freeze or listen to Aunt Beth?

Cold it was.

Her feet took her toward the lighted path of trees. She hugged her arms in an attempt to stay warm.

The one fancy hotel in Santa Clarita was decked out for the holidays. But it wasn't the view that snapped her out of her crappy mood, it was the fact she could see her breath.

Determined to stay outside long enough to look flushed and energized when she returned to the reception, Grace forced her legs to carry her to the end of the garden to stare at the water fountain.

"This is stupid," she muttered to herself.

She rubbed her arms absently as a strange heat tickled the back of her neck.

The sensation of someone watching her was unshakable. She imagined there were hotel guests looking down from their rooms and wondering what kind of fool walked around in the cold, in a dress . . . without a coat.

"Me." *I'm the fool.*

She shifted from foot to foot and slowly turned to determine if she could locate the eyes on her. Her head tilted up, as if she were looking for stars. The spans of hotel windows, all four stories of them, were in various stages of open blinds. Most were closed, but a few were wide open with the lights on in the rooms. Yet no one peered down.

Grace let her gaze sweep over the landscape and behind her toward the hotel. Several sets of automatic glass doors lined the hotel halls that wrapped around to the ballrooms. Several people meandered about inside, but none seemed to have noticed her.

She was about to give up looking for the person behind the heat on her neck when she saw him.

He leaned casually against an inside pillar on the other side of a floor-to-ceiling window. He wore a suit, minus the tie. Grace tried to place him. Was he at the wedding?

No.

She would have noticed him the second he walked into the room. Tall, which considering she was as vertically challenged as they came, didn't take much. Rugged . . . as in sharp features and shoulders that filled the suit jacket really . . . really well.

Grace realized she was staring and averted her eyes back to the fountain.

Despite the fact she could still see the vapor her breath created in the night air, she didn't feel quite as chilled as when she walked out. That alone told her the man continued to watch.

She knelt down to adjust the strap on her shoe solely so she could confirm her suspicion.

He hadn't budged.

In fact, she was pretty sure he smiled.

Grace stood tall to the extra three inches her heels allowed and turned away. She'd normally be a little freaked out about a man staring at her from inside a building. But she was standing out in the cold like an idiot, and if she'd seen someone doing the same thing, she'd probably stop and stare, too.

Lucky for her, the doors leading to the reception were opposite of where Mr. Stare Happy was perched.

Men in hotels were not the kind she wanted to meet. They were either there on business, visiting someone, or cheating on their significant other. Nope, nope, and nope.

She checked over her shoulder right before sliding back into the ballroom.

Stare Happy wasn't there.

Good!

Although she had to admit, the man was good-looking. From what she could tell from her distance.

The music had switched to something fast, and the dance floor was crowded.

Erin approached, confusion on her face. "There you are. I've been looking for you."

Grace waved a hand toward the direction of the door. "I've been . . . I was . . . never mind. What's up?"

"They're about to cut the cake."

"Right. Cake . . . got it." There was a wedding going on, and a lively one at that. The last thing she should be doing is wallowing in self-pity about her lacking love life.

Once the cake was cut and the bouquet was tossed, her responsibilities to the bride and groom were over, and she could do what every other self-respecting bridesmaid did at a reception . . . get hammered or hook up.

Considering most of the people in attendance were family or close friends she knew too much about to consider a one-night stand, it looked like she had a date with a bottle of champagne.

But first . . . cake.

~

The sound of a horn blaring outside dragged Grace from the far depths of sleep.

5

Thick paste had taken the place of saliva in her mouth, and she heard every beat of her heart between her ears.

Sun filtered through the windows of her condo with such brilliance she knew she'd missed most of the morning.

She tested her head slowly, moving it to the side to catch the time.

Ten thirteen? How did that even happen?

Slapping her lips together, she tasted a little too much of what she'd eaten, or more importantly, drunk, the night before. And the need to pee was dire.

Moving more quickly than her brain liked, she staggered through her bedroom to the adjoining bathroom. Two minutes later she stood in front of the mirror while water rushed into the sink.

Her hair stuck out in every direction, her eyes were bloodshot, and her lips were as dry as the Mojave Desert.

"That last glass was a mistake," she said to her reflection.

Her feet still throbbed from the dancing. She'd made sure to spend the remainder of the evening dancing with anyone with a pulse. And then, when the night came to an end, because her condo was only a few blocks from the hotel in the heart of Santa Clarita, she left her car in the parking lot and walked home.

In short, her feet hurt like hell.

So did her head.

She flipped on the hot water in the shower and let it steam the room while she brushed her teeth. Even coffee didn't sound like the right thing to add to her digestive system.

By now her brother and Parker would be on a plane. One solid week in Maui, courtesy of her parents. Lots of money spent so they could stay inside a hotel room and exercise the heck out of each other.

She smiled through the headache and stepped into the shower.

Thirty minutes later, with her thick, wavy hair pulled back in a short ponytail and a big pair of sunglasses hiding the lack of restful sleep under her eyes, she headed out for the short walk to the hotel to gather her car. Halfway there, the scent of java had her making a detour.

The coffee shop was wall-to-wall customers on a late Sunday morning. By the head count of people carrying shopping bags from the mall across the street, it looked as if most of the people there had been up for hours holiday shopping.

She rubbed the back of her neck through the turtleneck sweater she'd put on. Her headache was starting to fade.

Thank God.

The line inched slowly. As it did, her need for a large shot of caffeine grew.

And sugar. She needed sugar.

Finally, her turn came.

She looked at the menu as if she was seeing it for the first time. "Cappuccino," she blurted out. "Double shot."

The barista typed her order into the register.

"With pumpkin spice. Can you do that?"

"Yeah."

"The pumpkin is sweet, right?"

"Yeah." The kid behind the counter wasn't amused.

"Can I get that in a large?"

He narrowed his eyes. "Do you want a latte?"

She shook her head. "No. Double shot cappuccino with pumpkin spice is fine."

"Is that all?"

"With whip cream."

He sighed. "How about an extra-large pumpkin latte, double shot, with whip cream?"

Someone behind her cleared their throat.

"Fine."

He rang her up.

"And a blueberry scone."

"Is that all?"

"Yes."

"Full milk or soy?"

"Nonfat."

Whoever had cleared their throat behind her now laughed.

Grace refrained from looking around to see the face behind the laugh, paid, and stepped aside.

She pulled her cell phone from her back pocket while she waited for her coffee. Her mother had sent two text messages. Erin had left one. All were in regard to helping with moving the wedding gifts over to Colin and Parker's place and cleaning up the mess they'd left behind the day before.

"Double shot nonfat pumpkin latte with whip cream with a blueberry scone and a complimentary side of diabetes," the barista called out.

Grace glanced up, saw a familiar face. "Very funny, Leah."

Leah pushed her order across the counter. "Let me guess, big Saturday night?"

"My brother's wedding."

"Oh, that's right. How was it?"

"Beautiful. Of course. They both said 'I do' at the right time."

The guy at the register shouted out another order.

Leah looked over her shoulder. "Come by next week during lunch. I want to see pictures."

"I will." Grace grabbed her coffee, pastry, and dignity and headed for the door.

"Nice to see you're more appropriately dressed for the outdoors today." The deep baritone voice came from her right. She took one step before realizing the words were meant for her.

Slowly, like something out of an old cartoon, she turned to the man behind the voice.

Mr. Stare Happy relaxed in a chair with his arm leaning on the table. Unlike the night before, when she couldn't see his face clearly to tell for certain that he smiled at her, there was no mistaking it now.

He was smiling . . . if not *laughing* at her.

She feigned innocence. "Have we met?"

A flicker of amusement passed over his lips. "The hotel . . . last night?"

What was up with his voice? It vibrated the entire room. It was deep and salty like a jazz musician in a New Orleans club. Like a deep purr of a lion.

"You were at the hotel last night?"

He blinked and snickered.

She lifted her coffee to her lips to hide any expression that might leak through.

"And you were walking the gardens in a thin dress without a jacket."

The sugar in her coffee reached all the right spots and gave her the words she needed.

"Oh . . . was that you who opened the door for me?"

His eyes narrowed. "No."

"You weren't at the wedding, right? I think I would have remembered you at the wedding."

Mr. Stare Happy's smile slid from his lips. "No."

"Were you one of the waiters? There were so many—"

"No. I'm not a waiter. I saw you . . ." He stopped talking and reached for his cup before standing.

When he did, she was struck by the size of him. Close to her brother Matt's height, but not taller than Colin. Still, since she was five three and wearing a pair of Keds, Mr. Stare Happy dwarfed her.

She looked over the edge of the sunglasses she hadn't bothered taking off. She did a complete sweep of the man with the lion's voice and came to rest on his amused eyes. "I'm sorry, last night was a blur. My brother got married . . . there was champagne."

He reached a hand out. "Dameon."

Unable to stop herself, she chuckled. "With a voice like that, I'm not surprised."

"Excuse me?"

That was rude. Her little cat and mouse pretending to not recognize him was one thing . . . "Grace." She shuffled the bag to her hand holding the coffee and shook his hand. It was warm, and firm . . .

She swallowed.

He looked at their hands before he let her go.

"A pleasure meeting you, Dameon. I'm sorry I don't remember you from last night."

"Pleasure's mine," he said.

She nodded toward the door. "I gotta go. I left my car in the parking lot. Wouldn't want to get towed."

"Because of the champagne and the blur?" he asked.

She waved the coffee cup in the air. "Yes. Those two things." With the back of her hand, she pushed her sunglasses higher on her nose. "Enjoy your stay in Santa Clarita."

He watched as she retreated. "I will."

Even outside, she felt his eyes. Damn if she couldn't stop herself from making sure he was watching.

Their eyes met, much like they had the night before, and Grace smiled.

CHAPTER TWO

"Hudson?" Her boss, the head of the civil engineering department for the city, knocked on her office door once, called her name, and entered.

"Morning, Richard . . . thanks for knocking this time."

Richard was thirty years her senior and still lived in the dark ages when it came to working with women in the office who weren't clerical.

He pushed past the door and dropped a two-inch-thick file on her desk, displacing the paperwork she was currently working on. "We have a new developer coming into the city. Bought a bunch of land in and around San Francisquito Canyon."

Grace opened the file, glanced at the first page. From the thickness of the preliminary file, she knew it wasn't a small job. "Looks extensive."

"It is. Thought it was time to give you something with more meat in it."

"Define *meat*." She had a bad feeling that Richard's meat would mean unpaid overtime. She already had a full fifty hours' worth of work on her desk every week and had only recently shaved her days down by a half an hour. She was the only female civil engineer in their department. For five years she'd been proving herself to Richard. To have him insinuate that she needed to prove herself yet again was insulting.

"Several acres. Residential and commercial with a ton of infrastructure and open space considerations."

None of which sounded like any meat she hadn't yet chewed.

"Possible zoning changes," he added.

"Sounds like work for a team and not one person."

From the tip of his balding head to the redness of his gin-blossom nose, Richard stared down at her.

"A team starts with one person." He leaned over as if to take the file. "But if you don't think you can hack it . . ."

She placed her hand over the file. "I didn't say that."

He righted himself. "Good." Turning to leave he added, "Become familiar with the file before we meet with the developer."

"When is that?"

He cleared the door.

"Two hours."

Her head shot up in alarm. "What?" That was insane. "How long have you known about this meeting?"

"A week."

Yeah, she didn't buy that. "And you waited till now to give this to me?"

Richard gave her a look out of the corner of his eye. "You were a little busy *wedding planning* and taking extra time off."

Oh, that was rich. Half of the people that worked in their building had been at the wedding. It helped that Colin was a supervisor for the public works department and knew just about everyone in the city. Between him, her firefighter brother Matt, and their retired law enforcement father, the safest place to be in Santa Clarita had been the hotel ballroom.

Yet here Richard was snarling about her involvement as if it was a *girl problem* he couldn't understand.

"Fine." She glared at the file. "You can close the . . ." She was talking to herself. Richard was gone.

"Two hours," she muttered.

She crossed her office to close the door and knew her entire plan for the day had just flown out the window.

12

Only after she sat back down did she realize she'd just been completely manipulated into taking on more work. Not that she had much of a say in things. But this time, Richard practically made her ask for it. Which meant when she wanted to leave the office at five like most of the staff, he would use that against her.

She opened the file and started skimming the highlights.

~

"Tell me why it is you're here again? I can do this without you."

Dameon stared out the picture window that had a ground floor view of one of the busiest streets in the city. It was much more congested than he expected it to be on a Monday.

"Because small towns want to know who they're doing business with. They don't like working with corporate entities. They like working with people."

"Santa Clarita isn't that small."

No, it wasn't. He'd spent the weekend driving around and getting a feel for the place. Less than forty miles from the center of Los Angeles, the Santa Clarita Valley boasted a suburban atmosphere with a large dose of country living. The outlying boundaries of the city were filled with small family ranches complete with horses and other barnyard animals. The old west atmosphere was felt in the heart of the older sections of the city. He'd purposely booked a room for the weekend just so he could come to the meeting armed with knowledge of the area you couldn't find in a scouting report or online.

He'd driven through the Santa Clarita Valley several times in the past year and a half while the properties were being purchased. Now was when the work began. And a good relationship with the city and the people who approve things . . . was key.

"No. It's not small. But it has everything to make this project work. We'll get things off on the right foot today and I'll leave you to it."

He finished talking at the same time the door of the conference room opened and a man walked in.

"Hello, gentlemen. Sorry to keep you waiting." He looked between the two of them. "I'm Richard Frasier. I believe I spoke to you on the phone."

Dameon stepped up and offered his hand. "You spoke with me. Dameon Locke."

Firm handshake. Always a good sign.

"Pleasure to meet you."

"This is Tyler Jennings, my project manager."

Richard smiled, shook hands, and looked over his shoulder. "We're just waiting on Hudson. Hold on." He glanced out the door and looked both ways before leaving the door open and pulling out a seat. "Please sit."

Dameon took the man's lead and made himself comfortable. No sooner did his butt hit the chair than he heard the distinctive sound of a woman's heels clicking their way through the door.

"Sorry to keep you wait . . ."

It was her.

The petite spitfire who had pretended she hadn't noticed him gawking through the window of the hotel. The lady who needed an IV of sugar after a night of drinking. The woman who made every single nerve ending in his body stand at attention and make him perfectly aware that he was a healthy, able, heterosexual male.

He lifted his ass out of the chair as she hesitated just inside the doorway.

Tyler shot to his feet.

Grace placed the folder she was carrying on the table and stared.

"It's just Hudson. You don't have to stand," Richard said as he remained seated.

"Thank you, but Richard is right. Please, have a seat." Her voice wavered.

If Dameon hadn't been on the other side of the table, he would have pulled out her chair. He realized in the workplace, that wasn't expected, and in fact, was often frowned upon. But with his libido drumming in his chest, all the lessons his mother taught him rushed forward.

"It's Grace, right?"

"Have you two met?" Richard asked.

Grace looked directly at him, her cheeks filled with color.

"At the coffee shop," he explained.

Silence sat in the room with both of them staring at each other until Tyler broke it. "Well, *we* haven't met. I'm Tyler Jennings. Mr. Locke's project manager."

Dameon watched as they shook hands and made sure he was next.

Her palm was cool, her face heated. "We seem to be bumping into each other a lot." He squeezed her hand one extra time before letting go.

Her eyes flared ever so slightly.

"It does appear that way, Mr. Locke. I never think of Santa Clarita as a small town, but sometimes it surprises me."

He waited until she took her seat before taking his. "Tyler and I were just talking about the size of your city."

She placed her hands over his folder. "Your company is based in LA. Is that where you live?"

"Yes." The question was personal.

"What made you choose Santa Clarita for this project?"

"Land availability, growth, and the ability to add something to a community without complete destruction of what is already there."

She didn't smile, didn't frown. Her lips were a straight line.

But when he smiled, there was this tiny spark in her eyes that gave away her thoughts. Grace Hudson wasn't completely unaffected by his presence. He'd sensed it through the window at the hotel, felt it in the coffee shop, and could practically taste it here.

"Well, now that we have that out of the way," Richard started. "Let's go over a few things so your time here isn't wasted, Mr. Locke. Then I assume Mr. Jennings will be working directly with Hudson from here on out?"

Tyler started to talk, but Dameon jumped in.

"No, actually. I'll be heavily involved in the beginning stages with your department."

Tyler nudged his foot under the table.

"You will?" Grace asked.

"Yes. I want to make sure everything goes smoothly. While I'm confident Tyler can take care of things in my absence, this is a significant project that will take several meetings to make sure that once we break ground nothing will clog us up."

Richard opened his file. "Let's get started, then."

CHAPTER THREE

Grace closed and locked her office door, dropped Dameon's file on her desk, and went straight to the thermostat to turn the air conditioner to the lowest setting it would accept.

He'd squeezed her hand . . . twice.

From that point forward it was shocking she could put two coherent sentences together.

And since when did the owner of a multimillion-dollar investment company get involved with city engineers?

Never. That's when.

From the look on Tyler's face, the project manager had been just as surprised.

Things were going to get sticky.

Grace rolled her shoulders and sat in her desk chair. She grabbed her phone and dialed Erin's number.

"Hello, you," Erin answered on the second ring.

"I need happy hour. Tonight."

"What? It's Monday and we just—"

"Tonight. And no boys. Leave my brother at home."

"He's working today."

Matt was a firefighter and worked twenty-four-hour shifts.

"Even better." Grace gave her the name of a local bar. "Five thirty?"

"Someone sounds frazzled," Erin said with a laugh.

"You have no idea."

~

"Mind sharing what that was all about?" Tyler asked as they walked out to the parking lot.

Dameon kept a steady pace to his car, the lift in his step directly related to the woman he'd just unsettled.

He liked having that effect on the opposite sex.

"What what's about?"

"You being *heavily* involved. That's how you put it, right? Heavily?"

"Just making sure everything goes smoothly."

Tyler snorted. "Has nothing to do with the Miss Sexy in high heels?"

He couldn't deny it.

"I'll have my schedule cleared for you and I to meet tomorrow afternoon. I want to know every single line item we need the civil engineering department to sign off on."

They stopped at Dameon's car.

He unlocked the doors with his key fob.

"Nice diversion without any denial or affirmation of my claim."

Dameon opened the door, shrugged out of his suit jacket, and loosened his tie. "You sure you're not a closet lawyer, Jennings?"

"You sure you're not a closet politician?"

They both laughed while Dameon slid behind the wheel. "See you back at the office."

He started his engine and glanced at the building where Grace Hudson worked. He would never have pegged the woman as an engineer. Let alone one who worked for the city.

Blessed is the man who has found a way to wiggle into a reluctant woman's life.

As he pulled out of the parking lot, Dameon considered himself royally blessed.

~

Erin's purse fell into the seat beside Grace. "It looks like you started without me." Erin slid into the chair and removed her sunglasses.

"It's been one of those days," Grace told her.

"Apparently it started before noon."

"It started on Saturday."

"At the wedding?"

Grace took a fortifying sip of her martini and a deep cleansing breath before starting in. "There was this guy . . ."

Erin's lips split into a grin. "It always begins with a man."

"Yeah, well . . . this one was watching me outside the window of the hotel. I'd stepped outside for a few minutes to get away from the constant yammering of Aunt Beth and her 'You're going to be too old to have kids if you don't settle down soon' bullshit. And this guy just kept staring at me."

Erin's smile fell. "Outside?"

"No, he was inside the hotel."

"Leering?" Erin was sensitive to the opposite sex and unwanted attention. Considering she was recovering from her ex-husband, who once used her as a punching bag, and then took it farther and tried to kill her for leaving him . . . yeah, Erin was quick to conclude any action from a man was a threat.

"No, no . . . nothing like that." Grace reached a hand across the table. "No. Dameon was admiring me. You know, like from across the bar, only I was outside and he was inside."

"So you met him?" Erin asked, her smile slowly returning.

Grace waved a hand in the air. "Not yet. I mean, I saw him . . . he's tall and pretty easy on the eyes. Wearing a suit. Which I looked past."

Erin frowned again. "Never trust anyone in a suit."

She laughed. Her father had the same line. "Anyway, he smiled at me, I pretended not to notice. He totally knew I noticed."

"What did you do?"

"I sucked in my stomach and walked away. Back to the reception. Figured that was the end of it. Cute guy making googly eyes. Game over. But no. Fast forward to Sunday. I'm looking three shades of hell frozen over and kicking myself for tipping that last taste of champagne in my glass. I left my car at the hotel so I have to go get it—"

"You saw him at the hotel again?"

"No. I stop for coffee and there he is. He starts up a conversation. I pretend I don't recognize him. Pretty sure he saw through that, but he plays along. This time he's wearing a turtleneck and slacks and looks even better than the night before. Which is bad, right?" She stopped to sip her drink.

"Why is that bad?"

Grace shook her head, swallowed. "He's in a hotel. So he's either from out of town or cheating on his wife or girlfriend."

Erin pulled back. "Sometimes you need to stay in a hotel because your house is being fumigated."

"In a suit?"

"You have a point."

The waiter walked up to the table. Erin ordered a glass of white, and he rushed off.

"Anyway . . . we shake hands, he tells me his name, I tell him mine. I walk away."

"What? No phone numbers?"

Grace lifted her index finger in the air. "From out of town." She put another finger in the air. "Or cheating. No. He didn't ask. I couldn't get out of there fast enough."

"I'm guessing the story doesn't end there."

Grace leaned forward, rested her elbows on both sides of her drink. "He was my eleven o'clock meeting. Big freaking investment company CEO from LA. Bought a bunch of property up San Francisquito, wants to develop it."

Erin's lips turned to an O. "He's totally stalking you."

Grace shook her head. "I don't think he knew I worked for the city. He seemed shocked when I walked in. And in reality, I was given the project two hours before the meeting. I had never heard of Locke Enterprises before today. So even if he knew I worked for the city, the file could have ended up on any of our desks."

"Good scammers investigate their prey before they engage."

Grace stared across the table and let Erin's words seep in. "I really hope you're wrong about that."

Erin's wine arrived and she took a taste. "What happened at the meeting?"

Grace reached across the table. "He did this thing." She waited for Erin to grasp her hand and squeezed it . . . twice.

Erin pulled back. "Oh . . ."

"Right? Totally flirting."

"Yeah. The double squeeze is always an invitation."

Grace sat back, brought her drink with her. "I didn't bite. Completely inappropriate to go there." She fished the olive out of her glass and bit into it.

"So, if you're not taking his flirty-double-squeeze handshake and running with it, what's the problem?"

"He's super hot and oozes confidence. And I have to work with him."

Erin started to chuckle.

"It's not funny. I have to act like I don't notice. I have a feeling if I give him so much as a sideways smile he's gonna sniff at my heels until I give in."

"Assuming this guy is legit and didn't know you worked for the city and isn't *sniffing*, as you put it, just to use you to get what he wants with his project . . . why exactly would you not 'give in'?" Erin asked over the rim of her glass that did a shitty job of hiding her smile.

"I've gotten used to being employed."

"Once he's through the city's red tape . . ."

"It's going to take months, years. And I'm sure by then he'll realize I'm not his type."

"How are you not his type?"

Grace took a few minutes to look up Mr. Locke on her phone to learn a bit more about the man. "He's society-page rich, and I live in a condo down the street. Different worlds."

"Have you forgotten who you're talking to?"

Grace caught her breath. "That doesn't count."

Erin pointed to her chest. "I'm society-page rich, as you put it, and I love your brother and wouldn't trade him in for anything." Erin and her sister had come into half the controlling stock of a company that was worth billions. Their share had made them incredibly wealthy over the past few months. "Money doesn't have to be a factor."

"True. But to be fair, you and Matt got together when you both thought you were scraping along like the rest of us. Guys like Dameon Locke can snag any arm candy they want. Even if she only wants his money. When men like him play in my field, it's to prove they can."

"I really want to tell you you're wrong," Erin said.

"But you know I'm right. When you were married to the rich prick, you knew the game." Erin had been born with money and walked away from all of it to escape her ex. Technically, she was a widow, but she didn't like the title, so everyone referred to the man as her ex. Calling herself a widow was met with sympathy from outsiders. No one was sorry the man was dead.

"There are nice guys out there with money."

Grace lifted her hand and signaled the waiter. "While you're writing a list of their names, I'll be looking for Dameon's faults. I'm always looking at the good and miss the red flags, even with them waving in front of my face."

Erin grimaced. "Dameon is a name I think of when I watch scary movies with vampires or the devil."

"See!" Grace pointed at her. "Fault. I thought the same thing."

"On the other hand . . . Dameon and Grace has a fabulous sound to it."

CHAPTER FOUR

"You work too much."

Dameon looked up at the underside of his mother's kitchen sink with a wrench in one hand and a towel in the other. "You mean like I'm doing right now to replace this crappy faucet? I should have gone with my instincts and hired a plumber."

"Your father always did the repairs around here and you promised to do it when he left us. So don't go pawning off your chores on someone else."

The faucet was older than him and just as stubborn as his mother. "I'm under here, aren't I?"

"I'm not talking about minor house repairs. I'm talking about that fancy office job that's killing you."

"Who says I'm dying?" Damn bolt was rusted and wouldn't budge. He'd been at it for thirty minutes and only managed to twist the thing in four complete rotations. And from the threads on it, he was going to be at it until morning.

"When was the last time you went to a doctor?"

"I'm not sick."

"How do you know if you don't go to the doctor? Every time I see Dr. Menifee he gives me another pill."

He switched to a locking wrench and braced his foot on the opposite counter for leverage. Dameon didn't know what hurt more, his arms from keeping them elevated above his head, or his back that rested on the straight edge of the sink cabinet.

"Oh, yeah . . . what did the good doctor prescribe this time?" He counted to three in his head and gave the wrench all he had.

"C ohhh enzyme something or other," his mom said.

Her words didn't register, and the bolt moved.

"Yes!" He positioned the wrench again, and this time the bolt gave way. As it did, bits of rust fell into his face. He closed his eyes and kept his lips sealed as he worked the rest of the bolt free.

"Did you hear what I said?"

"No, Mom . . . I'm having a party under here."

His mom's face popped into his field of view. "Oh, did you get it?"

"Yes, I did." And without so much as one f-bomb escaping his mouth. That had to be a first.

"I'll put the chicken in the oven, then. And by the time it's all done, I'll be able to do the dishes."

He wanted to argue, say he couldn't stay for dinner, but knew it would be a waste of his breath.

"Skip the salt on the chicken," he told her.

"Oh, did your doctor say it's bad for you, too? That's how it started with your father, you know."

"Not me, you." His mother was only sixty-five, but she often acted like she was eighty. And outside of her blood pressure soaring into the high zone, his mother was healthy as a horse. Truth be told . . . he knew nothing about horses or their overall health.

An hour later, the new faucet was in, his back was out, and Dameon had a beer in his hand.

Lois, his mom, stood in front of her sink turning the water on and off repeatedly. "So fancy," she told him.

"I could really show you fancy if you let me fix up the place."

She pulled the spray handle down and turned it on once again. "*This* is fancy."

"You know what I mean."

"Your father left me quite comfortable. Save your money for you. Or help your brother out."

Just mentioning his younger brother had Dameon picking up his cell phone. "If Tristan ever wants a job—one he would actually do—he knows where to find me." They both knew that would never happen. Tristan was allergic to work. He'd worked for Dameon for less than two weeks three years ago, and said he couldn't hack it. Now he lived in what looked like a hostel with a dozen other pot-smoking surfers just outside of San Diego. What he did for money, Dameon could only guess. At least he didn't harp on their mom for support.

Lois brought the chicken to the table and put her hand over his. "Your brother is finding himself."

"At the end of a joint? Chances are, he isn't going to find anything."

She walked back to the stove and brought the rest of their dinner. "That stuff isn't that bad."

"It's making him lazy."

Lois took her seat and put a hand under her chin. "It always made me hungry."

His hand that was reaching for the chicken stopped midway. "Excuse me?"

She looked him straight in the eye. "I did grow up in the sixties. Don't be so shocked. In fact, it was your father that offered me my first joint. It was *illegal* then." She whispered *illegal* as if the walls were listening.

Dameon blinked. "I know."

She grinned like a teenager with a secret. "I remember it being fun. Your father used to like to—" She stopped midsentence and pinched her lips together.

Much as Dameon wasn't sure he wanted to hear what she was about to say, he found himself asking, "Like to what?"

Lois smiled and looked at the ceiling as she often did when talking about his dad. It had been five years since he had a sudden heart attack and died within twenty-four hours. It had been a blow to all of them.

His mom lowered her voice to a rough whisper and leaned forward. "It made him *horny*."

Dameon squeezed his eyes shut and thought for sure his ears were bleeding. "Okay, then . . . thank you for that."

"Well, it did." Her voice was back in its normal range. "We had the best sex—"

"Mom! Please. I'm glad to know you and Dad were happy flower children, but if you want me to eat, save the descriptions."

His mom started laughing.

It didn't take long for him to join her.

When they both stopped, he continued to fill his plate.

"I miss him every day."

He reached over and patted her hand. "I know."

"It's why I don't want to change stuff around here."

"I know that, too. But eventually—"

"Eventually. But not today."

He took a sip of his beer and dug into the food. Good as it was . . . it needed salt.

"How is this work you're married to?"

Same questions . . . different day. "Work is good. And I'm not married to it."

"So you're dating?"

He poked his fork into another bite of chicken and waved it in the air. "I won't tell you about my sex life, and you won't tell me about yours."

"So you *have* a sex life."

He was *not* stepping in that minefield. "Mom."

"Sex isn't love. What about your love life?"

"If there was someone special in my life, you would know."

She reached across the table, picked up his beer, and took a drink. "That's what I thought. You're married to your work."

Next would be the reminder that she wasn't getting any younger and she wanted a daughter-in-law and grandkids.

Dameon stood from the table and retrieved a fresh beer from the fridge. He popped it open and handed it to his mom.

Instead of saying no, which she normally did, she took it from him and tilted it back for more than a sip.

He waited for the inquisition and guilt.

Lois picked up her knife and fork and silently cut into her food.

Seconds passed.

Only the chime of the grandfather clock in the hall filled the room.

No harping. No more questions.

No banter whatsoever.

What he saw on his mother's face was worse.

Sadness.

If there was one thing Dameon hated more than anything, it was letting his mother down. Wasn't that why he crawled under her sink because she asked? Why he would find a job, even if it was delivering lunch to the employees, for Tristan if he ever grew up.

An image of Grace flashed in his head, and his mouth started moving. "I did meet someone."

His mom's eyes shot to his faster than a bullet left the chamber of a gun.

"We just met, so don't get too excited," he said.

"What's her name?"

Was he really going to say this? "Grace."

That sadness melted away with his answer. "That's a lovely name."

"She's clever and confident." He thought of Grace in that dress, freezing her butt off outside the Hyatt. "Beautiful."

"How long have you been dating?"

To lie or not to lie?

He channeled his inner politician instead. "It's new, Mom."

Thankfully that's all he needed to say.

"This makes my heart happy."

It would make her heart equally unhappy to know the complete truth. And since his mother didn't venture too far outside her neighborhood and friends, he wasn't worried she'd stumble upon the facts.

～

Now that the wedding was over, it was time for Grace to dive into Christmas.

With a glass of wine to help with the spirit, she pulled the plastic tabletop tree out of a box she had in the small storage space in her single car garage. She plugged it in, grabbed the decorations, and within fifteen minutes her decorating was complete.

Pathetic . . . but complete.

She looked around her condo and took in the space.

It had everything she needed. A small kitchen that cooked for one. There had been painfully few men who had spent the night, and even fewer that were worth cooking breakfast for. She had space for a dining room table for four. A living room with a sofa, a chair, a floor lamp, and a coffee table. The TV lived mounted on the wall. She had two bedrooms. One doubled as her home office and guest room, but the bed was full of boxes and stuff she'd accumulated before and during the wedding planning that had yet to find a permanent place. Most of it could probably be tossed, but that would require work, and Grace had no desire to clean it up. She had two bathrooms, one in the hall and one in the master bedroom. She had a small balcony that overlooked the courtyard of the complex. And since she was on the third and top floor, she didn't hear neighbors, and her ceilings were vaulted, giving the illusion of more space.

She'd bought the condo with a little help from her parents shortly after getting the job with the city. Within two years she'd paid her parents back for their loan, even though they said she didn't have to. She could walk to work if she wanted to, but could count on one hand how many times she'd actually done that. The mall and all the restaurants around her were easier to get to on foot. Especially this time of the year when the parking lots were stuffed with Christmas shoppers. The only drawback was carrying bags home.

Her space was perfect.

Her brothers had opted for houses on the other side of town, but she stayed much closer to where her parents lived. Not that anyone lived far away. Only traffic dictated the time it took to get from one place to another. And traffic in an expanding city like Santa Clarita was a problem.

That was where she came in.

Men like Dameon Locke and their companies wanted to plop subdivisions and strip malls in and often didn't think about the impact on the roads. The houses would sell, of that she had no doubt. The business properties in outlying areas, however, didn't always fill up. With all the new tax and employment laws making small businesses struggle, there were lots of shut doors. But that wasn't her concern. She concentrated on roads and zoning and infrastructure to handle the expansion. Bridges and drainage and even the impact on the schools to a lesser extent. She at least needed to identify the potential issues and make sure someone was on it.

"And why are you thinking about work on a Friday night?" she asked herself.

She set her half-full glass of wine aside and slid off the couch. Maybe a couple of Christmas pillows would add to her decorations and make the space more inviting. Not that anyone came over, but maybe if the right guy . . . Her thoughts shifted to Dameon.

Tall, broad shoulders, with a devil that lived in his brown eyes. Not brown . . . more like honey with a hint of gold. And that voice. Just thinking of it had her tongue moistening her lips.

Grace moaned and reached for her purse. "Enough of that."

She put on a sweater and boots that complemented her jeans but weren't needed for any unwanted weather. While it was cool, it wasn't raining or snowing . . . or any of those other weather things that happened elsewhere in the country this time of year. It was Southern California, and it hardly ever rained until late December.

Well, except the year before when the clouds parked over the region and dumped for months.

Not this year. At least not yet.

Grace grabbed her purse and slung it over her shoulder before heading out the door.

She hesitated as she walked by the coffee shop where she'd stumbled upon Dameon just five days earlier. He wouldn't be there, of course, since he lived in LA. Grace still patted her back on how she'd managed to gather that information. Stealth. Yeah . . . that's what she was. He had no idea that she was thinking about him. And there was no way the man was thinking about her.

Except there was the double squeeze.

She dismissed the thought and pulled open the door to her favorite restaurant, or more to the point, favorite bar, and walked inside. People were lined up out the door. Grace walked past all of them to the open seating. She zeroed in on a barstool sandwiched between two couples.

"Hey, Jim," she greeted the bartender.

"Hey, Gracie, how you doin' tonight?" He placed a coaster on the counter as he walked by with someone else's order.

"Better than you, this place is slammed."

"It's the holidays. The usual?"

She nodded an affirmative, and he scrambled off to fill her order.

One look to each side of her and Grace realized she'd be talking to herself. She pulled out her phone and did what just about every single person did on a dateless Friday night. She opened up Instagram and started scrolling through posts. The first images to pop up were Parker's. It looked like the honeymooners had managed to get out of the hotel room long enough to take some beach pictures. But the image of her brother in a grass skirt standing with a bunch of tourists shaking their asses was what had her laughing out loud.

Jim dropped off her martini. "You eating tonight?"

"Chicken wings."

Jim winked, placed a napkin on the bar, and walked away.

She looked up long enough to realize everyone at the bar was deep in conversation or busy watching one of the many sports that played on the monitors mounted on the walls.

From Instagram she went on to Facebook. Some of the same pictures she'd seen on one app were on the other, courtesy of having the same friends as she did followers.

She picked up her drink and took a sip at the same time she clicked on "Friend Requests."

Dameon Locke's image, name, and page had her sucking in a breath instead of swallowing her drink.

She came up sputtering, dripping vodka down her shirt.

Grace managed to set the drink down without spilling more and reached for the napkin. Her throat burned, and people around her started to stare.

Jim came to the rescue with a glass of water. "You okay?"

After coughing several times, she managed a thumbs-up and a deep breath while her eyes watered.

She looked at his name for several seconds. Before accepting anything, she moved to his page.

It was public and looked like a giant advertisement for Locke Enterprises.

After a good minute she concluded that Dameon hadn't friended her. Locke Enterprises had. Which wasn't shocking since she, too, had a public page and often talked about the new things happening in the city.

Someone in his office was obviously in charge of these things.

The debate in her head that followed was a tennis match of should she accept or should she deny. A corporate gesture being denied felt wrong. The CEO of the company asking to be a friend, even on social media, felt equally erroneous. Saying no was petty. She closed her eyes and hit "Confirm."

"Whatever. It's nothing," she said to herself. She tried her martini a second time after putting her phone away.

CHAPTER FIVE

Grace walked out of the bar with the vodka buzzing her head and the chicken filling her belly in search of something festive.

Half of the mall was outside, with hundreds of white lights strung between the buildings. An explosion of red and green, gold and silver adorned every possible open space to remind shoppers that it was time to help the businesses get into the black. Maybe not in such an obvious way. More by way of encouraging people to spend more money than they should to make others happy one day a year.

Her family did a Secret Santa and a white elephant gift exchange. One where they picked a name and the other didn't know who got it . . . and another where outlandish, crazy gifts were bought and wrapped without names. That was always a good time. Everyone was given a random number, and the person with number one opened any gift of their choice. From there a person could steal the gift from number one, or open something new. It became quite a fight and often ended up with a tug-of-war over the best, or funniest, gifts in the mix.

Grace was on the hunt for a gift for Erin.

The woman could buy whatever she wanted for herself, so the gift had to be personal and thoughtful. And that was hard. But Grace was determined.

Inside Pottery Barn, Grace found holiday pillows to pump up her space. She browsed the store, attempting not to knock over the many breakable items while maneuvering around other customers. She set the pillows on a nearby table to check the price of a battery-operated candle.

No sooner had she picked up the glass holding the candle than her phone rang.

She fished it out of her purse and lifted it to her ear. "Hello?"

Forty-five bucks? Seriously?

"Grace?"

Smoky voice filled with sexy could only be one person.

The glass in her hand started to slip. She managed to catch it, but as she did, the glass bit into the waxy surface of the candle, completely screwing up the stupid thing. "Dameon?"

"So you do remember my voice."

Standing in the middle of a traffic pattern of customers, Grace held the glass vase to her chest and candle in her hand while juggling her phone. "It's not exactly forgettable."

"So I'm told."

Grace moved aside for a woman with a huge bag filled with stuff. "How did you get my number?"

"Facebook. I'm calling you from Facebook."

She pulled her phone away from her ear to look at the screen, put it back. "Seriously? Who does that?"

"I could call you directly, if you like. What's your number?"

Another shopper walked by and picked up one of her pillows. "Those are mine," she shouted.

The lady dropped it with a scowl.

"Where are you?" Dameon asked.

"Christmas shopping. Like everyone else in this town."

"You sound frazzled."

"You called me from Facebook. No one on the face of the earth does that."

"I'm unique."

Her vision was starting to clear. "Why are you calling, Mr. Locke?"

There was a pause. "I like it better when you use my first name."

Grace unloaded her armful of overpriced goods made in third-world countries on the table holding her pillows and purse. "This is highly inappropriate." Erin would call him a stalker and confirm it with facts.

"You accepted my friend request."

"Are you listening to yourself right now? I thought it was a corporate gesture."

"It's a personal page," he said.

"That's filled with your corporation's accolades."

He paused. "My mother does think I'm married to my work."

Grace placed one hand on her hip. "If that's your personal life, then your mother isn't wrong."

"I'll tell her you said that."

This conversation was bordering on ridiculous.

"Why are you calling, Dameon?"

"That's better." He sounded so smug.

"Mr. Locke," she corrected herself.

"We're back to that?"

Grace closed her eyes and shook her head. "We never got past that."

"I want to take you to dinner."

There were few times Grace found herself without words.

This was one of them.

"Are you there?" he asked.

"I'm here."

"So?"

"No."

Silence filled the line.

Finally, he said, "I didn't know you worked with the city. Not at the hotel when we saw each other through the window. Not at the coffee shop. You felt something."

"I didn't." Her denial was too quick. Even she heard the lie in her voice.

"You were scattered and blushing in the meeting. Don't try and pretend."

Grace licked her lips and ignored the stares of those around her walking by. "This isn't appropriate, Dameon."

He paused, and she knew she'd let her true feelings be known. "Maybe not. But it is."

This conversation needed to end. He was doing a very good job of getting things out of her she didn't want revealed. "I have somewhere to be, Mr. Locke. Why don't you try calling during business hours, since that's the context in which I know you."

That husky voice rumbled when he laughed.

It was the first time she'd heard it, and it made quite a dent in her belly. "Okay, Grace. I'll call you on Monday."

"That's better."

"I'll talk to you then," he said.

"Not on a Facebook phone line."

"I'll call your office."

"Good."

He laughed a second time. "Good night."

Why did that sound personal? Like something a lover would say sheepishly over the phone.

"Good evening," she said instead.

Even as he hung up, he was chuckling.

Five minutes later, she exited the store with a half-broken over-priced candle and the desire for two pillows she couldn't afford.

～

"It's called practice," Grace told Erin as she tugged on a pair of bowling alley–issued shoes.

Around them, lanes were filled with families and couples and even a few single bowlers who were obviously born for the sport.

"Our league doesn't start until January."

Grace had talked her brothers and their significant others into joining a league. Because there were an uneven number of them, they decided to have the girls on one team, and the boys on another. Matt was trying to convince one of his friends to join their team, but if he didn't succeed, they'd do without and use a blind player score.

"I know." Grace plopped her foot down on the ground and stood in her awkward shoes. "But I like to win. Or at least beat my brothers."

"Then you probably should have invited someone else to be on your team. The last time I bowled had to be at a birthday party when I was ten."

Grace moved to where the house bowling balls sat and started sifting through them. "There's a thing called a handicap." For the next ten minutes, Grace explained how league bowling worked so that everyone had a chance to win. Obviously, the better bowler you were, the chances of you winning increased so long as your team improved as the weeks went on.

". . . and if nothing else, we have happy hour somewhere else while getting some exercise," Grace concluded.

"I'm just happy to be out." Erin had spent the greater part of the last two years of her life hiding from her past. In doing so, she isolated herself from social situations. Despite her best efforts, her abusive ex-husband had found her and attempted to end her life. The man damn near succeeded, but in the end, it was her ex that found himself on the wrong end of a gun. Unfortunately, it was Erin who had squeezed the trigger. She was in therapy and working through her demons. Thankfully, she had Matt at her side.

Grace loved her brothers. Matt was one of the good guys.

When Erin's therapist had suggested she join social clubs to keep busy and find where she fit in her new world, Grace had suggested bowling.

Everyone jumped at it.

While the clock ticked down their five minutes of practice before they started their game, Grace picked up her ball and pictured where she wanted it to land on the lane.

"You were in a league before?" Erin asked as the ball left Grace's hand.

Five pins fell.

Grace rolled her shoulders and stood aside for Erin to practice while the pins were reloaded.

"In college. I played for two seasons. Even came away with a third place trophy."

Erin's ball ended up in the gutter. "Ugh."

"It's okay. We're just starting."

Grace stepped up again, lifted the ball to her chest, and remembered some of her tricks. Palm up. This time the ball hit the head pin and knocked down nine of them.

Erin's turn had three pins falling over.

"The guys are going to depend on muscle. We're going to out skill them." Grace shifted her feet a tiny bit to the left and aimed for the right side of the head pin.

When all ten pins fell with a satisfying roar, she did a little happy dance. "Sweet."

Erin smiled. "I'm glad I'm on your team."

"I love besting my brothers."

"Looks like you're off to a good start," Erin said.

Grace watched while Erin threw the ball. When it ended up in the gutter, Grace moved beside her and lifted her hand, palm to the ceiling. "You're crossing your body when you toss the ball. Start by holding your ball palm up, and just try and hit the second arrow on the lane."

"There's arrows?"

Grace pointed out the spot and waited while Erin threw another ball.

Six pins down.

"That's better."

Erin turned back to her with a huge grin.

As their practice session ended and their game began, they kept talking. "Guess who called me," Grace said.

Erin sat at the table waiting for her turn. "Does his name start with a *D*?"

Grace nodded. "The guy is ballsy."

"I have a feeling he'll be calling your office a lot. Mr. Double-Squeezer."

That had her laughing while she waited for her ball to return. "He didn't call the office."

"Wait, you gave him your cell number?"

Grace went into him calling via Facebook. Sure enough, Erin called him a stalker.

"I think he's determined and resourceful," Grace countered.

She left one pin standing and sat down for Erin's turn.

"All the qualities of a stalker."

Grace paused. "Am I that hard up for male attention I'm ignoring the obvious with this guy?"

"You haven't exactly been dating in the last six months."

"I've been concentrating on my work." And avoiding the male species altogether.

When Erin finished her turn, she sat down and picked up her cell phone. "What's this guy's name again?"

"Dameon Locke."

While she looked up the man on the internet, Grace took her turn.

"Ohhh! He is really good-looking."

Nine pins down. "I know. It's unnerving."

Erin leaned back and read up on him. "Pretty successful for thirty-five."

"I know. The land his company purchased is not a tiny lot."

"Did you look him up?" Erin asked, waving the phone in the air.

"I didn't have to. His business profile is sitting on my desk." She turned back to the lone pin and concentrated hard. It fell with one solid plop.

Erin didn't move. "Never married . . ."

"What about a girlfriend?" Grace asked.

"I'm looking."

Grace hadn't gone that far. Refused to for fear of what she'd find. "You do that, I'll get us a couple of beers."

"M'kay."

The bar was packed and it took forever. When she returned, Erin was deep into whatever she was reading. She glanced up and patted her hand on the table. "Listen to this. Locke Enterprises is only six years old. Which means Stalker Man started it when he was twenty-nine."

"Ballsy. I told you." Grace sat and drank the foam off her beer.

"Before that he was a general contractor. I found an article where he credits his father for his success."

She leaned forward. "Did his dad have money?"

Erin shook her head. "I can't find anything about him."

"Anything about a girlfriend?"

"Nothin'. The guy is virtually off the grid. Very few articles."

"That's good." And it was. The man obviously had means but didn't go out of his way to flaunt it.

"Oh, that's interesting." Erin kept reading.

"What?" Grace moved around to the other side of the table so she could see what Erin was oh-ing over.

"Looks like Locke had some seed money early on and recently that bank account expired."

Grace looked at Erin's phone and took it from her hands. An image of Dameon next to another man in a suit posing for a photograph at what looked like some kind of cocktail party. "Wonder what happened."

"Lots of businesses begin with investors. Often more than one. They tend to be on a board of some sort that has some say in the company. If this Dameon of yours parted ways from his extra cash flow, it means one of two things: there was trouble, or Stalker Man no longer needs the other company's money."

Grace skimmed the article. "What do you think it was?"

"I don't know. What I do know is the next couple years will determine if Locke Enterprises can do it alone."

She lowered the phone and looked at Erin. "You know a lot about this stuff."

Erin shrugged. "This is my father's life. I guess some of the conversations I overheard during the years stuck."

Grace couldn't help but think that Dameon needed everything for his latest project to get off the ground. And quickly.

And that made her question his motives for flirting with her even more.

"Maybe you have it right. He's a stalker." She handed the phone back to Erin and stood. "Whose turn is it?"

~

The bed dipped with the weight of someone sitting on the edge. A hand reached out and touched her leg. "Honey?"

Grace opened her eyes. It was late, or really early. The sun wasn't up. "What's wrong?" She was in her childhood bedroom that had been converted into a guest room.

Nora, her mother, turned on the bedside light, her eyes wide with fear. Very few things put that look on her mother's face.

Grace shook the sleep from her head. Her mom was dressed, but not in her usual state. It looked like she'd tossed on a shirt from her hamper and an old pair of jeans. "What happened?"

"It's Erin."

Grace froze, hanging on the next words that came from her mother's lips.

"Her husband found her."

Grace scrambled up in bed. Terror clenched her chest. "No. No. No."

"We have to go," her mother told her.

Grace flung back the covers and realized she was naked.

Only she didn't sleep naked.

This was wrong. Something wasn't right.

"Where are my clothes?"

"You don't need them. C'mon."

Not right.

Was she dreaming?

"Mom, I have to put something on."

Nora was standing now, looking down on her. "Erin's dead and he's coming after you."

Grace shot straight up in bed, her hands clutching the blanket. Short scattered breaths racked her body.

She was in her own bed, and light was peeking through the shades.

She closed her eyes and dropped her head back on the pillow. "Just a dream." Some of it, anyway.

Grace had been at her parents' house when they were woken in the middle of the night to hear that Erin was held inside her home by her husband. Grace and her parents had scrambled into clothes and rushed to the Sinclair ranch, where Erin lived in Parker's guesthouse. By the time they arrived it was all over.

Erin had been loaded into an ambulance and rushed to the hospital while everyone else stood outside huddled together in shock.

It could have been her.

Grace could have been the one in that ambulance or worse . . . dead on the floor with a bullet in her head.

Tossing back her blankets, Grace padded barefoot into her bathroom and turned on the light. A pale version of herself stared back.

"You're smarter now, Gracie."

Or was she?

CHAPTER SIX

Grace arrived to work on Monday forty-five minutes early. She had every intention of leaving at five sharp, if not earlier, so she could get over to Colin and Parker's place now that they were home from Hawaii.

Parker was anxious to open the wedding gifts and wanted her there. Spending time with family was a lot more inviting than being alone in her condo.

She switched on the light in her tiny office, one she'd acquired less than a year before, when one of the senior staff vacated it and she was next up for a private space. It wasn't big, and certainly not a corner office. But it was hers and she loved having a door she could actually shut.

This early in the morning, however, her door was wide open since she was the only one there.

After removing her sweater and tucking her purse into her desk drawer, Grace pushed aside Dameon's file and attacked an earlier project that was going to take her out of the office at ten. At one there would be a group meeting she had to attend. Maybe in all of that she'd miss Dameon's promised phone call.

Slowly, employees arrived, and the office outside her door hummed with activity.

Evan, another engineer in the office, poked his head around the corner with a sharp knock on the wall. "Hey, Grace?"

She looked up. "Yeah?"

"Mind going to the ten thirty without me? Richard piled a new project on my desk, and I need to do a site check."

"Glad to know I'm not the only one," she replied.

"Excuse me?" Evan stepped all the way in.

"Nothing. Fine. I'll make notes and bring them back in, and we can go over everything later."

Evan smiled. "I owe ya one."

"I'm keeping track," she yelled after him as he walked away.

By nine forty-five she was slipping down the hall and out of the office. The sky had turned gray and the temperature had dropped. Since her job often took her out of the office and onto jobsites, she had two pairs of shoes in her trunk: tennis shoes and a pair of rubber boots for sloppy weather. She had the ever-beautiful white hard hat and orange vest that were mandated whenever there was heavy equipment or construction in process.

After filling up her gas tank and stopping for a real cup of coffee instead of the brown liquid they passed off as coffee at the office, Grace made her way across town.

She arrived at the proposed site ten minutes early and parked her car on the shoulder of the busy road.

Runoff on Sierra Highway had washed out several roads and driveways the previous winter. Most of the landowners jumped on repairs as soon as the rain stopped.

Not the owner she was meeting with today.

Mr. Sokolov, the owner of the mobile home park, had packed dirt and gravel over the ingress and egress of the only road into the place. Between the residents' complaints and the fire department flagging the property, Mr. Sokolov was being forced to pave the road to current city standards.

He wasn't happy.

At the first meeting, he'd done a fair amount of bitching and moaning about cost.

While Grace understood financial limitations, it wasn't her job to lower the cost to the landowner. It was hers to come up with an engineering plan to make the road safe for everyone involved.

Knowing she was visiting the site, she'd thought ahead and wore slacks to work. She removed her high heels and tucked her toes into her tennis shoes before exiting her car. As she pulled her arms through her sweater, she scolded herself for not putting a warmer coat in her car.

With a clipboard in one hand and site plans in another, Grace walked over the gravel path in question. No one was there to greet her.

She pulled out the plans she and Evan had worked on together and walked the site to see if they'd missed anything. Ten minutes later, Mr. Sokolov drove onto the property and parked in a red zone. He pushed out of his Mercedes wearing sunglasses and a frown.

From the passenger seat, another man, almost as round as the first, joined him.

Mr. Sokolov looked around before his eyes landed on Grace. By now she was walking toward him.

"You with the city?" he asked.

Grace moved in front of him and extended her hand. "We met last month, Mr. Sokolov. Grace Hudson."

He looked at her and her hand like she was kidding. "Where's Evan?"

Grace dropped her hand and tried to let his slight go.

It wasn't easy.

"Evan couldn't make today's meeting."

Mr. Sokolov finally removed his unneeded sunglasses and stared down at her. "I've been dealing with Evan."

Grace looked to the man at Sokolov's side briefly. "You're dealing with the city engineers, of which I am one."

Somewhere in his early fifties, he was as round as he was tall, which wasn't more than five nine. Stocky as opposed to just overweight. His friend beside him wasn't much different from his scowl to his girth.

Mr. Sokolov's gaze dropped from Grace's eyes to her chest. He lingered there long enough that Grace knew the gesture was meant to make her uncomfortable. In any other situation she would have called him on it. Instead she kept her eyes on his face and waited for him to look away.

"Do you have an office here where I can spread out the plans and show you what we've come up with?"

He smirked, and she knew she'd chosen the wrong words. "I own the place, little lady, I don't live here."

"Hudson. My name is Miss Hudson. Not little lady." He was dancing on her last nerve.

"Right." He moved past her toward his car and tapped the hood. "You can *spread* them here."

Let it go, Grace.

She unrolled the plans. "Would you mind holding that end?" she asked both of them since neither had moved to do so.

Reluctantly, Mr. Sokolov's companion, who they failed to introduce her to, did so.

All three of them peered down at the drawings and calculations.

The sketches were minimal, but the dimensions were precise. The only reason they were looking at the city drawings instead of her looking at his was because if he didn't cooperate and do the job himself, the city was going in to do it for him and charge him accordingly. This was a public safety issue, and the warnings had gone out months ago and were ignored. This meeting was the last attempt to get the man to cooperate before they took action.

"As we pointed out when we met last month, the road has to significantly increase in size to accommodate the use and efficiency of the location."

"Which is bullshit. The road has been the same size since I bought the place," he argued.

"And had the road been maintained with the right material, it may have withstood last year's storms and we wouldn't be having this conversation."

He glared at her. "What are you suggesting?"

"Nothing." She made her point before placing a finger on the drawing. She explained the depth of the excavation, the amount of rebar that needed to be placed, and the weight of concrete or asphalt needed.

He asked where exactly the crossing needed to start.

She walked over to the approximate point and stopped.

Mr. Sokolov sputtered something she didn't quite hear, and his friend finally spoke. "Isn't that excessive?"

"Not when you have to get emergency response vehicles in and out of here in bad weather."

"Last year was an anomaly."

"And when years like the last one happen, the city is forced to go back to the drawing board and make sure we're prepared for the next one."

"Stick it to the little guy."

As she saw it, there was nothing *little* about Mr. Sokolov.

"You have thirty-three residents in this community. Many are retired and elderly. First responders are called here no less than four times a month. The fire department needs access."

"This is going to cost a fortune."

The man sang the same tune he did the first time she was on-site.

"It will cost more if you don't hire someone yourself," she assured him. "We don't shop contractors. We hire big crews to come in, do the job, and hand you a bill." And considering the lack of respect he was showing, she'd have no problem suggesting overtime to get things done faster. After all, it did smell like rain was on its way.

"You're enjoying this," he accused her.

"I'm doing my job." Between the cold and the adrenaline the conversation was pumping in her system, Grace shivered. She walked back to the car, rolled up the plans, and handed them to Mr. Sokolov.

He slapped them against his thigh and said something to his friend in a language she didn't understand.

When the other man laughed, she assumed an insult had ensued.

"You have a week." She gathered her papers.

"What the hell?"

"You've had months, Mr. Sokolov. The first letter was written to you in May and every four weeks after that—"

"I told your office I didn't receive any letters."

"Yet you managed to get the one where we told you action was imminent."

He glared and leaned forward. "You're calling me a liar."

She held her ground, lifted her chin. "Just stating facts, Mr. Sokolov. If you fail to meet the timeline we've laid out, the city will expedite a crew and begin right after the New Year. Weather permitting."

"I need more time."

"We're already into our rainy season." She held her hand up as if catching raindrops. "The city will not be held responsible for a lack of action. One week. We'll expedite permits since Evan and I have already been on-site and know what needs to happen. Keep in mind our holiday hours." Grace looked between the two of them and hiked her purse higher on her shoulder.

Mr. Sokolov moaned.

"Gentlemen," she said with a nod before turning and walking away.

～

Grace's hands shook as she left Sokolov and his leering friend. A mile down the road she pulled over to catch her breath.

No matter how hard she tried to stick her chin in the air and put on a brave face, sometimes the indignant and sexist behavior of the men she had to deal with got to her.

This was one of those moments.

She knew this would be a fact of life when she entered the engineering field. Dealing with the Sokolovs of the world who didn't take her seriously, and probably called her a raging bitch behind her back the moment she left their sight, was a fact of life.

But damn it to hell, it sucked. Her male counterparts didn't suffer the same behavior.

She'd lay down money that no one ever stared at Evan's crotch while he was trying to talk to them.

She needed backup.

In cases like Sokolov, where the disrespect was a 9.5 on the Richter scale, Grace needed a little help from her friends—or in this case—her family.

She picked up her phone and called her brother.

"Well, good afternoon," Colin greeted her with way too much cheer for what she'd just gone through.

"Hey." She took a deep breath and tried to collect her thoughts.

"I've been home twelve hours. What took you so long?"

That had her smiling. "I love you."

"I love you, too. What's wrong?" Her brother knew her.

"When are you back to work?" Colin was a supervisor of the public works department for the county. And even though this particular issue didn't fall into his department, some of his crew would be called on to build the crossing the city was forcing Sokolov to comply with.

"Wednesday."

"Okay . . . good—" Her phone rang through with another call. Since she was on the company phone, she needed to take it. "Hold on. I have another call."

"Kay . . ."

She switched the call over. "This is Hudson."

"Grace?"

She blew out a breath. "Dameon." His voice gave him away.

"You don't sound good."

"Well, thank you, Captain Obvious." For whatever reason she had no issue putting Dameon in his place. "Hold on."

She clicked back to her brother. "Sorry . . . I need you to stop by the mobile home park on Sierra Highway. The one that flooded out last year . . ."

"Is there a problem?" Colin asked.

"You have no idea—" Her phone buzzed, reminding her she had Dameon on hold. "Damn it. Wait."

She clicked over. "Can I call you back?"

"Is that your way of asking me for my phone number?" Dameon asked.

Grace hated the fact that she smiled. Hated it so much that she put Dameon on hold and went back to her brother.

"The guy was a complete douche. Stared at my chest and called me *little lady*. I need some backup on this one."

"What the hell?" Dameon's voice filled the line.

Grace pulled the phone away from her ear and stared at it. "Shit, shit, shit . . ." She switched the call again, put it to her ear. "Dameon?"

Her brother answered. "Who's Dameon?"

She was going to lose it any second. "No one. Uhm . . . let me call you back."

She dramatically pressed end to the call with her brother and put the phone back to her ear. "Forget I said that. It wasn't meant for you."

"Who were you calling for backup?"

Grace found herself answering on autopilot. "My brother." She closed her eyes and shook the fog from her head.

"Okay . . . good."

After blowing out a deep breath, Grace pulled in her emotions. "What can I do for you, Dameon?"

"You can start by telling me who was disrespecting you."

"What are you going to do? Go beat him up?"

"Maybe."

She squeezed her eyes shut and pounded her steering wheel with her free hand. "I'll leave that to my brothers. But thank you."

"Your brothers would do that for you?"

"Lots of cement boots in the bottom of the ocean," she said, joking.

Dameon laughed. "All right, then. That makes me feel better."

"You really don't have any right to feel anything on the subject." And she had no right to have butterflies tickling her stomach with the conversation.

"Yeah, well . . . I do."

What did she do with that?

Ignore it.

"What can I do for you, Dameon?"

"I wanted to set up a site meeting to go over a few things before the holidays suck away all of your time."

His request wasn't out of line, even if his flirting was.

"When were you thinking?"

"Friday."

"This Friday?"

"Unless you were free on Saturday. Then maybe we could have dinner and discuss the project."

Grace was vaguely aware of the traffic whizzing by her car as she idled on the side of the road.

"I believe I have Friday afternoon free. I'll have to confirm when I'm back in the office."

Dameon sighed over the line. "Great. Have your people call my people and set it up."

She laughed. "I work for the city, Dameon. I don't have *people*."

"Even better. You can call me back directly. Do you have a pen?"

"Why?"

"For my phone number."

"I have your office number," she told him.

"I'm leaving the office. I'll give you my cell."

She grabbed a pen and flipped open the notepad that sat in the passenger seat. "Fine."

He rattled off his number.

"I'll get back to you."

There was a pause in the conversation. "Try and have a better day," he said.

"I will." She hung up and dropped her phone in her purse.

This day needed to turn around . . . fast.

CHAPTER SEVEN

It was potluck at the honeymooners' house.

Grace walked in the door with a bottle of red wine and a grocery bag full of everything needed to make a walnut-cranberry salad.

She didn't bother knocking since her parents' car was parked in the driveway.

"Ho, ho, ho," she greeted anyone within earshot.

She saw her brother first.

Colin kissed her cheek and took the bag from her hand. "You look better than you sounded earlier."

She rolled her eyes. "Don't get me started."

They walked around the corner to the great room that held a kitchen, a dining room, and a den. Her mom stood beside the sink cutting vegetables, and her dad was playing tug-of-war with Parker's dog, Scout. "Hey, Dad," Grace called out.

"Hold on," he said. "I almost got him."

From the determination on the dog's face, her dad wasn't getting anything. "Good luck."

Her mom smiled and kept chopping. "Hi, sweetheart."

Parker walked out of the master bedroom looking just as relaxed as Colin. "Someone got a tan," Grace told her.

Parker lifted her arms and looked at them. "I almost feel guilty," she said.

"I don't," Colin teased.

Parker blushed and came in for a hug. "We had the best time."

"I don't want to hear about your sex life." Grace's comment pulled a chuckle out of her mother.

"I can get away Friday afternoon for that issue you have on Sierra Highway," Colin told her.

"Around three?"

"Works for me."

The front door opened again, and she heard Matt and Erin walk in.

"Looks like the party started without us," Matt said before kissing their mom on the cheek.

Grace handed her brother the bottle of wine. "Not unless you open this," she told him.

Matt grinned. "Hello to you, too."

"Where's Austin?" Erin asked.

Parker's younger brother still lived with her . . . and now Colin. Parker had been responsible for taking care of him and her younger sister after their parents died a few years back.

"Working the Christmas tree lot again this year."

Grace's gaze moved to the tree in the den that flashed with colored lights and brightened up the room. "When did you guys have time to do that?" she asked.

"We didn't. Austin and Mallory put it up while we were gone. Wasn't that sweet?"

Matt had worked the cork free of the bottle and poured some for Grace.

"My siblings never put up a tree for me," she complained.

"Where would we put it? Your patio?" Colin asked.

"He has a point," their father said. He'd given up the rope to the dog and sat on one of the barstools at the kitchen island.

Colin handed out beers to his dad and brother, and Matt opened a bottle of white for Erin.

"Is Mallory coming?" Erin asked.

"She has finals."

Grace had been in Parker's kitchen enough to find what she needed to make the salad. As they all danced around the kitchen preparing dinner, the conversation swirled.

Out of nowhere, Colin asked, "So who is Dameon?"

Hearing his name brought Grace's attention away from what she was slicing. "Uhm . . ."

"How do you know about Dameon?" Erin asked. "You told him about Dameon?"

"No, I—"

"I don't know about a Dameon." Parker pushed her shoulder into Grace's arm.

"You've been in Maui," Grace reminded her.

Colin reached over Grace's shoulder and snagged a tomato. "If Erin knows about Dameon, he must be someone."

"He's not!"

"Instant denial is always a sign of a lie," her father chimed in.

"Give it up, Gracie . . . who is he?" her mom asked.

"Oh my God. Seriously, he's no one." Her family was like a dog with a bone.

Silence ensued and all the eyes were on her.

She set the knife down with a sigh. "He's a guy."

"We figured that," Colin said with a laugh.

"A client. He's a land developer . . ."

Still the room was silent.

Then Erin spoke up. "Who called you from Facebook."

Now the room started to buzz.

"He did what?"

"Can you do that?"

"Who calls someone from Facebook?"

The questions came so fast she couldn't answer them all. Instead she stared at Erin. "Thanks, *friend*."

Erin lifted her hands in the air. "Hey, I think he's a stalker."

That's all anyone needed to hear.

Everyone started talking at once.

Grace stood back and took a big drink of wine.

It wasn't until her father asked for Dameon's last name that Grace ended the conversation. "Enough," she shouted.

Even Scout stopped licking himself and turned to stare.

"Dameon is *not* a stalker." She put her wineglass down. "He is a guy I met completely by accident before I knew he was a land developer and showed up at the office. And before you ask . . . no, nothing happened. We met in a coffee shop."

"And at the wedding," Erin corrected her.

"He was at the hotel, not the wedding. And we didn't meet then. We just . . ." She stopped talking, knowing what she was about to say would get everyone going again.

"You just what?" her mom asked.

"Noticed each other."

Parker sighed and leaned against the counter, all smiles. "You mean like *across the crowded room* noticed?"

In that second, Grace remembered him standing inside the hotel watching her.

"Someone is blushing," Matt teased.

"Am not!" She looked at Erin.

Erin shrugged her shoulders and nodded.

Grace put the back of her hand to her warm cheek. "It's nothing, okay? He's a flirt." She picked up the knife again and started working. "Not to mention it's completely inappropriate. He's working with the city on permits and zoning changes for his massive project. It's a conflict of interest."

"The denial is strong with this one," Matt said in a deep Yoda voice.

Grace picked up a walnut and tossed it at her brother.

"Does he wear a hard hat or a suit?" her dad asked.

"A suit."

There were several sighs.

"Can't trust a man in a suit," her dad affirmed.

"Then it's a good thing he's nothing, cuz he wears them. Now can we please talk about someone else? Like, hey, Matt . . . when are you going to make Erin an honest woman?"

If there was one thing about her family, it was their ability to dish it out. And since Erin had added just enough fuel to the fire to make Grace squirm, it was her turn to make sure the woman felt a little of the heat.

~

"Third quarter was shit, and the fourth is even worse."

Dameon sat with his executive board staring down at the financial report. He ignored the tension crawling up his neck and asked the hard questions. "What's the projection for the next six months?"

"Damn, Dameon . . . since when do we only look six months ahead?" His CFO and longtime friend, Omar, tossed the report down and stared.

"Since Maxwell bailed and the cushion his bank afforded us went with him. We knew it was going to be tight. The question is, how tight?"

Omar glared. "Our asses are going to squeak when we walk."

Dameon leaned forward. "But are we still standing?"

"We're standing, but the ground is shaky. We need the Rancho project to finish and start bringing in revenue if we're ever going to get the Santa Clarita project going. Even then, I don't know that we're going to have the funds for the scale we originally proposed."

Locke Enterprises had a dozen other commercial projects going. All in various stages from acquisition to construction. Rancho was half the scale of the Santa Clarita project, but the largest of the ones close to completion.

"We need the Santa Clarita project to get us back where we were," he reminded them.

"We don't want to be like Fedcon with half-built projects in the middle of the desert," Tyler added.

Fedcon was a well-known developer that went belly-up in the middle of a three-hundred-home subdivision out past Lancaster. The houses sat in various stages of construction for five years until another developer swept in and made a killing.

"We're not going to let that happen," Dameon said. "If anything, I want us to be the ones who come in and take over lost projects that make sense."

Omar turned to Chelsea, who ran the public relations and marketing departments. While it sounded vast, the reality was that she managed less than five employees.

"I have a suggestion on the Rancho property," Omar started.

"I'm listening."

"I know the original idea was to hold on to the properties and triple net lease the commercial space. But at this time, a clean flip might give us what we need to see the black for another year. At least get us breaking ground in Santa Clarita."

Much as Dameon didn't like the idea, he had to give it merit. They'd made a significant amount of money flipping properties from the beginning. Only after they started holding on to them in order to generate a steady flow of money did Locke Enterprises start to rise. With that rise meant more staff and bigger budgets.

Chelsea tapped her pen on the papers in front of her. "Another idea would be to bring in an investor."

"So they can pull out after we exceed the depth of our coffers?" Dameon asked. "I'd like to avoid that."

"With the right contracts and lawyers, we can circumvent any of those issues," Omar told him.

Yeah . . . Maxwell had been more of a handshake deal with very little written down. That's the problem when you join forces with your college friends who have family money. One bad argument and it was game over.

And over a woman, no less.

"Omar, I need numbers that show our status if we had stayed the course we started last January. Chelsea, I want a list of interested parties as well as the going rate for what we have out there in Rancho. I want reality, not dreaming numbers." He pointed to the closed door. "There are a lot of people out there that depend on us to pay their bills. And I really don't want to be handing out pink slips this time next year." He paused. "And as much as it pains me to even ask for it, I'd like a list of potential investors."

His team seemed to like that the most since they all smiled at each other.

Dameon called the meeting over, and Tyler and Chelsea left the room.

Omar hung back. "We're going to make this work," he assured Dameon with a pat on the back. "We started this with grit and guts."

Dameon laughed. "We started it at a bar, drunk off our asses." Omar had been an accounting major and had switched to business finance. Maxwell was the aforementioned trust-fund kid who was taking business classes because his father told him to. And Dameon had already gotten his contractor's license and was getting a degree in business so he didn't have to pound nails for the rest of his life.

By the time Locke Enterprises was born, it was money Dameon had earned flipping a dozen homes and one apartment complex that started it all. But the nest egg he'd built wasn't enough to get to the next level. Which was where Maxwell came in.

Maxwell didn't like to work. He was a silent investor who met with Dameon and Omar once a month to either pick up or drop off a check. Until last year.

"I think we need more drunk nights at a pub," Omar suggested.

Dameon dismissed his thoughts and faked a smile. "Maybe so."

CHAPTER EIGHT

Grace arrived at the Locke jobsite thirty minutes before her scheduled time with Dameon. She knew on paper what the scope of the project was, but had yet to get on the property to take a closer look. She'd changed into jeans and a sweater and wore a long coat to ward off the cold winds that were blowing in the first real rain of the season. Precipitation hadn't yet fallen from the sky, but it was coming.

She hoped it would hold off a couple more hours.

The ranch property where she had agreed to meet Dameon looked as if it had been abandoned for at least a year. "No Trespassing" signs were posted, but that didn't mean people adhered to them. She'd been at her job long enough to know not to go poking around the house until someone else was there. The homeless were known to squat in abandoned properties, especially ones like this, that were away from prying eyes and anyone who might call the police.

She took one look at the lock holding the gate closed and decided to walk across the dirt road and through the brush to where it met the wash that flowed out of the canyon.

This had once been a thriving ranch community. But through the years and the ups and downs of the real estate market, some owners mortgaged themselves into bad situations that forced them to sell. Slowly, many of the properties had fallen into disrepair. The livestock became a novelty and not a norm. Some owners used part of their properties to store RVs and boats. Even if the zoning didn't allow for that kind of thing, the owners got away with it because no one complained.

Why would they? Everyone was just trying to hold on to what was theirs.

Grace tried to imagine a subdivision and what it would do for the area. She couldn't help but feel that some of the homeowners would balk at the idea. They came out there for solitude and privacy. On the other hand, it would increase the value of their homes if the area was developed.

Ultimately, it wasn't for her to approve or disapprove of any project. Just to point out the engineering of them. And from an engineering standpoint if something wasn't feasible, the landowner needed to change his or her plans.

She heard tires eating up the gravel road and saw a truck pull alongside her car.

She peered closer. When Dameon opened the door of the truck and hopped out, she couldn't have been more surprised. She took him for a luxury sedan kind of man.

Dameon noticed her and lifted a hand in greeting.

In addition to driving the truck, he was wearing a pair of jeans and a sweater. He reached into the cab, pulled out a coat, and was shrugging into it as she approached.

She had to tilt her head back to look at the man. And looking wasn't a hardship. Dark brown hair, strong jaw . . .

Stop it, Gracie.

"Good afternoon," she greeted him with as much professionalism as she could muster.

He grinned as he shut the door and reached out to shake her hand.

For a moment, she hesitated. Actually fearing his touch for what it would do to her senses. But then denying a handshake was like a slap in the face.

Sure enough, the moment their palms touched, her body became very aware of the man.

To make matters worse, Dameon closed her hand between both of his. "You're freezing."

"It's not exactly warm out here."

He did the squeeze thing with her hand before letting it go. "At least you're wearing a coat this time."

She couldn't help but smile. "I have gloves in my car."

Once she dumped her purse in the trunk and put her keys in her pocket, she gloved up and grabbed her clipboard and pen.

"Tell me, Dameon, what do you hope to accomplish today?"

He opened his mouth, closed it . . . put a hand in the air and didn't utter a word.

In that moment, she knew he was not thinking about the jobsite.

"With the property," she clarified.

"Right." He dropped his hand. "The land. For a minute there I thought you'd changed your mind about dinner."

She turned away from him to hide her smile. "That is not why we're out here."

When he was silent, she glanced over her shoulder.

"Right." He walked in front of her in the direction she'd just come from. "We really need to know the scope of infrastructure to carry out our plan. What pitfalls and problems you foresee that we haven't taken into account."

For the next thirty minutes they walked the land, and Grace found herself doing all the talking. She pointed out the road improvements. Considering much of the canyon off the main road was gravel and dirt, it was a given that a big part of the build would be concrete. None of the homes were on sewer. The city hadn't built the area with that in mind. The small strip mall that was half occupied was as close as the sewer system ran. "But your desire is to add a commercial space at the far end. That's going to require tying into the city system."

Dameon nodded several times. "Some of the properties have wells."

"And almost all of them are used for irrigation, if at all. While the water table is high through this area, that doesn't mean the wells capture much of anything. I wouldn't count on them. Not unless we have ten years of heavy rain."

They both looked up at the sky that had turned dark gray and threatened exactly what she had said. "And speaking of rain, this is a bigger ordeal." She pointed to the wash.

"The watershed from the canyon," he said for her.

"Right. We'll need soil reports, but I can tell you now, this is a big reason why this canyon hasn't been developed to the extent you're trying to do." She glanced at him out of the corner of her eye. He was scanning the landscape as if he knew exactly what she was going to say. "You need to give the water a place to go. The people who live in the homes on the other side of this often go for weeks at a time without crossing it. The residents out here have tractors and big trucks for a reason."

"We're going to need bridges and culverts to deal with the drainage," he said.

"I hope whoever you paid to scout this area knew what they were doing."

"They did." He looked at her and smiled.

She moved her gaze to her feet and avoided his eyes.

"What about the zoning changes?" he asked.

"I'm sure you're aware that this is residential with an agricultural overlay, giving the residents the right to have farm animals or grow their own grapes."

"I don't see a lot of farming here."

"No, but many have a handful of chickens, the occasional horse or goat. But they can have cows or alpacas or any of the like if they choose. If you attempt to take that away from the neighbors that are here, you're going to get kickback. And chances are you'll lose. Not to mention it's going to take time to work the system."

"We really want to break ground by spring." His voice had dropped and his eyes didn't stop taking in the landscape.

"Removing the agricultural overlay in the housing development you're putting up is doable. Or you can leave it and put it in the HOA that barnyard animals are against the rules. Which brings us to the next concern. The amount of homes you're proposing." She stopped walking and looked at the space around them. "In the past ten, fifteen years, houses have sprung up like weeds. Each subdivision crammed in closer to the next. As people inch out in areas like this, they're looking for more space."

"More space means less profit."

"I know." She lifted a hand in the air. "But if there's one thing I've learned about this community, it's that change comes slow. Maybe not as slow as mid-Texas, but slower than, say, the valley. Dividing these lots up will have to go before the city council."

"Our team didn't think that was going to stop anything."

"It won't stop. But if you don't want to get tied up, and that's why you wanted this meeting today, you come in with a compromise plan if in fact there is pushback on lot size. Ask for the world, but be prepared to scale it back. Unless you want to be attending city council meetings for the next two years."

Dameon stuck his hands in the pockets of his jacket and lifted his face to the sky. "We don't want that either." The first droplets of rain started to fall. "I have a set of plans in the truck I'd like you to take a look at," he said.

"Okay."

They picked up their pace as they walked to the cars.

It didn't take long for Grace's hair to turn to wet curls.

He grabbed the plans out of the truck and fiddled with a set of keys as he attempted to find the right one for the bolted chain-link fence.

"Let me hold that," she said, taking the tube with the plans from under his arm.

By the fourth key, the rain was taking a steady beat.

Grace pulled up her collar to try and keep dry.

Finally, Dameon sprung the lock free, and the two of them half jogged to the front porch of the house.

She shook off the water and waited while Dameon repeated the process to find the correct key for the front door.

Once inside, they both did their best impression of a shaking dog. Grace wasn't sure who laughed first, him or her.

Dameon stopped laughing and stared at her. The kind of look that was going to be followed by something that shouldn't be said, or happen.

She turned around and took in the space. Seventies construction with low popcorn ceilings and orangeish carpet that should have been put out of its misery twenty years ago. Someone had left a couch in the middle of the room that reminded her of Grandma Rose's motif. Brown flowers and dark green accents. "This is perfectly awful," Grace said, looking at the sofa.

"My mother would love it," Dameon said from behind her.

"I thought the same thing about my grandmother."

The room opened to a kitchen that had a large enough counter to spread out the plans. "This will work." Grace opened the canister and removed Dameon's drawings.

He walked to the window and pulled open the blinds to let some light in the room. "I should have kept the power on," he said.

"And encourage squatters?"

He moved to the sink and turned the faucet. Nothing happened. "This is as good a space as any to house the construction office in the first phase." As he spoke, he opened cabinets and walked through the room.

"Is this the first time you've been here?"

"Yup." He walked down the narrow hall.

Grace found herself following him. "How does anyone do that?"

"Do what?"

"Buy a house without seeing it?" She knew it happened. But she'd never felt at liberty to ask someone like Dameon how they did it.

"We bought the land. The house is incidental." He looked above his head and then opened a closet door in the empty room. "And most of the time, they're not in this good of shape."

"Really?"

"Yeah. This was a repo. The owners defaulted on the loan. It went to the bank. Banks hate owning real estate. Most never recouped after the housing market crashed."

"So you came in and bought it sight unseen."

"The land value out here is cheap. Once we're done with it, it will be worth money again. I know the existing neighbors are going to voice opposition, but chances are my PR department will tell them the facts about how we're going to add value to their homes." He skirted past her in the narrow hall and opened another door. "Ohhh," he said, looking inside.

"What?" Grace ducked her head through the doorway. A king-size bed sat in the middle of the room. There wasn't any bedding covering the stain-filled mattress. She turned her nose.

"Do you ever look at a bed in an old house and wonder what stories it can tell you?"

She realized she was standing entirely too close to the man when she had to tilt her head back to look him in the eye. "No," she said. "I look at fireplaces and front windows and wonder how many Christmas trees had been put up and family stories were exaggerated once the adults reached the bottom of the wine bottle." She stepped back.

"I like that much better than my thoughts."

Grace walked back into the kitchen and shrugged off her coat. She wasn't warm, but the weight of it dripping from the rain was making her colder.

Dameon's coat followed hers, and they stood next to each other looking at the plans.

Grace attempted to ignore the fact his shoulder kept brushing hers. Did everything she could to not pull in the scent of rain and masculinity that surrounded him.

She forced her eyes to look at the plans and not the man at her side. Swallowing hard, she realized neither of them had spoken in several seconds.

Dameon's hand scooted closer to hers on the plans, and that's when her brain engaged.

"I've seen these before," she told him without looking up.

She pointed out her concerns and put just enough space between them that she didn't feel the heat of his body.

Time slipped by as she sketched in what she knew he was going to need, at least at this stage. She spent more time poring over the plans than she normally did. It helped that Dameon seemed to be on top of the city's expectations. It quickly became obvious that he didn't sit behind a desk all day long.

Grace wrote side notes on his plans with check boxes that needed to happen first.

"I think you have enough to keep you busy until after the holidays," she told him as she stepped back.

Outside, the skies had turned nearly black. And with the sun dipping low as late afternoon approached, the house was getting dark.

Dameon rolled up the plans, and she handed him the tube to put them in.

"I really appreciate your help."

She reached for her coat. "It is my job."

He took the coat from her hand and opened it for her to step into. The gesture was seamless for him by the looks of it. For Grace, it wasn't something she was accustomed to.

She fumbled her way into the coat and felt his hands linger on her shoulders.

For one brief second she enjoyed his touch.

There must have been something she did to encourage him, because he lowered his fingers just enough to graze her arms. With her back to him, she heard him sigh.

"What can I do to convince you to go to dinner with me?"

She closed her eyes and remembered who she was standing with.

With a twist of her body, his hands had no choice but to fall away. "Dameon—"

"Just dinner. It would be a favor to me. Otherwise I'm going to get on the freeway with everyone else at this hour."

"You really want me to believe the words *just dinner*?" His eyes were saying there wasn't anything "just" about it.

"Maybe more than just dinner. But we have to start somewhere." He took a step closer.

"We have no business starting anywhere." Yet her feet weren't moving away.

He slowly lifted a hand to her face and pressed his palm to her cheek.

She found the room lacking oxygen as she pulled in a sharp breath.

"Your lips say one thing," he said as his thumb traced her lower lip. "But your eyes . . . these eyes are singing a completely different tune." He moved his thumb to her temple.

"I think I read that line in a book somewhere," she whispered. *Move, Gracie . . . get out of his space.*

"Are you suggesting that I'm wrong?" He moved closer. "That if I pressed my fingers to the back of your neck"—he did what he was threatening to do—"that you wouldn't look up at me and open your lips just enough to ask for a kiss?"

She pushed her lips closed, her eyes locked with his.

A small laugh escaped him and he leaned down.

Back away!

Grace opened her mouth. A denial sat on her tongue but wouldn't come out.

Suddenly, the front door of the house crashed open.

CHAPTER NINE

Grace jumped and Dameon twisted around to stand in front of her, shielding her from whatever or whoever had opened the door.

"Gracie?"

With her heartbeat well past her chest and up into her head, she looked around Dameon to the fury of Colin. "What the hell?" She dropped her hands that had grabbed ahold of Dameon's waist and stepped in front of him.

Dameon's arm came out and stopped her.

She pushed his hand aside. "He's my brother," she all but yelled at him.

"Are you okay?" Colin asked.

"Don't I look okay?"

Colin's gaze moved between her and Dameon and back again. "Who's this?"

"What do you mean, 'who's this'? What are you doing here?"

"You didn't answer your phone."

She patted her back pocket and remembered she'd tossed it in her purse that was sitting in the trunk of her car. "It's in my car."

"We were supposed to meet at the Sierra Highway site." By now the heat in Colin's voice had started to ebb.

Grace lost some of her fire as well. "Oh, damn, that's right. I got sidetracked."

"When you didn't answer, I used Friend Finder and saw your phone was up here." Colin had stopped looking at Grace altogether and was staring at Dameon. "In the middle of nowhere, where anything could happen."

"I'm capable of taking care of myself, Colin."

"Considering everything that's happened in the last year, you'll have to forgive my intrusion."

Any heat that was still lingering in her body left. She knew exactly what he was referring to.

Dameon took a step forward and reached out a hand. "I'm Dameon Locke."

For a half a second, it looked like Colin wasn't going to take it.

The men grasped hands and shook. Only Colin didn't let go. "So you're Dameon. I've heard a lot about you."

Oh, no . . . this was not going to happen.

"Oh? Is that right?" Dameon gave her a sideways glance.

The handshaking continued with white knuckles from both of them.

Grace placed her hands over theirs and pushed hard. "Enough."

Their hands broke free, but she couldn't tell who let go first.

Colin found her eyes. She knew she flashed a huge warning for him to shut up, but he was ignoring her.

"So, this is the stalker?"

Her eyes rolled back and she turned to Dameon. "I didn't call you that. Erin did."

Dameon looked at her, his lips holding the slightest grin. "Who's Erin?"

"A friend," she told him.

"Our brother's girlfriend. Who has had her share of stalkers and is pretty good at identifying the like," Colin said.

Grace swiveled so hard she nearly lost her balance. Two strides and she was in her brother's face. "This macho big brother trip was cute when I was sixteen. Now knock it off! Dameon and I are here going over plans for his project. I'm doing my *job*."

"That's not what it looked—"

She lifted her foot and slammed it on her brother's toes.

"Oh, damn, Gracie, that hurt." Colin limped back a step.

"Be happy it wasn't your balls." She stood as tall as she could. Which wasn't much, in light of the fact she was wearing tennis shoes and not heels. "Now . . . thank you for your concern, but kindly shut the hell up."

Colin grunted and put one more dagger in his look at Dameon.

"Next time keep your phone with you," he told her.

She really couldn't hold that against him. "Next time, knock."

He leaned over and kissed her cheek. "Love you."

"Love you, too."

Dameon spoke from behind her. "I'm sorry we met under these circumstances."

She wanted to melt into a puddle and seep into the carpet just to escape the awkwardness of the moment.

"I'm glad to have a face with the name," Colin said.

Grace lifted a fist in Colin's direction and he retreated. "Goodbye, Colin."

She watched as he walked through the rain and climbed into his truck. After he backed out of the driveway, she released a sigh.

"That was, hands down, the most entertaining encounter I've had in at least a decade," Dameon said, laughing.

Thank God he was laughing. She wanted to crawl into a corner and die. "I'm so sorry."

"Is your family Italian?"

"No."

"Are you sure?"

"No, I'm not. But no one has claimed it." She finally dared a look in his direction. Even with the fading light, she saw his grin.

"So, you told Erin about me."

"You're going to make this more awkward, aren't you."

He shook his head. "No. I'm going to hold on to that fact and let it settle for a while."

"Good."

"You wanna tell me what Colin was talking about when he mentioned this last year?"

"It's really not my story to tell and edges on gossip." Not to mention it was still raw for her.

"Considering your brother wanted to yank my hand out of my arm, I'd like to know the context of his concern."

She reminded herself that Dameon was first and foremost a client. And aside from the fact that he had nearly kissed her . . . and she'd nearly let him, he did have some right to know a few things.

"Erin was getting a divorce from her abusive ex. Went so far as to change her name and identity to get away from him." Grace glanced up and saw Dameon's smile fade. "He did in fact stalk her, found her, and nearly killed her."

"Oh, God."

"Erin was living in the guesthouse on Parker's property. Parker and Colin are the ones who just got married. Colin was home then, but by the time they knew what was happening it was too dangerous for him to go in."

"What happened?"

"Erin managed to get ahold of the gun he used against her. She survived. He didn't."

And before Grace even knew of the drama, Erin's ex had manipulated his way into Grace's life. It still made her sick every time she pictured the man. He'd kissed her. In fact, he was the last man who had kissed her.

"Are you okay?" Dameon stepped forward.

"It wasn't that long ago. We're all still raw. Colin's a good guy. He's just protective."

Dameon walked back toward the kitchen. "Rightfully so."

He tugged his coat on and retrieved the plans. "You sure I can't talk you into dinner?"

"Dameon . . ."

"Next time."

"Dameon . . . this isn't . . . we shouldn't—"

He opened the door and placed a hand on her back. "But we both know we almost did," he said close to her ear.

~

Traffic leaving the Santa Clarita Valley wasn't nearly as bad as the cars moving in the other direction. It still it took him over an hour to get to his condo and drop his wallet and keys on his kitchen counter.

Dameon could not stop thinking about Grace. She was a hundred percent different from the women he usually pursued.

She was so damn smart and witty. The need to laugh when in her presence was constant. The scene between her and her brother played like a boomerang video in his head.

And she'd told her friend about him.

When women told their friends about a man, that man was being thought about. Which was exactly what he wanted when it came to Grace.

He crossed to his liquor cabinet and decided he wasn't in the mood to drink alone.

It was past time he had a night with the guys.

Omar picked up on the second ring. "Please don't tell me you're calling because we have problems."

Dameon laughed. "I need that night at the bar. You in?"

"You buying?"

"O'Doul's in thirty minutes?"

"Be there in twenty." Omar hung up and Dameon jumped in the shower.

Twenty-five minutes later he waved at Omar from the doorway of the busy Irish pub. Christmas lights twinkled above the bar, and Irish music drifted in between the noise of the people. With dark wood and salty patrons, O'Doul's was the kind of place no one who wanted to be seen went to. It was a simple place with decent beer on tap and lots of Irish whiskey.

He greeted the bartender by name and moved to the empty stool next to Omar. "I see you started without me."

"I wasn't sure if this was a beer night or shots."

He pulled his jacket from his shoulders and placed it with Omar's. "Let's start with beer."

Omar signaled the bartender, asking for another.

"So, what prompted this impromptu night out?"

Dameon took his seat. "There's a woman."

"And two shots of Jameson, Tommy," Omar added.

Dameon had to laugh.

"I knew there had to be a girl involved. Who is she and why haven't I heard of her before now?" Omar cut right to the chase.

"Her name is Grace and she's an engineer with the city of Santa Clarita."

Omar stopped his beer midway to his lips. "*That's* why you're going out there all the time. I knew there had to be a better reason than you micromanaging the team."

Tommy gave Dameon his beer and brought over two shot glasses and filled them. "Throw some fish and chips in for me, will ya, Tommy?" Dameon asked.

"Make it two," Omar added.

"Settling in for a long haul, are ya?"

"There's a girl," Omar said.

Tommy O'Doul was somewhere in his sixties and had owned the pub since it opened thirty years past. "Is this a celebration shot, or am I leaving the bottle so you can forget her?" he asked.

"Celebration shot," Dameon told him.

Omar's hand darted out and stopped Tommy from taking the bottle. "But you can leave the bottle since Dameon is buying."

"What do you think this is, a date?"

"You did call and ask me out," Omar said with a laugh.

Tommy waved them off, left the bottle, and walked away to put in their food order.

"Okay, keep talking. You obviously have things to say."

"Have you ever met someone you just can't stop thinking about?" Dameon asked before taking the first drink of his beer.

"Yeah. Then I sleep with them and forget their name."

He rolled his eyes. "Which is why you are the first person I thought of when I wanted to come here tonight. I knew you weren't busy."

"I'm busy when I want to be," Omar defended himself.

"Grace is different. She's like this tight ball of confidence and humor. She's trying so hard to deny our attraction."

"Wait, what? Someone is denying the great Dameon Locke?"

"Yes . . . no, not really. She thinks it's wrong since I'm working with the city right now. Conflict of interest."

Omar rested an elbow on the bar and tipped his glass Dameon's way. "She has a point. A conflict for her, not you. You said she was an engineer?"

"Yeah."

"Not to sound sexist, but that's odd, isn't it? Most of the engineers we've dealt with are men. Stoic, humorless men."

When Dameon took a second to think on it, Omar was right. "Analytical personalities. Comes with the job, I guess."

"But not your Grace?"

"No . . . I mean, yes . . . analytical when she's talking about her job and the project. Her mind is going a mile a minute. Like a ticker tape rolling constantly." Dameon tipped his beer back. "But funny."

"And hot, I'm guessing."

The memory of tilting her head back, and the heat in her eyes. "Yeah. Not like Lena." He'd dated Lena off and on for about a year. "Petite, curvy . . . has a girl-next-door thing going."

"That doesn't sound like your type at all."

"Yeah," he huffed. "She has a job."

They both laughed, and Tommy stopped by and dropped off silverware.

"I have two problems, though," Dameon said.

"Other than the fact that her boss might hold it against her if she's seen messing with a client?"

"Okay, three problems."

Omar pushed the shot glass Dameon's way. "Problems require whiskey."

How could he argue with that? They saluted each other and knocked the liquor back. The back of his throat warmed all the way to his stomach.

"The first is her brother." Dameon reenacted the scene at the house from the door barging open to the big brother's handshake and unmistakable instant dislike. "The other issue is her friend thinks I'm a stalker."

"How did that happen?" Omar asked.

"I've been trying to figure that out. I saw Grace at the hotel. But we didn't talk then. The next morning, she walks into the coffee shop, hungover, and I approach her. Monday morning, she walks into the city office and . . ." He stopped. "I did call her from her Facebook page."

Omar nearly spit out his beer. "You what?"

Now that Dameon said it aloud, he realized how the facts stacked up against him. "Holy shit, no wonder her friend thinks I'm stalking her."

Tommy pushed a hot plate in front of both of them and looked at the bottle of whiskey. "You boys nursing this, or are you drinkin'?"

Omar put a finger in the air, signaling another round.

Tommy winked, poured, and walked off.

"First . . . stop using Facebook."

"I figured that out." It had felt genius at the time.

"You need to make good with the brother. And in my experience, if the girlfriends don't like you, you're running uphill the whole time." Omar popped a fry in his mouth, picked up another.

"The girlfriend is dating her other brother."

Omar picked up the second shot. "The whole fam damily is hating on you. You've got some ass kissing to do if you want in with this lady."

Dameon reached for the shot. "Do you know how long it's been since I needed to have anyone approve?" He was pretty sure it was high school and a sixteen-year-old's father was involved.

". . . or you can call Lena."

Just thinking of that put a bad taste in his mouth that a bite of his dinner didn't repel. "I'll start with the brother."

Dameon was formulating a way to do just that as he took the second shot Omar was offering.

CHAPTER TEN

Grace was back in Dameon's house.

Rain fell on the roof like the march of a wartime drum. Nothing natural about it.

His back was to her, but her belly warmed in anticipation of him turning around.

She wanted his kiss even if she shouldn't. And in here . . . in a dream she knew was a dream but could taste the scent of him, she could let Dameon hold her.

Grace placed a hand to his back, and the lights flickered.

He didn't move.

Cold bled through his coat.

He turned, suddenly, and Desmond's hand was on her throat.

Grace woke with a start, her hands reached for her neck. "Not Dameon."

Desmond Brandt, better known as Erin's ex, resurfaced in Grace's dreams.

She rolled out of bed and walked to the bathroom. A flick of a switch and bright light attacked her eyeballs. Grace ran a hand over her neck, still felt his fingers lingering there.

"Stupid," she called her reflection in the mirror. She'd been stupid to ignore his obvious lies. All because he was good-looking and worldly.

Even the memory of him kissing her, something she wished she could erase from her hard drive, brought the feeling of his fingers on her neck.

Then Miah, a beat cop she'd known since high school, and his partner showed up. They were on a routine walk at the far end of the mall. They spotted her with Desmond and everything in his demeanor had changed. He must have felt exposed or nervous. He made a hasty retreat, and the next day Grace learned who he really was. A week later, the man was dead and Erin was in the ICU.

And it could have been her.

She could have been the dead one.

The investigation that followed Desmond's death found pictures of her and Parker with the words *first* and *second* written over the images. The police had been reluctant to tell her the findings, but when they did, it was her father who'd sat down with her and explained what they meant.

"He was a sociopath, Gracie. And if he'd gotten you alone, there's no telling what he would have done."

"Why are you telling me this now?"

Her dad squeezed her hand, and rare tears hovered in his eyes. "Because I can't lose you. You have to be more careful. You're too old for me to ground so you're not seeing the juvenile-hall-bound punk in school anymore."

Grace ran cold water in the sink and shocked her system by saturating a washcloth and rubbing it over her face. She was being more careful all right. To the point of avoiding men in the romantic sense completely.

Until now.

Back in her room she noticed the time.

Three in the morning.

She walked the short hall to the living room and turned on a dim light in the kitchen.

After pouring herself a glass of milk, something her mother always did when she had trouble sleeping, Grace sat on the sofa and pulled a blanket over her lap.

Dameon and Desmond, their names almost identical, but that was where the similarities ended.

Two weeks following the night he died, Grace starting having nightmares. More memories of what had really happened than the one that woke her up tonight.

Having grown up with two older brothers, she'd learned to stand up for herself. Prided herself on being able to pick the bad ones out of the bunch. With Desmond, she never saw it coming. He'd casually approached her while sitting in a bar. She thought she was waiting on a Match date that never showed up. Later, when the police had finished their investigation, she'd been informed that he had created the entire setup using a fake profile. He knew where she was going to be, and knew she was never going to meet her "chosen date."

She'd deleted every dating app she had been on and didn't look twice at men who tried to pick her up in a bar. She'd sworn off the gender altogether.

Grace closed her eyes and tried to squeeze the whole memory from her brain.

Maybe Erin was right about him. Maybe that was why she'd suddenly started having the nightmares again. Maybe Dameon wasn't as innocent as he claimed to be.

Or maybe her memories of Desmond were screwing with her because she was attracted to someone for the first time in nearly six months.

~

It was Sunday, and Grace joined Parker, Colin, Erin, and Matt on their annual walk through Santa Clarita's version of Santa Claus Lane. The homes were decked out in every conceivable Christmas decor, with lights streaming across the street to each other's houses. There were Grinch themes and Disney motifs, fake snow, and trees that appeared to explode out of rooftops. The air was crisp with the scent of a recent rain that simply added to the whole experience.

She knew the minute she walked up to the group that someone was going to mention Colin's run-in with Dameon. If there was one thing her family was notoriously bad about, it was keeping anything to themselves.

To everyone's credit, it took nearly five minutes of hellos and cheek kisses before the first word was uttered. They stood in a circle while Erin pulled on a scarf from the back seat of her car.

"What's this I heard about a compromising position between you and a client in an abandoned house?" The question was from Matt.

The silence that followed gave Grace everything she needed to know. Everyone had already talked about it.

"Thanks, Colin," she said.

He smiled as if he'd proudly accomplished a mighty task. "I'm pretty sure it was you who told each of us to step in if we ever saw you dating someone who wasn't right."

"Was I a part of that conversation?" Erin asked, closing the door of the car.

"No. It was in the hospital waiting room when you were in the ICU," Parker told Erin.

Grace had said those exact words as she was deleting the dating apps on her phone. Her entire family, including her mom and dad, had been there, too.

"First of all, Dameon and I aren't dating. And second—"

"I know what I saw," Colin interrupted her.

"And second . . ." She paused to make sure everyone was listening. "There isn't anything *wrong* with the man. But I want to swing around to the part about *we aren't dating* again."

"I saw how he was looking at you, Gracie. If you're not dating . . . or whatever you're doing, it isn't for his lack of trying," Colin pointed out.

"Even if he was, what's wrong with that?"

Parker tucked her arm into the crook of Grace's and started walking toward the Christmas lights. "Nothing's wrong with that. We're all just a little gun-shy."

Considering the nightmare that had woken her up in the middle of the night, she couldn't be too upset about her family's reaction.

"If you have anything negative on the man, be sure and bring it to my attention. Right now, it seems like everyone is a worried ninny looking out for the fragile single woman in the group."

Colin walked up beside Parker and dropped his arm over her shoulder. Matt and Erin came up behind them.

"My counselor said it was normal for everyone to be overly protective for a while and to try not to take it as a personal insult," Erin told her. "It comes from a place of love."

Parker squeezed Grace's arm and leaned close. "We just love ya."

"I'd feel better if we knew more about the man," Colin said.

"How about you invite him to a family dinner?" Erin suggested.

"Guys, I'm telling you. We're not dating. Yes, he asked me out. But I have enough trouble at the office with Richard and his backhanded slights and suggestions to add an actual anything with a client to fuel his fire."

"I thought Richard had backed off," Matt said.

"He stopped asking me to get his coffee a long time ago. Now he just piles on the work and insinuates that if I can't handle it he will give it to Evan or one of the other *men* on the team."

"That's shitty," Parker said.

They turned the corner, and the entry to the neighborhood lit up the street.

"I can say something to him on Friday at the Christmas party," Colin offered.

"I only see that backfiring on me. But thanks. I can handle Richard."

"Offer stands."

Grace smiled at her brother, then turned to stare at the giant nutcrackers that framed the street. "This gets bigger every year."

"It's crazy!" Erin said.

And just like that, the conversation steered away from Grace and Dameon and onto power bills and electrical grids.

~

Dameon was in his office with spreadsheets and projections sitting in front of him. He'd be lying if he didn't admit to himself that he was nervous. His company had experienced rapid growth over the past four years, equating to more employees, bigger office space, and an increase in overhead. Without Maxwell's investment, they had very little wiggle room. During their growth, Dameon had the opportunity to step back and spread out his personal involvement on each individual jobsite and delegate the daily operations to people he trusted. Could he continue to work like that? One misstep and he'd have to downsize.

His phone rang from his secretary's number. He put it on speaker. "Yes, Pauline?"

"There's a Mr. Hudson on line one. I asked if he had a reason for the call. He insisted you'd take it."

Dameon started to tap the pencil he was using against his desk. "I've got it. Thank you."

His finger hesitated over the call. This had a fifty-fifty chance of going bad. He clicked into the call and put Colin on speaker. "This is Dameon," he answered.

"Good morning. This is Colin, Grace's brother."

"Yes, good morning. I was trying to find a reason to call you myself. Thank you for beating me to it."

"Is that so?" Colin asked.

"Friday was a bit awkward and I wanted to clear the air."

"How did you plan on doing that?"

Colin was a ballbuster, Dameon had to give him that. "I'm not really sure," he said honestly. "Grab a beer, prove by example I'm none of the things that were assumed about me."

It took Colin a minute to respond.

The silence made Dameon want to add something, but instead he let the moment linger.

"Are you suggesting you're not pursuing my sister?"

"No. I'd like nothing better than for Grace to let me take her out. She's determined to make me work for it. Thinks she'll find trouble with her boss."

"If I told you she has legitimate reasons to feel that way, would you back off?" Colin asked.

Dameon actually had to think on that. "I wouldn't want to cause her any problems at work."

"Good."

"But that doesn't mean I'd give up." And why was he having this conversation with her brother? "I may have to lie low until my company is through the city's red tape."

"That's part of the reason for my call."

He waited. "I'm listening."

"The city hosts an annual holiday party. It feels more like a networking event than a personal office gathering. Many of the city's brass attend. I thought perhaps if you came you could talk to the other departments, city council members . . . you know, the people who have to give you a green light on your project. Perhaps it would expedite or at least give a face to your name when it's time for their signatures."

Dameon couldn't help but feel like he was missing something. "That sounds like a perfect idea. Is there a reason why you'd help me with that?"

He really wanted to hear that Grace had put him up to it.

"I'm a nice guy," Colin said, nearly laughing as he did.

"Who practically took my hand off when we met," Dameon called him out.

"I have reason to be jumpy."

"You're referring to the incident with Erin and her late husband?" Dameon asked.

"Grace told you about that?"

"She did."

Again, there was silence.

"Then you understand my suspicion of anyone pursuing my sister in less than normal ways."

That didn't sound right. "I'm not sure I'm following you."

"You reached out to her on Facebook, right?"

"I did."

"That's strange, don't you think?" Colin asked.

"A lot of people use Messenger for texting."

"But you called her."

"Okay, yeah. But in my defense, I like your sister. And I'm pretty sure the feeling is mutual."

He heard Colin sigh. "Don't you see the similarities?"

"Between calling Grace on Messenger and Erin's husband trying to kill his wife? No, Colin, I don't see the similarities."

"No. I don't mean that. I mean between you using Facebook to contact Grace and Brandt using a dating app to approach her."

Dameon was completely lost. "Who is Brandt?"

"Desmond Brandt. The man who tried to kill Erin and who manipulated his way into Grace's life."

Dameon's jaw slacked. "What?"

Colin started to stutter. "Oh . . . no. She didn't tell you that part, did she?"

All the fragmented pieces of the conversation swirled like leaves blowing in the wind. Finally, they settled into a neat little pile. "You're telling me that the dead man used Grace to get to his ex?" The hair on his neck stood on end.

"Sh-shit. Not exactly. But, oh, damn . . . Grace is going to kill me."

"What do you mean, 'not exactly'?"

"Oh, no . . . no more from me. You're going to have to get the details from Grace."

"At the Christmas party you're suggesting I go to."

"Right. That. Only it probably wouldn't be a good idea to mention this phone call at the party."

"So I just show up at a random party without an invitation . . . How does that take away from my stalker reputation with your family?" Especially now that he knew the depth of the stalker concern for Grace.

"You're a resourceful man, I'm sure you can find an invitation if you try hard enough."

Yes, he was all that. "Tell me one thing, Colin . . . Did he hurt her?"

Dameon held his breath while he waited for the answer.

"Not physically. But she's not completely the same since it all happened."

Even that hurt Dameon's heart.

"Can I ask you something?" Dameon asked.

"Yeah."

"If you thought I was anything like this man, why ask me to this party in the first place?"

"To determine for myself if you are."

That answer Dameon could live with.

CHAPTER ELEVEN

There was a reason Monday memes found themselves on coffee cups, T-shirts, and social media.

Mondays sucked, especially when the weekend slid by without enough restful sleep to make up for a shitty workweek.

Grace sat in a twice monthly meeting with the engineers. Richard was at the head of the table, she and Evan took one side, while Lionel, Adrian, and two interns sat on the other. Because they often worked jointly on projects, they regularly held meetings where they could all talk about the progress or issues and iron things out in a group setting. They all had their strengths in different areas of engineering, and it was here that work was delegated.

She'd made a conscious decision to wear outfits that afforded her the ability to put on high heels on days like this. Wearing the extra few inches gave her the boost she needed to look her colleagues, or better yet, her boss, in the eye.

Richard had started with Lionel and Adrian before moving on to Evan.

"Where are we with the Sierra Highway situation? Are we breaking ground or did the landowner cooperate?" Richard asked.

Evan looked at Grace. "I think Grace has this one," he said.

"I told him he had to the end of business today to give us the name of the contractor he was using. But I wouldn't be surprised if he found some stall tactic to give him more time."

"He's had months," Evan said.

"I know. The man is combative," Grace told them.

"Aren't they all when the city is coming down on them?" Adrian asked with a smirk.

"Too much for you to handle, Hudson?" Richard asked.

Evan sat forward. "That's not what she said, Richard. The man's an asshole. No respect for any of us. I agree with Grace on this one. He's going to stall."

"I gave him a firm deadline. I've already drawn up what needs to happen. All I need is the okay to move forward and get a crew on this." Grace said her piece and waited for Richard's okay.

"Put it in January's budget," Richard said.

Grace felt a little victory knowing she could take it to the next level.

Evan went on to talk about one of his lead projects that was wrapping up and another that needed more hands.

Richard approved and turned to Grace.

Like the others, Grace started with the most pressing and ended with the most recent. That being Dameon's site. She talked about the scope of the project and the pieces their department would be involved in. "I know that Dameon wants to break ground on this by spring. In order to accommodate him, I'm going to need more hands on this. The relocation of the commercial space is a job all by itself."

After everything she said, Richard only had one question. "Dameon? You mean Mr. Locke."

She cautioned herself to not hold her pencil too tight or risk breaking it. "Yes, Richard, I mean *Dameon* Locke." She found herself in a staring match with him.

Evan, her right hand, offered his assistance. "I can work on the commercial buildings."

"Thanks, Evan." She tore her eyes away from her boss and looked at Adrian. "Didn't you do a soil report recently for San Francisquito Canyon?"

"Been over a year now," Adrian said.

"Can you find it for me? Might save some legwork."

"No problem."

Richard finally spoke. "Looks like you have it all under control, Hudson."

His tone said he wasn't happy. "It's always good to get a jump start on the New Year." Having accomplished what she wanted out of the meeting, Grace sat back and rested her hands in her lap.

Evan followed her back to her office and waited until the door was closed before saying what both of them were thinking. "What the hell is up with him?"

"Don't tell me you're just now clueing in."

"Okay, he's always a hard-ass but today was over the top."

"Starting with he always addresses everyone before me. He constantly attempts to make me sound inadequate or inappropriate. He calls everyone in this office by their first name, and I'm Hudson." She plopped down in the chair behind her desk.

Evan took the chair on the other side. "Call him out. Start talking gender discrimination."

She rolled her head back. "I'm not playing that game. I don't know if it's gender or personal." Which was a complete lie. She'd never done a damn thing to Richard that he would hold against her. "Besides, once you go down that road, finding a job after is near to impossible."

Evan shrugged. "Why do you think I keep my personal life personal?"

Grace huffed. She'd known for years that Evan was gay. "You don't have to pretend with me."

"I know. It's just easier to keep it separate."

She pushed her chair closer to her desk. "I have a feeling he'd be more comfortable with your sexuality than my plumbing."

He laughed, leaned forward. "Look on the bright side, the man will retire long before us."

"If I can outlast him. I have to admit, I've done a few online searches." Though there was no guarantee she'd be treated any better somewhere else.

"Can't blame you." Evan waved a hand in the air. "Hand over the Locke drawing. I'll make a copy and look at your notes."

Grace walked over to her files, pulled the shelf with Dameon's plans, and found the ones Evan needed. "Thanks. I appreciate you stepping up."

"No problem. You've been on the Sokolov crap without me. Far as I see it, I owe ya."

She rolled the plans and handed them over. "You don't owe me."

"Debatable." Evan headed for the door, hesitated. "Are you bringing a plus-one on Friday?"

"You know I haven't dated in months."

"Cryin' shame. That dead guy is not an indicator that you're not picky or smart about your dates."

"Am I that transparent?" She thought she'd done a decent job of hiding her feelings.

"Educated guess. You've had lots of plus-ones and are always quick to point out their replacements. I haven't seen that from you since . . ."

"I know. I'm just not ready."

He winked. "Don't give the dead guy any power, Grace. You're too young to start collecting cats."

That made her smile. "I don't even have one, let alone a collection."

Her phone rang, cutting off their discussion. "Bye, Evan." She lifted the receiver. "Grace Hudson," she said.

"Good morning, Grace." Dameon's voice was smooth silk.

"Good morning."

Evan looked over his shoulder as he left the office.

She placed her hand over the receiver. "Shut the door."

He walked out, and Grace turned back to her phone call.

"Am I interrupting something?" Dameon asked.

"No. It's okay."

"Good. Listen, I'm going to be in town tomorrow. I'd like to discuss some things."

"I'm pretty busy tomorrow."

"What about your lunch? Maybe you'll let me buy."

She lowered her voice as if the walls were listening. "Is this your way of taking me out when I keep saying no?"

He hesitated long enough to answer her question. "You have to eat."

"I actually have a thing . . . tomorrow. At my lunchtime."

"A thing?"

"It's important."

"I'll drive you to your thing."

"Dameon."

"I'll settle for your cell phone number."

She shook her head. "You have my work cell."

"Do you really want me calling that after work hours? I'm not sure if your phone is ever audited, but . . ."

The man was persistent.

"Fine." She rattled off her number.

"It has never taken me so long to get a girl's number."

That made her grin. "I'm sure they throw them at you often."

"I wouldn't say that."

She pushed aside the meeting notes. "Unless there's something pressing, I really need to get back to work."

"I'll be on the lookout for something pressing."

"Why does that not surprise me?"

"Because you're smart. Have a nice day, Grace."

She was getting used to hearing her name from his lips.

"Goodbye, Dameon."

She hung up and picked up the folder she'd been working on before the meeting with a smile.

When her personal cell buzzed on her desk with a text message, she knew who it was before looking.

Making sure this is you.

You're incorrigible.

He sent a winking emoji.

Yeah . . . it was probably best that those types of text messages weren't on the city phone. Richard would probably shit a pumpkin if he saw anything flirtatious.

CHAPTER TWELVE

Dameon had three days to secure an invitation to the holiday party, leaving him few options. He watched Grace exit the office building at noon sharp.

"If you're going to be accused of stalking, might as well do it." He really felt like a perv.

Instead of climbing into a car, she headed toward a strip mall.

Following her would be a dead giveaway, so instead he drove the short distance and caught a glimpse of her entering one of the businesses. He parked his car and walked a little farther than where he had noticed Grace disappear into a storefront. As he moved closer, he slowed his pace. It was one of two doors.

The first one was some sort of check-cashing location. He glanced inside and didn't see any sign of her, so he moved to the next and saw her kicking off her shoes.

"A nail salon? You gotta be kidding me." There was no way he could pretend to bump into her inside a freaking nail salon.

She sat in a lounge chair and put her feet in the water.

Dameon stared.

He realized someone inside the shop was watching him, so he pushed inside. *Act casual.*

"Grace? Is that you?"

With the call of her name, her head shot up. "Dameon?"

"I thought that was you." Several sets of eyes moved his way. There was a woman sitting at a counter with her hand inside some kind of light. One of the employees wheeled a stool by Grace's chair and adjusted the water pouring in.

"What are you doing here?" she asked.

"I was, ah . . ." He pointed a thumb out the door. "Just at the . . ." Shit, he had no idea what was in the shopping center to say he'd been at. "So this was your *thing* today?"

Suddenly it was Grace in the hot seat. Her cheeks turned red. "It's important."

"Do you have an appointment?" The question came from one of the employees.

"I'm sorry, what?" The question caught him off guard.

"An appointment." He shook his head.

It was Dameon's turn to feel heat in his cheeks.

The woman getting her nails painted started to laugh.

He looked up at Grace, who was hiding a smile.

"I can sit you next to your friend," the employee insisted.

"I'm sorry. I don't . . ."

"She wants to know if you want a pedicure," Grace explained.

God no.

He looked around, completely out of place. "Uhm."

"Well, you can't just stand there," Grace told him.

"Can we talk?" he asked.

Grace looked at the empty seat beside her.

Son of a bitch.

"Yeah, okay." Someone somewhere was cutting his man card in half.

The woman smiled, lifted the armrest on the chair, and encouraged him to sit.

He toed off his shoes before slipping into the seat.

He noticed Grace's smile before she removed a remote from a pocket on the side of the chair.

"This is how you spend your lunch hour?" he asked.

"It's close, and noon is always a good time."

He started to sit back while the employee turned on the water. That's when it occurred to him that he needed to take off his socks and roll up his pants. Which had to be the stupidest thing he'd done all year.

Once he knew his dress pants weren't going to get wet, he put his pale feet in the water. One toe in and he yanked it out. "Hot."

The employee stuck her whole hand in the water, looked at him with a *you gotta be kidding me* expression, and then turned the dial.

"It's cold outside." And he wasn't used to taking his shoes off in public places unless he was buying new ones.

The woman at Grace's chair pulled one of her feet out of the water and started removing the polish from Grace's toenails.

Dameon tested the water again, deemed it comfortable, and sat back.

"Let me guess. You've never done this before?" Grace asked.

"Men don't do this kind of thing."

The seat doubled as a massage chair, and Grace's whole body arched as the roller ran down her spine. Dameon tried not to stare at her chest as it heaved forward.

"I see guys in here all the time," Grace told him.

"Really?" Because he didn't know anyone with a penis that had pedicures.

"All the time."

"Why do I get the feeling you're pulling my leg?"

Grace spoke to the woman doing her toes. "Nell, you get men in here every day, right?"

Nell nodded and smiled.

"So what did you want to talk about?" Grace asked.

Dameon wiggled his toes in the water and pressed a button on his remote. The chair started moving forward, which didn't seem right. "Uhm . . . how do I get this thing to go back?"

Grace reached over and pressed the right button. The words on the remote were worn off from years of use. "Sit back," she told him before putting the chair in motion.

Suddenly his body was heaving just like Grace's. It actually felt kinda good.

He wiggled his shoulders side to side. "That's not bad."

"An hour of stress release," Grace told him as she leaned her head back and closed her eyes.

He was insanely happy there was zero chance of anyone he knew seeing him in there.

"I'm moving to town," he announced.

Grace's eyelids shot open. "You're what?"

"Mainly weekends. Probably be a few weekdays once things get rolling. Called DWP and had the water and power turned back on at the house."

"In the canyon?"

He nodded. The employee at his feet tapped the space where Grace had placed a foot and looked at him. When he didn't move, she gently tugged on one of his legs until he had a foot perched like Grace. She drizzled some kind of cream on his toes, grabbed a pair of nail clippers, and went to work.

"Dameon," Grace said his name, pulling his attention back to her.

"Yes. The house with the grandma couch. I thought it would be more convenient than me driving back and forth to the city or staying at the hotel. I already own the place, might as well make use of it. I'll set up the back bedrooms as offices, use the den as workspace."

"So you plan on sleeping there?"

"Yeah." What was the woman doing now? It looked like she was clipping skin away from his toenails, but he didn't feel a thing. He pointed down and asked, "Is that normal?"

"Yes," Grace said. "What brought that on?"

"I thought if maybe I experienced the area for more than an hour at a time, I might better grasp what's going to work." All of which was true, but not the main reason he had a small crew of workers at the house that morning to clear out the left-behind bed and odds and ends throughout the place.

"That's going above and beyond, don't you think?" Grace asked.

He stopped looking at his feet and directed his attention to her. "Maybe. I need this job to go smoothly, Grace. Not going to sugarcoat it. If there was a place I could meet all the essential players that I'm going to be dealing with over the next year to make this project happen, I'd jump on it."

"You sound nervous."

He decided it wouldn't hurt to give her a few facts. "I'm responsible for a lot of employees. My main investor pulled out. And while my company has the funds to do this, it would be a huge weight off my shoulders if I could network with some of the players."

"You mean schmooze."

"Yeah," he said with an unapologetic nod.

"Is that what you're doing with me?"

He lost his smile. "No." There were a lot of things he wanted to do with her, but schmoozing wasn't on the list.

"So you're sitting in here getting a pedicure, *not* schmoozing?"

The chair started pounding his back. "I'm here doing this because you won't say yes to dinner."

Grace rolled her eyes.

Nell laughed but didn't comment while she worked on Grace's feet.

"C'mon, Grace . . . you're my only friend in town. You must know someplace this circle of people spend time." The employee moved on to his other foot after all but pushing the first one back in the water.

"There's a holiday event this Friday," she told him.

He tried not to smile and give away his excitement. "Oh? Who's going to be there?"

"You never know who will show up. With free food and alcohol, a lot of the people you're going to deal with will be there."

"How do I get an invitation?" he asked.

"It's not that formal, but I can put your name down. Different investors have been known to come. The who's who of the community will be there."

His foot was plopped back in the water, the other one was lifted out. Next thing he knew, the woman was scraping it with some kind of sanding block. Each pass made him jump.

Grace started to giggle.

"It tickles," he told her while trying to stay still through the torture. "What are you doing, anyway?" he asked the woman at his feet.

"Scraping dead skin."

He didn't like the sound of that. Worse, he didn't like the feeling of that. He turned his attention back to Grace. "So, you'll pass on the time and place of this event?" he asked for confirmation.

"I'm happy to." Grace leaned back and closed her eyes as the woman at her feet poured lotion on her leg and started to rub.

"Are you going to be—"

Her palm in the air stopped him midsentence. "No talking during the best part."

Much as he wanted to keep going, he found his leg oiled up and hands running up and down his calf.

The best part didn't last nearly as long as he'd have liked.

"Yes, I'm going. It's the only office party we have, even if it's a free-for-all event."

"Is it formal?"

"You mean black tie?"

He nodded.

"We're not that kind of city."

Nell started applying a bright red polish on Grace's toes. For one brief, fanciful moment, Dameon imagined her foot rubbing the side of his while they were tangled up in sheets.

"So you'll go?"

He blinked away the vision of her lying next to him. "What? Yeah. Of course. Wouldn't miss it."

"You want polish?"

Dameon looked at his feet and the woman waving a clear nail polish in the air.

"No. I'm good."

Grace started to laugh. "Men get polish, too."

"I call bull on that," he said.

She kept laughing.

His feet were dried and his pants rolled back down. The woman thanked him and walked away.

Dameon waited until Grace's toes were painted and carefully tucked into a pair of sandals. He stood and reached for his wallet as he approached the desk where he'd noticed the other woman check out a few minutes before. "Both of us," he said, pointing to Grace.

He thought he'd get an argument from her, but found silence.

She looked at him with innocence. "What? You yammered through my stress relief. The least you can do is pay for it."

That's the sarcasm he was growing to appreciate from the woman.

Nell told him a price and he handed her his credit card.

The transaction went through and he put the card back in his wallet.

He started toward the door.

Grace stopped him. "You need to give them a tip."

"Oh, of course." He reached for his wallet again and whispered, "What's appropriate?"

She smiled. "Ten each."

Considering the bill was less than fifty, he thought that was a bit much.

"And it *is* the holidays," Grace added.

He removed two twenties and handed one to each employee.

The cash disappeared quickly with thank-yous and smiles.

He opened the door for Grace and followed her out. "I just over tipped them, didn't I?" he asked.

Grace giggled. "Yup."

"And men don't go in there, do they?"

"Well . . . it's cheaper than a podiatrist when you're on a fixed income," she pointed out.

He cringed. "That's what I thought."

He walked beside her.

"I'm sure my brothers have had pedicures."

"Really?"

"No. They wouldn't be caught dead in there." She started to laugh as if she'd been holding it in for the last hour.

It was worth it, he decided, just to hear her happy. "I'm never going to live this down, am I?"

She placed her hand over her stomach with laughter. "Nope."

They stopped at the edge of the strip mall.

"This was fun, but I need to get back to work."

Dameon wanted to pull her in for a hug. More, he wanted to kiss her. He shoved his hands into his pockets instead. "I'll see you Friday."

"I guess so. I'll text you the information." Her eyes were searching his. "I gotta go."

"Right."

She turned away.

"Wait."

"Yeah?" She looked at him again.

"Where's the best place to buy a bed in town? I can use Grandma's sofa, but the bed needs to be replaced."

"There's a mattress store on the Old Road."

He knew where that was. "Thanks."

"No problem."

She turned again.

"Oh, and Grace?"

"Yeah?"

He glanced down at her feet. "I like the red."

And just like that, her cheeks matched the paint on her toes.

CHAPTER THIRTEEN

Concentrating at work became a chore when Grace kept remembering the maze of expressions on Dameon's face during his virgin pedicure. Absolutely priceless. She wished she had known it was coming so she could have set up a secret camera to record it.

Before it slipped her mind, she sent Dameon a picture of the invitation that went out to the masses for the holiday event and called to leave a message for the coordinator to add his name to the list of attendees.

She no sooner hung up the phone than her cell buzzed.

I feel the need to attend a boxing match after today.

She laughed, texted him back. Do you feel like a girl now?

What can I do to convince you to keep today a secret?

Grace sat back in her chair and looked at her drying toenails. My price is steep.

Name it!
Never mind. I'll hold onto the information to lord over you.
I see how this works. Blackmail.

She couldn't stop smiling. We all have our ways and means. Now go away. I have real work to get to.

Grace stared at her phone, knew she was flirting, but couldn't seem to stop herself.

Thirty minutes before quitting time, Richard walked into her office without so much as a knock.

No hello, no excuse me, he jumped right in with his demands. "I need you to go by the Sierra Highway site today."

She looked outside. The sun was already low on the horizon. "Why?"

"Mr. Sokolov called my office, said he had a plan that doesn't require the city to step in."

Grace felt her pulse rising. "I told him end of business yesterday."

"He said you told him he had until next Monday."

"Richard . . . he—"

"If it will save us time and upfront money, we're going to do it." He waved to the clock. "You have time."

No, actually, she didn't.

"He said five o'clock." Richard walked away, putting any argument she had to rest.

She dropped her pen onto the desk and pushed the chair back. A stream of words ran in her head but didn't escape her tongue.

Not only was she not dressed for an on-site meeting, she hadn't brought the right coat to be traipsing outside. Especially once the sun went down. Even though she lived close enough to change, there wasn't enough time if she was going to make it to the site by five. Not during rush hour.

She powered down her computer, grabbed her sweater and purse, and left the office.

Grumbling all the way across town, Grace arrived at five minutes past five. Instead of parking on the street, she pulled into the mobile home complex and parked on the side of the road.

Sokolov's car wasn't there.

She removed her cell phone from her purse, glanced at the time to see that it matched her car's, and swiveled in her seat.

The wind had picked up, and the sun was long past warming up the day.

She was going to give the man ten minutes and then she was out of there.

Two cars drove past. Their lights shined inside her car, but kept going.

One minute to her self-imposed deadline, the dark sedan pulled in behind her. She was actually disappointed. Unable to avoid the man, she stepped out of her car.

It wasn't full dark, but it was getting awfully close.

Mr. Sokolov pushed out of his car and pulled at his pants as if making room in the crotch. The man was disgusting. "Nice to see the city jumping to meet with me," he said instead of a simple hello.

She wanted to contradict him, but he had a point.

"Do you have plans for me to look at? Or a contractor for me to meet?"

Because standing in the cold, dark mobile home park with a man she loathed wasn't going to last long if he was there stalling.

"I had my guy write something up."

"Let's see it."

"You're an impatient little thing, aren't you?" His voice felt like acid down her spine.

She crossed her arms over her chest, cell phone tight in her hand.

"It's late, Mr. Sokolov."

"Okay, okay . . ." He rounded his car, opened the door to the back seat, and pulled out rolled-up papers she assumed were plans.

He unrolled them on the hood of his car and used his cell phone as a flashlight.

Grace set her phone on the hood and used both hands to hold the plans in place.

Even though she didn't have her drawings with her to compare, she knew at first glance the scale wasn't right. "You've shrunk the scale," she said.

"These are almost identical to what you gave me."

She pointed to the guidepost she used as the cornerstone of the plan. "This is where it needs to start." She moved her finger to where his plan began. "Not here."

"That's not what you told me before." He was so close she could smell the tobacco on his breath.

"There's nothing here about material or infrastructure."

"We'll get to that later." He stood too close, so she sidestepped away.

"There is no later. This meeting was to offer a solid plan and the name of the contractor you're using." Her gaze moved around the plans. She flipped the giant paper to see an empty one underneath. No name or contractor's license number anywhere to be seen. It was as if he scribbled the drawing himself.

"We're *negotiating*." He'd moved closer, his eyes kept in constant contact with her chest.

Grace stood as tall as she could and marched in the gravel to the same point she had a week ago. She touched the pole. "Right here. This is where it starts." She stormed a couple of yards away to where his plan indicated. "Not here."

"There's got to be something we can do to make this work," he said. "Some way to work this out." He reached for his back pocket and removed his wallet.

Did he really think she'd take a bribe?

"It is the holidays and I'm guessing the city doesn't pay as well as the private sector."

Grace shook her head. "Don't insult me." She kept her distance. Her heartbeat alone told her it was best to keep the man where she could see him.

He waved his wallet in the air. "The sooner you realize the way the world really works, the better, little lady."

"I've had just about enough of you and your overinflated ego."

His half-cocked smile slid. He shoved his wallet back where he found it and rolled up his plans. "You're making a mistake."

She marched back to her car, ready to swing if he attempted to touch her.

As she passed, he sucked in a sharp breath, jolted, and slapped the plans against his legs.

The action made her jump and nearly stumble.

She glared at him, and he started to laugh.

"Someone's on edge," he said.

Inside her car, she immediately locked the doors and turned over the engine. Gravel spit in all directions as she drove away.

Half a mile down the road she looked at her hands shaking against the steering wheel. "Calm down," she told herself. He was trying to scare her, and he'd succeeded.

And that pissed her off.

She needed to vent. Yell at someone who would take her side.

She thought of Parker. But Parker would tell Colin, and Colin would turn caveman. Or tell Matt, who would make it two cavemen. Worse, they might say something to their dad. Retired cop or not, her dad would bring in his friends, and next thing you know the whole thing is blown up and she'd be branded a problem employee once word got out.

Thinking rationally was how she needed to proceed. Mindful action. Calm action.

But all she wanted to do was scream *asshole* at the top of her voice.

She pressed the wireless call button on her steering wheel.

The car made a noise but didn't ask for a command.

She did it again,

While she drove down the busy street, she fumbled in her purse for her cell phone. Her hand reached it and she pulled it out to see if the battery had died.

Realizing it was her work phone, she dropped it in her lap and dug for the other one. Not feeling it, she slapped the space around her purse in the passenger seat.

Her mind flashed to her setting it down to look at Sokolov's shitty plans, and she started to panic.

Did Sokolov notice her phone? Did he grab it? Did it slide off his car and was in the middle of the road?

She needed to go back and look.

What if he was still here?

He wouldn't be, she argued with herself.

But the voice in her head said he might be.

She waited for a long line of red taillights at an intersection before grabbing her work phone.

Calling her family was out.

Calling her brothers' girlfriend and wife was out.

Before she lost her nerve, she found Dameon's number and dialed.

"Well, this is a pleasant surprise."

Just hearing the levity in his voice helped her relax. "Dameon."

"What's wrong?"

Was she that obvious?

Grace took a deep breath and steadied her voice. "It's nothing, really. Are you still in town?" She didn't give him time to answer. "You drove back to the city, didn't you? It's okay—"

"I'm still here," he interrupted her. "Where are you?"

"Soledad and Bouquet Canyon. Not far from you."

"I'm not at the house. What's wrong, Grace?"

"It's kind of a long story. I lost my phone. I'm pretty sure where it is, but I . . . I don't want to go back to get it alone. I'd ask my brothers, but they'd freak." She should just forget the phone and get another one.

"Why would they freak, Grace?"

Traffic started to move. Instead of heading up the canyon to Dameon's house, she turned into the long line of traffic headed toward the mall. "They just would. Can you help me out?"

"Where can I pick you up?"

"I'm headed home to change." She gave him her address. He told her he'd be there in twenty minutes. Grace thanked him and disconnected the call.

Ten minutes later she walked into her condo, dropped her purse on her coffee table, and sat down. She was still shaking. Partly because it was cold walking into her place, but she knew that wasn't all of it.

Adrenaline was dumping into her system like a flood.

She hated that the man intentionally intimidated her. And that it worked. For years, she'd made up for her short stature with confidence and the occasional attitude. Her father had taught her to punch with her elbow and not her fist for maximum effect. Having two older brothers meant she knew how to take a good ribbing and deliver one as well.

Yet it seemed like lately she'd lost her edge when dealing with disrespectful men. Richard wasn't anywhere close to what Sokolov had just pulled, but the lines were blurry as far as she saw it.

Something needed to change.

She stood to go splash water on her face and change when her doorbell rang.

Dameon stood on the other side, his chest heaving like he'd run up the stairs.

"You didn't have to rush."

He stepped inside and placed both hands on her shoulders. He looked her up and down. "Are you okay?"

"As soon as I calm down, I'm going to be livid." She tried to smile.

His hands slid around her and in the next breath, she was pressed up against his chest. Much as she should probably pull away, she didn't. Her arms wrapped around his waist, and any adrenaline left in her system spilled out.

She heard Dameon sigh. "I got ya."

He held her in the open doorway of her condo and she let him.

A light from across the courtyard went on and broke the spell. "Come in," she said as she pulled away.

He followed her inside.

She looked down at herself and back to him. Gone was the laughing, jovial man who was constantly trying to take her out. Replacing him was Mr. Concerned and Worried. His lips a straight line, his eyes searching hers. She pointed toward the back of her condo. "I, ah . . . need to change. Make yourself at home."

Dameon ran a hand through his hair and removed his jacket.

In her room, Grace looked at her reflection in the mirror. Her face was a mask of white, no color at all. No wonder Dameon was looking at her like that. She looked like she'd seen a ghost.

It took her less than five minutes to throw on a pair of jeans and a sweater. She ran a brush through her hair and splashed the required water on her face. Looking slightly better and feeling more grounded, Grace walked back into her living room and found Dameon in her kitchen. He'd found a bottle of whiskey and had poured some into a glass.

He noticed her and pushed the glass her way. "This will help."

She wasn't about to argue. "Thanks."

"Don't thank me, it's your whiskey."

That put a brief smile on her lips. The liquor was warm going down and molten once it reached her stomach. She finally released a breath that didn't feel jacked up in her throat. She sat on the barstool at her counter. "I needed this."

"Grace . . ."

She held up her drink. "I'm getting there." She took another sip of the liquor. "I'm afraid what I'm going to say will sound stupid."

"I haven't known you long, but *stupid* isn't a word I would use to describe you."

She grinned, looked away. "Half an hour before quitting time, my boss, Richard, walked into my office, said I needed to meet with a landowner at five. A real prick of a guy who hasn't maintained the road leading into his mobile home complex for years, and after last year's storms, it's impassable in the rain. He'd been warned multiple times that if he didn't get it fixed, the city was coming in to do it for him." She looked up to see Dameon staring at her. "I met with the guy last week, gave him his final warning. He was supposed to get everything in to us yesterday by five. Today is a day late. I'm ticked, but I go."

She took the last sip in her glass.

Dameon took the glass and poured more.

"I get there. He's not there. He shows up fifteen minutes late. He rolls out his plans. Bullshit stall tactics I knew were coming. He's all *little lady* this, and *I'm sure we can work something out.* He stands a little too close . . . you know, intimidation tactics. I put some distance between me and him, point out once again what we need, and he starts waving his wallet in the air as if he's offering me a bribe."

Dameon continued to stare, his jaw tight.

"I'm pissed and I've had it with this guy. I tell him I'm done and walk back to my car. But my dad is a retired cop, so I give him space. Give myself space. I walk by and he does this jump thing." She mimicked Sokolov's movements. "I nearly screamed. It's dark and cold and the guy's an asshole. I get in my car and I leave. And I'm pissed that he got to me. Like I shouldn't scare so easily. I'm even more livid that he knows he got to me. And it's then I realize that I left my phone on the hood of his car. I don't even know if he noticed it. For all I know it's on the ground and been run over a hundred times by now."

Her eyes met Dameon's.

And he was pissed. Nose flaring, short breaths, white-knuckled fist gripping the neck of the whiskey bottle to the point she thought it would break pissed.

He released his hand on the bottle and laid it flat on the counter. "Let's go get your phone," he said in a voice so calm it was scary.

"It might not be there."

"We won't know until we look."

She stood, glad to feel steadier than when she walked in. After pulling a long coat from her closet, she grabbed her purse and keys. Dameon opened the door and waited for her. Once the deadbolt was locked, she let him lead her to his car. His hand stayed on the small of her back the whole time.

CHAPTER FOURTEEN

It took an incredible amount of restraint to keep his shit together. He knew when Grace called that something had to have gone down for her to cave and call him. Dameon knew he wasn't at the top of her speed dial . . . yet. She further showed him how scared she was when she let him hold her. And now, when he was calmly driving in the direction she told him and paying attention to the speed limits when he wanted to pull a Mario-Fucking-Andretti to get there, he was showing restraint. And Grace sat quietly in the passenger seat of his truck. He hoped the bastard had hung around. He'd gladly ask Omar for bail money to drive his fist into the man's face.

Men who went out of their way to intimidate women were some of the lowest creatures out there.

"Are you okay?" he asked.

"I was going to ask you the same thing."

He could lie. "I'm not a violent man," he told her.

She sighed. "Good."

"But I really want to break something right now."

She reached out and placed her hand on his arm. "You can't. If he's still there, you can't."

He wasn't about to make that promise.

"Dameon, I didn't call my brothers because that's exactly what they'd do."

"Have I told you how much I like your brothers?"

"You've only met one," she said.

"What's your other brother's name?"

"Matt."

"I like Matt. Nice guy. Takes care of his family." He glanced in his rearview mirror. "How much farther?"

"Before you get to the last light, there's a dark driveway on your left. Dameon . . ."

He pushed the speed limit since traffic had eased up.

"Dameon?"

"Yeah?"

She squeezed his arm. "Promise me."

"I have a younger brother. He's kind of useless now. Never really grew up. But when we were kids, we had each other's back. If someone messed with him at school, they messed with me. That sounds a lot like how you describe your brothers."

The first light cooperated, the second one didn't.

"Dameon, I'll lose my job."

He turned his head and looked at her. He wanted to tell her that if she lost her job, he had her back. But that's not what she wanted to hear.

"I won't make you sorry you called me," he told her.

That seemed to be enough for her. He turned into the gravel drive at a slow pace.

"He's not here," Grace said with a sigh.

At least Dameon didn't have to worry about breaking his word with her.

"Our cars were parked over there." She waved a finger in the air. "Stop here and leave your lights on."

He put the truck in park, left the engine running, and jumped out.

Grace briskly walked across the drive and concentrated on the ground. "We were here." She spread her arms out. "I put the phone on top of his hood right about here."

They searched the ground in silence.

Dameon looked far beyond where Grace said she'd last seen it. He walked around his truck and to the edge of the drive through the dry ditch. When he looked back at Grace, he imagined her there with the asshole who scared her. The place was dark. The closest mobile homes were equally dark, as if the residents weren't there or used blackout blinds to stop the headlights from shining in. Who would hear her if she screamed? Someone would, but would they do anything?

Dameon's mind went beyond the darkness and conjured up a whole lot of what-ifs. What-iffing was a waste of time, but he couldn't seem to stop himself. He noted the name of the mobile home park. He wouldn't ask Grace who the man was. Dameon would figure that out easily enough.

"I don't see it."

Dameon pulled his cell out of his pocket. "I'll call your number."

"Good idea."

He found her contact and pressed it. They both stood motionless and listened.

"Did you have the ringer off?" he asked.

"I don't think so."

It rang several times before going to voice mail.

"You're sure you left it on the hood of his car?"

"Positive."

"Maybe he grabbed it," Dameon said.

"If he did, he won't bother giving it back. Probably toss the thing in the garbage or roll over it on purpose."

Dameon hoped that was all he would do.

He put his cell away and walked back to her side. "Guess we need to go shopping."

"The last thing I want to do during the Christmas rush." Her gaze still scanned the ground.

"Did you try using the app for finding your phone?"

Grace looked at him as if he were a genius. "I didn't even think of that."

Someone pulled into the driveway and slowed down as they drove by.

"Let's stay warm in the cab of the truck."

They climbed in and he hit the dome light. He searched the internet for finding a lost cell phone and followed the directions someone had taken the time to spell out.

Grace gave him the information he needed. A map of the area came up and pinged their exact location.

"But it's not here," Grace said.

Dameon jumped around a little online. "It says it will locate your phone the last time it had a charge. Was the battery dead?"

"Half a charge if not more."

He kept searching.

"I'm going to take another look."

Before he could argue, she jumped back out of the truck and scanned the ground.

Dameon dug up another possibility. One that involved someone taking the sim card out of the phone in that location, therefore disabling the finding apps.

He killed the engine on the truck and joined her a second time. They both dialed her number and listened for a buzz of a vibrating phone.

"I don't think it's here," Dameon said.

"You're right. Damn, this sucks." Grace waved her work phone in her hand. "I still have this."

"We can get over to the phone store and pick you up another one."

She shook her head. "Not tonight." Grace glanced at her watch. "It's already after seven. I'm starved."

He paused. "Are you suggesting we get something to eat?"

Their eyes met, and she smiled for the first time that night. "I'll buy you dinner. It's the least I can do for putting you through the paces today."

"You don't have to ask me twice."

"Do you like prime rib?" she asked.

"Love it."

"I know just the place. Away from the mall and not crowded during the week."

"Sounds perfect."

He opened the passenger door and waited for her to get in.

~

Grace wasn't ready to be alone. She knew she was breaking the rules, but she'd crossed that line when she called Dameon in the first place. So what's dinner with the man going to do?

The Backwoods was an old-school steak house complete with dark wood and red tufted seats. The bar looked like it had been plucked out of an old west saloon, and the floor was littered with sawdust. The drinks were stiff and the prime rib filled the whole plate.

Dameon opened the door and waited for Grace to walk inside. It was a simple gesture, one that some women shunned and others expected. For Grace, it was unassumingly nice. She'd grown up with brothers who were taught to open doors and stand up for girls. At the same time, her parents told her to depend on herself. She'd chosen a profession that was testosterone charged because it was what she knew. As long as she held up her end, she'd be treated with respect. Apparently, that ended at home and didn't follow her into the workplace.

The hostess smiled as they walked in the door. "Hello."

Grace knew the woman but had forgotten her name. "Is Carrie here tonight?"

"She is."

Carrie was a friend from high school that had been working there since she was old enough to serve alcohol.

The hostess grabbed two menus and walked in front of them.

"Do you know everyone in this town?" Dameon asked.

"That's what happens when you live in the same place your whole life."

They were placed in a half-moon booth, giving her and Dameon the opportunity to sit closer to each other than if they were in individual chairs with a table separating them. They both shrugged out of their coats and scooted into the booth.

"I didn't think these places existed anymore," Dameon confessed once the hostess left.

"They do. I know a few around here for different types of food. You can get fancy closer to where I live, but the quality for the price can't be beat here." Not that The Backwoods was cheap, but it wasn't anything compared to downtown LA where Dameon lived.

She couldn't help but wonder if this felt hick to him.

If it did, she'd rather know now.

Carrie walked up to the table with a huge grin. She leaned over to hug Grace. "I haven't seen you for at least a month. How are you?"

"Busy, like always. How's Cody?"

"Turns five next month. Hard to believe." Carrie glanced at Dameon.

"Dameon, this is Carrie. We met in tenth grade."

Carrie smiled with a nod. "Lovely to meet you," she said.

"Likewise," Dameon said.

"Oh, that voice. Are you in the movies or do radio?"

He laughed. "Afraid not."

"Well, you should. Don't you think, Grace?"

"I'm sure he'd have a long career doing voice-overs," Grace said.

Dameon actually looked a little embarrassed by the praise.

"What are you two drinking?" Carrie lifted a notepad and poised her pen to write.

"Is Adam behind the bar?" Grace asked.

"Yup."

"Tell him it's me and I want an old-fashioned."

"Make it two," Dameon said.

"Coming right up," Carrie said with a wink.

She walked off and Dameon leaned closer. "She seems nice."

"Carrie's good people. Her little boy is adorable."

"How is it growing up in a place where everyone knows you?"

"There's well over two hundred thousand people in this valley. Not everybody knows me."

"Why do I doubt that?"

"It helps that my dad was a cop in this town. That's a close-knit group all by itself."

"Does it get you out of tickets?" he asked.

She shook her head, then nodded. "When we were new drivers, my dad would tell his friends to pull us over if we sneezed wrong."

Dameon laughed.

"We were so paranoid about getting a ticket that our friends never wanted us to drive anywhere. The funny thing was my dad's friends weren't nearly as bad as my mom's. The PTA moms in this town knew who just got their driver's license and were constantly reporting if they saw something they didn't like. It's easy to spot a police car. But everyone and their brother drives an SUV in this town." The busboy dropped off a basket of garlic bread, and Grace dug in. "We didn't get away with anything."

"Kept you safe, I bet."

"It did. I look back and realize I'll do the same thing if I have kids." Although she'd started to lose faith that kids would be a part of her world if her relationship status didn't change. "What about you? Did your parents helicopter you growing up?"

"Nothing like yours. My dad was a contractor, worked with his own team doing remodels and the occasional small complex. His reach wasn't nearly as big as your family's. Mom helped with his bookkeeping and back office work. She was involved in some of the school stuff we were in, but I don't remember the PTA being a thing."

Carrie arrived with their drinks, murmured something about getting an order out, and disappeared.

Grace swirled her drink with the cocktail straw. "So that's how you got into investing? Your dad?"

"My dad taught me construction. But I thought he worked too hard. He said he kept his business small because he didn't need the stress that went along with the money of making it big. But apparently his stress level was up there anyway."

"Oh, why?"

Dameon picked up his drink. "We lost him five years ago. Heart attack."

Grace looked him in the eye. "Oh, God, I'm so sorry." She couldn't imagine losing her dad.

"Thanks. It was hard. None of us saw it coming. Hit my mom the most."

Grace sipped her drink. "I bet it did."

"I wanted to build more, be more, than my dad. My parents encouraged me, helped out in the beginning."

"Do you enjoy it?"

He nodded and tilted his drink back. "I do. I like the fact that I employ people and build things. Or my company does, anyway. With that comes responsibility for the people who work for me, and I never lose sight of that."

"That's good. Keeps you humble. I would think a lot of men in your situation forget where they started and make bad choices when they do."

Carrie stopped by the table again. Neither of them had opened a menu, not that Grace needed to. She ordered prime rib with her desired sides, and Dameon lifted two fingers in the air.

"You trust me with your cocktail and your dinner?" Grace asked.

"How soon we forget the pedicure."

Grace started to laugh, her eyes met Dameon's, and he laughed right along with her. They eased into a conversation that moved from pedicures to projects, and the stress of the day began to melt off her shoulders. They took their time eating and talking about their families. Dameon told her he wasn't close to his brother, which baffled her. She countered with the fact that there wasn't a week that went by that she didn't talk to her brothers if not see them. It helped that she was friends with their significant others.

They finished with coffee and skipped dessert.

With her full stomach and head slightly affected by their drinks, Grace found herself staring at Dameon and wondering how the hell they got there. Yes, she knew, of course, but despite the fact that she knew better than to foster anything more than a working relationship with the man, she kept wondering what if . . .

What if they had met outside of work?

What if he was as infatuated with dating her as he said he was?

What was really wrong with that?

"Someone got quiet," Dameon said, snapping her out of her internal monologue.

She dropped her gaze to her hands resting on the table. "I was trying to figure out a way to blame you for breaking my self-imposed rule."

"What rule is that?" he asked with a grin.

"Dinner and drinks with someone I'm working with."

"Ah. You make it sound like I'm part of the office staff."

Their eyes met again. "You're hardly that."

He reached over and covered her hand with his.

Her skin buzzed with the simple contact. And from the way Dameon's smile disappeared and was replaced by heat in his eyes, he wasn't unaffected by the touch either.

Silence spread between them, and for the first time all night, Grace couldn't think of a single word to utter.

The gentle touch of Dameon's thumb stroking the back of her hand had her trembling.

"Grace—"

Carrie walked up to the table at that moment, cutting Dameon's words off. "I'm so glad you came in tonight," she said, her cheery voice a full octave above the tone at the table.

Grace shrugged out of the spell Dameon was placing her under and turned to her friend. "Let me know when you need a night out, we can go for drinks or maybe a spa day." As Grace spoke, she slowly slid her hand out from under Dameon's.

"You don't know how much I would love that." Carrie set the bill on the table. "Nice meeting you, Dameon."

"Likewise," he said.

Carrie walked away, and Dameon confiscated the check before Grace could grab it.

"I said I was buying," Grace told him.

He placed a credit card in with the bill and set it on the table. "Not in my world."

She kept her hands in her lap to avoid the temptation of touching him again. "Is that a sexist thing? You can't let a woman buy your dinner?"

"No," he said, shaking his head. Then he stopped and looked her in the eye. "Yeah, probably. My mom would call it good upbringing."

Grace shrugged. "My dad would say the same thing."

Dameon paid the bill, and they said their goodbyes to Carrie.

Halfway to Grace's condo, Dameon brought her back to why they were out together in the first place. "Are you feeling better about tonight?"

"With Sokolov?"

"Is that the guy's name?"

"Yeah. And yes, I am. I'm sure after a good night's sleep I'll be ready to deal with the situation more rationally. I don't scare easy, but this guy got to me."

"Last time I looked, offering a bribe was illegal. You can always go after him legally," Dameon suggested.

She wasn't willing to go there. "I'll let Richard know what happened and make a stand when it comes to dealing with him in the future."

"I don't like the idea of you having to deal with him at all."

"I won't meet with him alone again." Once bitten, twice shy, she told herself. There was no reason to give the man another chance at scaring the crap out of her. If anything, those tables needed to turn in the other direction. "Thanks for coming with me."

Dameon turned his truck onto the street leading to her condo. "I'm honored you thought to call me, Grace."

She didn't know how to respond to that, so she sat in silence the rest of the way home.

Dameon found an empty parking space and pulled in.

"You don't have to walk me to my door," she said.

He cut the engine and twisted in his seat. "Humor me. I'll feel better knowing you're inside safe."

"I've lived here for five years."

"Humor me," he said a second time.

Grace nodded and stepped out of his truck.

She could see her breath in the cold night air. The bite of the wind had her walking faster. "I can't believe it's almost ten o'clock."

"It's been a long day for both of us," he said.

At her door, she pulled her keys out of her purse and turned to him. For the second time that night, she felt a wave of nerves as the evening ended. "Thank you, Dameon. For coming, for dinner . . ."

"You're welcome." He stood just out of reach and wasn't making any attempt to move in to kiss her.

She shivered.

"You should go in."

With a nervous nod, she fiddled with the key in the deadbolt and twisted the lock. She pushed the door open, and the warm air from inside rushed against her skin. She stepped inside and turned. "Good night."

"I'll see you Friday."

"Right."

"Good night."

She started closing the door.

"Grace?"

She stopped and looked up. "Yeah?"

"Just one more thing." Dameon stepped forward, reached up with a hand to her face, and pressed his palm against her cheek. Their eyes met right before he bent his head and removed any space between them. His lips were warm, and her heart raced with all the excitement of the first taste of the man. Dameon was kissing her, and heaven help her, she was stepping into his arms and tilting her head back to take in the whole experience.

He moved his head to the side and coaxed her lips open.

The man was entirely too good at making her break the rules.

Just as his kiss started to deepen and border on the kind of kiss that shouldn't happen in public, Dameon ended it.

She blinked her eyes open and found him smiling down. "I want to do that again . . . soon," he murmured low in his throat.

Words failed her, so she settled with a nod.

He traced the side of her jaw with his thumb before dropping his hand and stepping away. "Good night, Grace."

"G'night." She backed into her condo and closed the door.

She heard his footsteps retreating, and she leaned against the wall.

A slow smile spread over her face. The man took her breath away and had her aching for more than a good-night kiss at her door.

Dameon Locke was fast becoming an addiction she didn't want a cure for.

CHAPTER FIFTEEN

Grace gave herself credit for not barging into Richard's office at eight a.m. sharp. She waited until eight thirty. She gave him the courtesy of rapping once before opening the door and letting herself in.

He looked up in surprise.

"Good morning," she said, giving him the simple pleasantries of polite conversation even though he didn't afford her the same respect.

"Do we have a meeting this morning?" he asked.

She ignored his question. "Last night's meeting with Sokolov was a complete waste of time, as I thought it would be. The *so-called* plans he wanted to use looked like they'd been drawn by a ninth grader and didn't take anything we've spelled out into account."

Richard stared at her, completely void of emotion. "And you couldn't tell me this at Monday's meeting?"

His question took her aback. He was right. "He attempted to offer me a bribe," she blurted out.

He raised his eyebrows. "Attempted, or did?"

"He waved his wallet around and said there must be some way we could work this out."

"So he didn't directly say he'd give you money to approve his plan?"

"He was more subtle than that. I made it clear what we required and left." He also went out of his way to scare the shit out of her, but she left that out. Richard obviously wasn't seriously alarmed by her news.

"The last thing we're going to do is jump into some legal action on vague charges." Richard leaned back in his chair.

"I wasn't suggesting we do. I thought you should know what happened. And in the future, I won't be meeting Mr. Sokolov without someone else with me." Especially after the sun went down . . . but again, she left that out.

"Well . . . thank you for *informing* me." He scooted closer to his desk. "Now if you don't mind?" He motioned toward the door.

Grace walked away from her boss's office feeling like she'd just tattled to her teacher about a boy being mean in class.

Back in her office, she closed the door and slumped in her chair. The pile of work on her desk never seemed to go down, and the gratification of doing her job had started to bleed into puddles on the floor that needed to be cleaned up. What happened to the joy she once felt? The job hadn't changed. Her boss was always kind of a jerk. To her, anyway.

The institutional-style clock on the wall clicked away the seconds.

Every day the seconds turned into minutes, minutes into hours. And at five, the pile on her right was never any smaller.

Something inside of her had shifted, and Grace couldn't quite put her finger on what.

She opened the folder she'd been working on before being pulled away the night before and dug in. Luckily today was a field day. She'd be out of the office for several hours, giving her the space she needed away from her boss. Only a couple more office days, then the holiday party, and short work weeks for the rest of the year.

Her office phone rang, pulling her out of her thoughts. "Grace Hudson," she answered.

"Good morning."

Dameon.

Just the sound of his voice lifted her mood. "Good morning," she chimed back.

"I thought a call would be better than texting your work cell."

"That's probably wise."

"You'll let me know as soon as you replace it?" he asked.

"I will."

"Good. That way I can text you something completely sappy about how much I enjoyed last night. Not the reason it happened, but how it ended up."

She lowered her voice, not that anyone could hear with the closed door. "I really can't talk about it here," she told him.

"I completely understand. I wanted to let you know that I'm back in the city. But if you need me, I can get up there in thirty minutes."

"And when in the history of LA traffic does it only take thirty minutes to get here from downtown?" She had to laugh.

"Okay, thirty-five."

She snorted.

"I'll be back Friday."

The holiday party. The thought of him resting his hand on her back or repeating his kiss with someone from her office seeing them ran in her head. "About the party. We can't . . . I mean it's not a good idea for us to be too . . . familiar with each other."

"I understand discretion."

"Thank you."

"I have a phone number for you," he said.

"Whose?"

"Mine, at the San Francisquito house. The cell service out there is awful."

She laughed. "I could have told you that."

"Something that's worth looking into with the project."

"I couldn't agree more."

He told her the number and she jotted it down.

"I'll let you get back to work."

"See you Friday," she said.

"I look forward to it."

They said their goodbyes and hung up.

Soon the sound of the clock ticking reminded her to get out of her daydream and get back to work.

∿

Some things were just more trouble than they were worth. And keeping his office open and expecting any real work to get done between Christmas and the New Year was one of them. Half of his staff went out of town to visit family, and the other half had family visiting. His office party was set up for Saturday and then the doors would be shut until January second. It was an expense his accountant advised him against when he'd first opened the doors. But his employee satisfaction and retention was significantly better than the next guy's, and that saved him money in the long run.

This year, Dameon was looking forward to the week between the holidays so he could put some time into the ranch house. There were a few things he wanted to do to make it more livable when he was there. Nothing too extensive since the plan was to level the house and make way for the development. But where the place stood was in the third phase of houses, which meant it was a good year away from demolition. The fact that he'd be closer to Grace hadn't slipped his mind. And after the previous night, he especially liked that he'd be ten minutes away.

He'd driven back to the city after he'd dropped her off and finished the evening with a kiss. She'd been soft and responsive and looked up at him like a woman wanting more. That look had filled his dreams and put a smile on his face since he left her side.

Then his thoughts turned to Sokolov and the reason Grace had called him in the first place.

He had spent an hour looking up the property owner's full name and information on the mobile home park. Anything that was in a public record, he dug up, or would. Not that he knew what he would do with the information, but it felt good to know more about his enemy.

What he really wanted was a picture of the man. But there wasn't anything online to help him out.

Dameon put aside the small amount of information he'd gathered on the man to tackle the things he needed to finish before the end of the year. Unlike his staff, he'd be bringing work home with him.

Chelsea had given him a small file with names and portfolios of potential investors.

Just looking at it put a bad taste in his mouth. Last resort, he told himself.

A knock on his office door drew his attention away from his work. "Yeah?"

Omar popped his head in. "Got a second?"

"Yeah, what's up?"

He walked in waving a piece of paper. "What's up with the Santa Clarita project and this expense report?"

"I'm making the property livable."

"For who?"

"Me."

Omar stopped short, tilted his head. "Come again?"

"Part time. I will be working remotely one day a week. Stay there on weekends."

"This doesn't have something to do with a certain woman, does it?"

"She factors in. But I think it's the best way to really know what the community needs. Sometimes what's on paper isn't the reality. Like cellular towers. The place is lacking cell service. We're going to need a budget for that, or some kind of cooperation with one or more of the major carriers." All of which was true.

"And then there's the girl," Omar said again.

Dameon dismissed Omar's smirk. "Think about it. Every project we've done has been in developed areas that needed revamping or a small block of homes. This is the largest project we've done to date. And we're doing it without a net."

Omar nodded a few times. "We can get a net."

"Investors mean dividing the profits." And they both knew they didn't want that. Not that Dameon needed Omar to be on board with what he wanted to do, but having him understand made everything easier.

"You haven't led the company wrong yet," he said.

"I don't plan on starting now."

Omar turned to leave. Right before he walked through the door he said, "I hope she's worth the commute."

"She is," he whispered to himself as Omar left the room.

CHAPTER SIXTEEN

Normally Grace wouldn't spend a lot of time figuring out what to wear to a holiday party with a bunch of people she knew and saw almost every day. Her colleagues didn't require special clothing.

But Dameon was coming.

And whether she admitted it or not, she wanted to make him drool.

A red cocktail dress and black stilettos was exactly the thing to achieve her goals. Grace pulled her hair off her neck and into a loose bun and wore dangling earrings that sparkled, even if they were crystal rather than diamond.

The neckline of her dress plunged enough to show off her curves, but not so much as to be considered indecent.

After a final pass by her full-length mirror, she considered herself as perfect as she ever managed to get, and left her condo.

She arrived twenty minutes into the party and the room was already swimming with people. The line for the bar was by far the longest.

Peggy, who worked as a receptionist in the city building, beelined straight for her. "Ooh la la," she said as she looked Grace up and down. "Look who is dressed to impress!"

"My black dress is at the cleaners," she lied.

"And what, this was hanging in the back of your closet?"

"Actually . . ."

Peggy laughed. "Maybe Richard will finally call you by your first name."

"I'm not holding my breath." Grace looked around Peggy. "Have you seen my brother?"

"Not yet." Peggy joined her in watching the other people in the room. "Who's going to get drunk this year?"

They turned together and looked around the crowd. Every office had at least one or two lushes who made a name for themselves at the party. "I'm sure Pete learned his lesson last year," Grace said.

Pete had managed to get stumbling drunk and collided with the mayor's wife as he rushed to the bathroom. Their heads bumped, and he stepped on her high-heeled foot with enough force to bloody a toe. The worst part was he didn't stop to apologize or anything. He rushed to the bathroom and lost the liquor he'd been drinking. The following Monday he didn't remember a thing. When the mayor presented him with the clinic bill for X-rays and another for a new pair of designer shoes, Pete realized just how bad it was.

"Something tells me Pete will be the designated driver tonight if he comes at all," Peggy said.

Grace felt heat down her spine. The kind that meant only one thing. She turned her head to the right and then the left . . . that's when she saw him.

Dameon's eyes locked with hers as a slow smile crept over his face. He was too far away to say anything, but when he moved his lips, she could swear he said the word *wow*.

"Whoa, who is that?" Peggy said at her side.

"Excuse me?" Grace shifted her gaze.

"The guy who is devouring you with his eyes?"

She looked around, feigning innocence. "Who?"

Peggy nudged her with an elbow. "Nice try. I saw you staring."

Grace met Dameon's gaze again and widened her eyes as if to give him some kind of telepathic message to stop staring. He grinned and turned away. "That's Mr. Locke."

"Mr. Hotness. How do you know him?"

Grace felt her face growing warm. "He has a development that's getting off the ground here."

"Oh yeah . . . where?"

Damn if Grace didn't glance up to see him staring again.

"Up the canyon . . . you know what, he looks a little lost, I should make him feel welcome."

Peggy laughed. "You go, girl."

Grace reminded herself to walk slowly as she crossed the room to stand before Dameon. The last thing she wanted to do was call attention to the two of them together.

She reached out a hand when she stopped moving. "Hello, Mr. Locke."

It appeared he was trying not to laugh as he took her hand in his. "Miss Hudson. You look absolutely radiant." His hand squeezed hers before letting go.

Squeezing hands . . . really? She knew her cheeks were warm. She just hoped they didn't look like she was flustered. "Why thank you. Did you have trouble finding the place?" She kept her questions easy and generic in case anyone had noticed them.

"Not at all."

She motioned toward the line to the bar. "Why don't we get a drink and I'll introduce you to some of the community."

"I'd appreciate that." He indicated for her to walk in front of him.

The closer to the bar they moved, the louder the music grew. People were either trying to talk over it or leaning in close to hear what the other person was saying.

Dameon ducked his head closer to her ear. "You're killing me in that dress," he said in the deep baritone that only he could manage.

And because she couldn't help herself, she said, "That was part of my plan."

The line inched forward.

Dameon bent his head, his lips pressed together with a slight grin.

Yeah, speechless was a good look on the man.

When it was their turn at the bar, she ordered a glass of red wine, and he asked for a whiskey soda.

"Well, Miss Hudson . . . who should I meet first?"

"You can call me Grace."

"You sure?"

She motioned for him to bend down so she could speak in his ear. "You say Miss Hudson like I'm the naughty high school teacher."

He tilted his head back and laughed.

She saw Evan and pulled Dameon toward her colleague. "Evan." She tapped his shoulder. "I have someone I want you to meet."

Evan smiled and shook hands during the introductions. "Welcome to Santa Clarita."

"Your city is growing on me," Dameon said, his eyes glancing at Grace.

"Is that right?" Evan looked between the two of them, his grin a little too obvious. "You look fabulous, Grace. Is that a new dress?"

Okay, maybe introducing Dameon to Evan was a mistake. "I wore the same one last year," she lied.

Evan shook his head several times. "Nope. Last year you wore slacks and stilettos." He turned his attention to Dameon. "To be fair, Grace always wears spikes on her feet. And if I'm not mistaken, you were working right up to party time last Christmas and your shoes didn't match your outfit."

"Then I wore this dress the year before." Grace frantically looked around for someone else to introduce Dameon to.

"I would have remembered if you had. That dress is hard to forget."

Okay, now she was blushing . . . she felt her body temperature soaring.

"It's pretty spectacular," Dameon said, chuckling.

And on that note . . . "Okay, then. Onward." Grace tapped Dameon's elbow and started to move away.

"You're adorable when you blush, Hudson." Evan never called her Hudson.

"Slow down on the drinks, Evan," she said as they were walking away.

Dameon lowered his lips to her ear. "Is he my competition?"

That had to be the funniest thing she'd heard in some time. "Ah, no! Even if I was his flavor, he's like a brother."

"Got it. He's right about the dress."

They'd stopped a few feet away, Dameon standing entirely too close.

"Stop looking at me like that," she whispered under her breath.

"Like what?" His eyes widened and he took a sip of his drink.

She was surprised the ice hadn't melted in his glass for all the heat coming off the man.

Or maybe that was her.

"Like I'm lunch." She tried hard not to smile.

Dameon sucked in a deep breath and closed his eyes before looking away.

"That's better." Grace turned. "That's the mayor. His wife is a busybody, so exercise that discretion you said you had."

"Yes, ma'am," he said in her ear.

She moaned. This was going to be a very long night.

She introduced Dameon to three members of the city council, the mayor, and a well-known contractor in the area. There were owners of smaller businesses, from plumbers to concrete companies. Members of the school board were in attendance, and of course the rest of the engineering team in her office.

The smiles and glances her way simmered, and Dameon eased into conversations like he already knew the people he was with.

They were an hour into the evening before Grace noticed her brother and Parker join the party.

She left Dameon's side while he was talking with a city council member to greet her brother.

"I was starting to wonder if you guys were going to make it," she said as she hugged Parker.

"We were a little . . . busy," Parker muttered, her cheeks flaming red.

"Is that what we're calling it? Busy?" Grace teased.

Parker shrugged.

Grace reached up to hug her brother. "You need to give the woman some down time."

Colin pointed at his wife. "She started it."

"Don't pull that. You walked into the closet when I was getting dressed."

"You were wearing lace."

Grace tossed her free hand in the air. "I really don't want to know more about your sex life."

Colin winked at her and looked over her shoulder. "I see Dameon made it."

Parker peered closer. "Is that him?"

Grace nodded.

Dameon must have sensed people watching and turned around. After saying something to the people he'd been talking to, he walked toward them.

"Dameon, I'd like you to meet Parker. The newest member of the Hudson family."

They shook hands. "A pleasure."

"And of course, you've already met Colin."

Grace watched them shake hands. This time it didn't seem to be a struggle to determine who had more testosterone coursing through their veins.

"Nice to see you again," Dameon said.

"We'll see about that," Colin uttered.

Grace gave him *the stare*. "Be nice."

"How about we get the ladies a drink," Dameon suggested to Colin.

Her brother kissed Parker's cheek. "Red?" he asked.

She nodded and the men walked off.

As soon as they were out of earshot Parker leaned close. "He is so much hotter in person."

"Tell me about it." Grace lifted her glass to her lips, realized it was empty, and set it down.

~

Dameon waited until they were well outside of earshot before turning to Colin.

"What do you know about Stefan Sokolov?" he asked.

For a second Colin looked lost. "You mean the guy who owns the mobile home park?"

"That's the one."

"I know he's lousy at maintaining his property . . . why?"

Dameon looked around, leaned closer. "A certain person we both know had a run-in with him earlier this week. Scared her enough to call me."

The pleasant expression on Colin's face fell. "What do you mean, 'scared her'?"

"Just what I said. You know her better than me. I have a feeling she doesn't spook easy."

Colin looked toward his sister. "No, she doesn't."

"Do you know what this guy looks like?"

"No."

"If you find an image of the guy, will you pass it on?"

Colin turned back. "She called you?"

"She was concerned that you or your brother would take it too far if she called you."

"She's right about that."

They moved forward in line. "You didn't hear it from me."

Colin regarded him with a sideways glance. "Why tell me this?"

Easy answer. "Because my office is in LA and I can't always be in town. Regardless of what you might think of me, I only want to see that woman smiling. Not shaking in fear."

Colin patted him on the shoulder as they stepped up to the bartender.

~

It appeared to Grace that Colin and Dameon had made some kind of peace. Her brother wasn't snapping or cutting barbs at the man, nor was he attempting to make him uncomfortable.

The four of them found a table and grabbed some food from the buffet.

"I understand you're building a pretty big development in town," Parker said to Dameon.

"I am. Grace has given me a lot to consider about the build. Some things we already factored in and others we didn't."

"My sister knows her stuff," Colin said with pride.

"You mind telling my boss that?" Grace asked.

"Richard still playing hardball?"

She looked at her brother and nodded. "You'd think he'd grow bored after a while."

Colin looked around. "Is he even here?"

"I saw him earlier," she said. "These things aren't in his skill set, he probably left already."

Parker shifted the conversation. "So, Dameon, where do you spend Christmas?"

"My mom lives in Glendale."

"Any siblings?" Parker asked.

"A brother. Sometimes he shows up. My uncle and his family come in every other year. What about you guys?" he asked, his gaze moving to Grace.

"Our parents host. Mom loves to cook and we're all pretty good at helping out."

"Nothing more important than family," Colin said, his eyes narrowed on Grace.

She pushed her plate of food aside and looked up to find Richard staring at them.

"Looks like my boss didn't leave after all."

"I should probably be mingling," Dameon said.

"That might not be a bad idea."

Colin stood when Dameon did. "I'll introduce you to some of the guys I work with, not that they have time to do anything for your project, but they do know most of the people in town who could."

Dameon leaned close to Grace. "Don't leave without saying goodbye."

He walked away before she could respond.

Parker moved over to the seat Colin had just vacated. "He's charming."

"I know. It's unnerving."

"I don't get the stalker vibe Erin talked about."

"Me either."

Before either of them could say more, Richard walked by their table. Their eyes met and he looked away without saying a thing.

"Merry Christmas to you, too," she said in a tone only Parker could hear.

"Ignore him. His wife probably hasn't had sex with him since the nineties," Parker joked.

"In the nineties he had a different wife altogether."

As the evening wore on, the people in the room loosened up and the voices grew louder. Grace scouted the group to see if anyone was going to be the talk of the party after the holidays. Pete was out of the running since he'd already left.

"We haven't had a girls' night since before the wedding," Parker said.

"You've been a little busy."

"We need to plan one. Before the wedding it was all about the wedding. Before that it was all about getting Erin back to the living. I feel out of the loop. And outside of the Dameon gossip, I have no idea what's going on in your world."

Grace shrugged. "I work, I go home . . . wash, rinse, and repeat."

"That's not healthy."

"It beats meeting strangers in bars and learning later that they tried to kill one of your best friends." Grace didn't realize the weight of her words until after they'd left her mouth.

Silence stretched between them.

"I'm guessing that's not healthy either," Parker said. A frown replaced her smile from the moment before.

"I stopped trusting my instincts." Grace glanced around to avoid being overheard. "Which is why I'm glad *you know who* is here for you to meet. Erin put doubt in my head, and I haven't completely shaken it off."

"I expect that from Erin. Not you. But that's not really fair, is it?"

Grace shook her head. "It's completely fair. No one tried to kill me."

"We don't know that. And I'm guessing you've come up with that conclusion yourself."

More than once.

"You'd tell me . . . if something was off with *you know who*, right?" Grace asked.

Parker placed a hand on her shoulder. "If something felt off, I'd be the first to tell you."

Grace found herself staring at the back of Dameon's head from across the room. "I really hope he's not playing me."

Within an hour Grace caught Parker yawning and checking her cell phone. Truth was, she was pretty tired, too.

"We should find Colin and get you home," Grace told Parker.

"Am I that obvious?"

"Yes."

Colin and Dameon were talking with a group of men, half of them laughing at whatever had just been said. When they approached, the conversation came to an abrupt halt.

"Don't stop on our account," Grace said.

Colin shook his head. "Fishing stories, sis. The kind where the fish get bigger with every drink one consumes."

Grace poked her brother's arm. "Except you don't go fishing."

"It wasn't my story."

"Damn, Hudson. You clean up really nice," Lionel said at her side.

Grace turned to her coworker. "I'm guessing that's a compliment?" she asked.

"Don't go getting mushy on me. You're not my type," he teased.

She grinned. "You're right. There's more to my weekends than a sports bar and the beer on tap."

Lionel put a hand over his heart. "I'd be wounded if it wasn't so true."

The crowd laughed.

"Speaking of weekends," Colin said, turning to Parker. "I think I need to get my wife home since we only have the next couple days to do our shopping."

"I'm sure that's why you want to get her home," one of the other guys in the group said.

Grace waved them off. "Leave the honeymooners alone. They're entitled to putting a white flag outside the bedroom door when they need food and water."

Parker was laughing the hardest.

"I'll go get our coats," Colin said before walking away.

"Didn't you Uber here?" Parker asked her.

"I did."

"We can give you a ride?"

"No, you go ahead." Grace tried not to look at Dameon. "I'm not ready to go home quite yet."

When Colin returned, he said his goodbyes to the group, and Grace walked them out.

"See you on Christmas," Parker said as they hugged goodbye.

Colin was next. "It's cold out here, go back in."

"Love you, too," she teased.

He kissed the top of her head. "Love you, Gracie."

She walked back in and found Dameon hanging outside the banquet room doors.

"Are you leaving?" she asked.

"Not unless I can talk you into a nightcap away from all the noise."

She smiled. "I might be persuaded."

He looked like he wanted to touch her. "Please?"

"You twisted my arm." She pointed to the party room. "I'll get my coat and meet you at your truck. It's probably best we don't leave together."

"Give me a five-minute head start."

She walked into the room while he walked in the direction of the bathrooms.

There were a few people she wanted to say goodbye to, so she made her rounds.

She checked her new cell phone for the time. At the four-minute mark she put her coat on and passed by Evan. "Merry Christmas," she told him with a hug.

"Back at ya."

She walked out of the room and through the hall. She kept her phone in her hand as if she were watching for an Uber ride. Out in the parking lot she saw the red lights on a truck illuminating her way.

Dameon reached across the seat and opened the door. "Need a ride?" he asked, teasing.

She hopped in and reached for her seatbelt. "I feel like we're sneaking."

He laughed. "That's because we are. But after spending the night with your colleagues and hearing some of the stories about your boss, I get it."

"If I was one of the guys, he'd probably care less. But then there aren't that many female developers biting off as big of a project as you are." In all actuality, she'd worked with very few women in Dameon's situation.

"Where to?" he asked.

"Do you like martinis?"

"Who doesn't?"

She smiled at him through the dim light of the parking lot. "When you pull out, turn right."

"Yes, ma'am."

"Ma'am?"

He put the truck in reverse, placed his hand over the back of the seat, and caressed her shoulder as he did. "I've been stuck on the naughty teacher comment all night."

CHAPTER SEVENTEEN

Once again, Grace surprised him. They walked into a dimly lit bar with a woman playing the piano in the corner. By his guess, this was one of the finer places to dine in Santa Clarita. People were dressed up, and the bar was void of television screens. They found a table in the back, and Dameon helped her out of her coat.

When they sat down, he rested his hand on her arm. "I've been wanting to touch you all night."

"I shouldn't want the same thing," she told him.

He kept her gaze. "Are you worried someone will see us here?"

"Everyone I know that would care is still at the party, not to mention most of them can't afford this place on what the city pays."

"But you know about it."

"Well, of course I do. I'm single without kids. I'm sure you know the fancy places in the city."

"And a few dive bars."

"Nothing better than a good dive bar."

The waiter came over, they ordered their drinks, and he walked off. "So, this is a place where you don't know the staff."

"You're teasing me," she said.

"It's refreshing. I haven't dated a woman like you before."

"Oh? What's your normal type?"

He wasn't sure he wanted to answer that.

"I'll tell you mine if you tell me yours," she said.

"You really want to know about the exes?"

She leaned over. "Scared?"

Okay, fine. "Her name was Lena—"

"Lena?" Grace sounded surprised.

"She was Greek." He stopped there.

"Okay . . . ?"

"Now, you tell me yours."

Grace huffed. "His name was Robert and he was a putz."

"Define *putz*."

"He played video games on his phone at family dinners."

Dameon wasn't expecting that. "Was this in high school?"

Grace rolled her eyes. "Last year."

"It must have been serious if he went to family dinners." Dameon couldn't see Grace putting up with a grown man ignoring her family for a cell phone.

"Not with my family. We're very open, and dinners with the boyfriends and girlfriends are a must."

"Even as adults?"

"My dad's an ex-cop," she said as if that explained it all. "Tell me about Lena."

A picture of the woman popped into his head. "Lena never met my mother. She didn't play video games, but she spent a lot of time on her cell phone taking pictures of herself."

Grace grinned. "I know that girl. I'm guessing she was a knockout."

Should he lie? "She was easy to look at."

"And always needed to be told how beautiful she was."

He nodded. "Very insecure."

"So what happened?" Grace asked.

"I don't think this is going to paint me in the right light."

"Paint it anyway."

Dameon took a deep breath. "I was bored. We got along well enough in the beginning. As long as we were going to fancy places with fancy people she was happy. If I took her to O'Doul's, she'd pout and act as if it was beneath her."

"What's O'Doul's?"

"A dive bar close to my place. Great whiskey and the best fish and chips in the city." He shrugged. "I never once had a desire to take her to meet my mom."

"Well, you've already met Colin. And if I know Matt well enough, he'll find a reason to show up on your jobsite sooner or later."

"Is Matt going to bust my balls as much as Colin?"

"Of course," she said with a grin.

The martinis arrived and Dameon raised his glass. "To new friends."

Grace touched her glass to his and sipped. "I think we might be a little more than friends."

He set his glass down. "God, I hope so."

She sipped her drink again, and he reached out and touched her arm. "Do you have New Year's Eve plans?"

She shook her head. "I haven't even given it a thought. Sometimes Matt drags us out to the desert, but he has to work this year."

"The desert is a thing?"

"Oh, yeah. Big bonfires in freezing weather. Lots of dirt and motorcycles and ATVs. Do you ride?"

"I'm afraid to say I don't. Do you?"

She nodded. "We grew up out there getting dirty. But I don't own my own bike anymore."

"You owned your own motorcycle?" The woman never stopped showing him new sides of herself.

"Yeah. We all did growing up. After my dad took a bad spill, my mom pulled the plug on a lot of the desert trips. Matt and Colin go out more than I do."

He shrugged. "How hard can it be?"

"Don't say that to my brothers. They'll put you through the Evel Knievel course."

"Especially if they don't like me."

"Yeah, we should probably save that activity for later."

He wasn't sure he wanted her brothers responsible for teaching him to ride. "So back to New Year's . . . I'll pick you up at seven."

She stared at him, her lips in a flat line. "You're asking or telling?"

Much as he hated the words, he said them anyway. "I'm asking."

Those lips of hers lifted into a smile. "You know something, Locke . . . you're catching on really well."

"Is that a yes?"

She looked at the ceiling as if the answer was there. "Am I dressing fancy or dive bar?"

"Ladies' choice is next year. This year we're going five star."

Her eyebrows lifted in question. "Someone is optimistic."

They took their time with their drinks before Dameon paid the bill and drove her the short distance to her home. As he pulled into a parking space, he noticed her starting to fidget.

Before she reached for the door, Dameon took hold of her hand.

Their eyes met and he leaned forward.

As soon as their lips met, she sighed. He couldn't touch her the way he truly wanted to with a console separating them, but he could tilt her head back and taste her lips with the tip of his tongue.

Her response was her hand tightening on his arm and her kiss matching his.

She was bold in so many ways, but in this, a simple kiss in the front seat of a truck, she seemed to hold herself back ever so slightly. He ended the kiss before his body revealed just what she was doing to him.

When Grace opened her eyes, he could see the dazed look of them in the lights of the parking lot.

"I needed to do that here," he told her. "Because if I do that at your front door I'd be tempted to stay."

Her eyes opened wider.

"And I don't think you're ready for that."

"Dameon . . ." She said his name with a sigh.

"If it's okay with you, I'd like to wait a little longer."

She was smiling now. "I'd like that, too."

And because that was settled, he reached for her again. This time, she kissed him a little harder, a little longer, and she said his name in a throaty whisper that he could get used to hearing over and over again.

CHAPTER EIGHTEEN

Christmas morning, Grace took advantage of the crisp, dry weather and took a walk in an effort to work off the calories the day was going to bestow upon her. She listened to her soundtrack of fast-paced tunes that kept her moving quicker than she normally would.

By the time she walked back in her front door, her phone buzzed with a text from Dameon. She smiled instantly.

Merry Christmas and good morning.

She pulled a water bottle from her fridge and sat at her kitchen counter while texting him back. Good morning and Merry Christmas to you, too.

When will you go to your parents?

I help my mom cook, so I'll leave here in about an hour. The masses start showing up after eleven. What about you?

I'm leaving at noon and bringing the wine. My contribution to cooking is carving the turkey.

She smiled. A noble task.

I think that was sarcastic.

Would I do that? Grace asked.

The dots on her screen took some time flashing before his reply arrived.

Yes.

A keen observation on your part. I guess that's why you're the CEO.

Dameon replied with a laughing emoji.

I'm getting in the shower. Have a wonderful time with your family.

Grace held on to her phone and waited for his reply.

You, too.

~

You would think the short distance from downtown LA to Glendale would take less than thirty minutes.

But the key word is LA. And Los Angeles was known worldwide for its traffic problems. Add a holiday with no typical pattern from which to gauge a timeline and it was a crapshoot as to when you'd arrive.

Dameon arrived thirty minutes later than he'd told his mom he'd be there. Expecting a little bit of flak, he was surprised to walk through the door and hear her laughing.

"Hello?" he called out.

"In the kitchen," his mom replied.

That's when he heard a male voice.

Not just any voice.

Tristan.

Dameon wasn't prepared to spend the holiday with his brother, or any day for that matter. In the last conversation he'd had with his mother, she'd told him Tristan couldn't make it. Dameon took a fortifying breath and walked around the corner with a smile. "Merry Christmas."

"Dameon!" his mom exclaimed as if she were surprised to see him.

He placed his armful of bags on the end of the kitchen counter and accepted his mother's hug. "Sorry I'm late."

His mom hugged him tight. "Are you late?"

"Traffic."

She brushed off his comment with a second hug. When she moved away, she turned toward his brother. "Look who's here!"

Dameon moved forward and reached out his hand.

Tristan grasped it in the handshake their father had taught them both. "Good to see you," Tristan said.

"You, too." The words were polite, and honestly not felt. "I thought you couldn't make it."

Tristan let go and shrugged. "Plans changed."

Their mom placed a hand on both their arms. "The perfect Christmas present for me is to see both my boys in the same room getting along."

Dameon gave it an hour before someone was pissed off.

~

Grace started with eggnog. The homemade kind that took a full day to set in the refrigerator after it was mixed. The turkey was in the oven, and she and her mom moved around the kitchen in complete sync with each other as they prepared all the side dishes that they only cooked once or twice a year.

"Colin tells me you're having trouble at work," Nora said while shedding tears from cutting onions.

Grace had her hands full of bread crumbs and sage sausage she was mixing together to create stuffing. "I wouldn't call it trouble, I'd call it the norm."

"Richard's always been an ass," her father called from the couch where he sat watching a football game. "Thought he was better than anyone else because he went back east for college."

Her father and Richard had gone to high school together.

"You're comfortably retired and he still punches a time clock. Seems you made the better choice," Grace told her dad.

"That's because I married right. What number is Richard on? Three or four?"

"Four. But I didn't see the latest wife at the Christmas party so maybe the honeymoon is over."

Nora shook her head. "That's really unfortunate."

Grace grabbed a handful of her mom's diced onions and added it to her mix. "He's an ass. I can't imagine anyone marrying him. He probably has a schedule of when to have sex and who has to be on top."

Nora started laughing until she snorted.

"You know it's true," Grace said, laughing with her mom.

"Maybe you should start looking in the private sector for a job," her dad suggested.

"I've been thinking about it. It's hard to make the leap. I make a decent living."

"Not worth it if you're miserable." By now her dad had turned around to look at her from the sofa. The TV was flashing commercials.

"I'm not miserable," she said.

"You're not exactly happy either," Nora said.

"Maybe if you found the right man."

Grace's eyes shot to her dad's. "Let's get that conversation out of the way before Aunt Beth shows up. I don't want to hear about my uterus drying up all day."

Her mom moved to the sink to wash her hands. "We're just worried about you. You haven't dated since that unfortunate encounter with Erin's ex."

"Nothing wrong with going to see a shrink," her dad said. Emmitt was an avid believer in psychologists, psychiatrists, or anyone who could help you work through trauma.

"I'm pretty sure I don't need that."

"So you're dating again?" Nora asked.

An image of Dameon had her smiling. "I did meet someone."

That's all she needed to say. Her dad put the TV on pause, and the room filled with silence.

Her parents stared.

"Oh my God, you guys act like I've been in a convent for a year."

"Do you know how many names your father and I have heard from you since high school?"

Grace had been a serial dater up until the past summer. "Maybe I'm tired of the chase."

"Wait, is it that suit-wearing land developer guy?" Her dad frowned like he'd just eaten something rotten.

Grace knew this conversation wasn't going to go well. "His name is Dameon Locke, not *suit-wearing land developer guy*. And I really shouldn't be interested in him. With Richard up my butt, it's really not smart on my end."

Her father scowled, disapproval written all over his face.

"Not everyone in a suit is a bad guy, Dad."

"When are you bringing him over?" Nora asked.

Grace stopped what she was doing. "I've known him less than a month and I don't know when you'll meet him. Now stop, okay? You know I'm not stewing in self-pity after Desmond, so let it go."

Her mom leaned over and kissed her cheek. "We just worry, Gracie."

"I know. But I'm okay."

~

Tristan had their mom in stitches.

His brother was dressed for the beach: shorts, flip-flops, and long, sun-kissed hair. The only thing he was missing was a tie-dyed T-shirt to go with his bloodshot eyes.

"The dog surfs better than Seth." Tristan was going on about one of his friends and his surfing border collie.

Dameon listened while he peeled potatoes. With his mom distracted, he jumped in to help, otherwise they wouldn't be eating until late.

"Did you see this?" Lois brought Tristan's cell phone to show Dameon a picture. Sure enough, the drenched dog wearing a life preserver sat perched on a surfboard.

"That's impressive." *For a teenager.*

With the potatoes peeled, Dameon went in search of a pot.

"What's the dog's name?"

"Barnacle, but we call him Barney."

That had his mom laughing again. "So clever. Don't you think that's clever, Dameon?"

"Very funny." The cupboard he remembered his mom's pots to be in was filled with cookie sheets and pie tins. "Where are the pots for this?" he asked.

"Oh, let me do that." Lois moved to his side and grabbed a knife. "Why don't you pour some wine and sit and chat with your brother."

I'd rather cook and burn dinner.

"Yeah, bro. Tell me what's new in your life." Tristan leaned back in the chair he'd scooted next to the kitchen island.

Dameon wiped his hands dry on a towel and searched a drawer for a corkscrew. "Work is great. I have a big project breaking ground next year."

"No, man . . . what's new? You're always working. Do you have a Mrs. in the works?"

Dameon opened his mouth only to have his mom cut him off. "Dameon has a girlfriend."

"Oh yeah? What's her name?" Tristan asked.

This was not a conversation he wanted to have with his brother, who kept calling him *bro* and *man.*

"Her name is Grace," his mom said.

"That's cool. Is it serious?"

"It's new" was all Dameon wanted to say.

Tristan kept nodding.

"What about you, honey? Anyone special in your life?" Lois asked.

"I'm not ready for that. Let the older son settle down first, right, bro?"

Dameon wiggled the cork free with a pop. "Who wants wine?"

~

The bird was out of the oven, and the side dishes were in various stages of cooking or ready while sitting in the warmer.

Grace had moved on from the eggnog to wine.

The house was packed.

Her brothers and uncle were shouting at the game on the TV.

Erin buzzed around the kitchen as if she'd been there her whole life. The woman knew her way around a family dinner. And it looked like she'd baked enough goodies to feed the block.

"What are these?" Aunt Beth bit into something that looked like a macaroon.

"Divinity," Erin told her.

Aunt Beth purred. "It's divine. I'll give you that."

A roar came from the den. "Interference!"

"Do they think the players can hear them?" Erin asked.

Grace laughed. "Yes."

Aunt Beth washed the candy down with wine. "So, Parker . . . when are you and Colin going to give my sister a grandchild?"

Grace moved behind her aunt and pointed at Parker with a smile. *Hot seat*, she mouthed.

"Give the kids time, Bethany," Nora chided.

"Well, if Colin was anything like you, she'd already be pregnant." Aunt Bethany knew how to throw punches. It was well known that Colin "came early."

Grandma Rose, who sat picking at the sweets, looked up. "That was a shotgun wedding," she added.

Nora acted innocent. "Colin was premature," she told Parker.

"Not that anyone really cares," Grace said, smiling at her mom.

The buzzer on the timer went off, and she moved to the oven to switch the stuffing with the yams. Behind her, Aunt Beth moved on to Erin. "What's taking Matt so long with you?"

Grace happily buzzed around the kitchen now that there were two other women in the house Aunt Beth could focus her meddling attention on.

~

Dameon stood in his mother's backyard with his phone pressed to his ear. By the fourth ring, he was starting to lose hope that Grace was going to pick up.

When her voice filled the line, he sighed as if someone had tossed him a life preserver after falling off the *Titanic*.

"The voice of sanity," he said after her hello.

"A little tipsy, but sane."

"I'll take tipsy. Hi."

She laughed. "Hi, Dameon. You sound stressed."

He turned to look at the back door, making sure it was still shut. "My brother showed up."

"That sounds like a bad thing."

"He rubs me wrong. And I'm pretty sure he laced something with pot and got my mom high."

When Grace started to laugh, he found his mood lifting. "It's not funny."

She laughed harder. "Sorry."

"The turkey was half cooked and we've burned through all the wine in the house."

Grace was laughing so hard she snorted.

That had him smiling.

"Your turkey is raw and your mom is baked," she managed to say through laughter.

"I'm glad you're entertained." Dameon ran his free hand through his hair. "Tell me your day is going better."

"My Christmas is awesome. The food was perfect and Aunt Bethany is harping on Parker and Erin instead of me. I'm golden."

"I'm happy for you. And hey, the news of the week here is my brother is employed."

"That's good, right?"

"At a *pot* shop."

Grace started laughing again.

Dameon started to chuckle. "Seriously! He's thirty."

"If you love what you do for a living, you'll never work a day in your life," Grace said as if quoting someone.

"You're thoroughly amused, aren't you?"

"One hundred percent. Do you think you can get a family discount? I'll lace some of Erin's brownies for my aunt."

"I'll see what I can do."

"God, that's funny." She finally stopped laughing.

He placed a hand on his stomach. "I'm hungry."

For whatever reason, Grace lost it again, and the line was filled with laughter.

CHAPTER NINETEEN

The office was virtually empty when Grace walked in the day after Christmas. Half the staff was out of town for the holiday, and the other half rolled in close to noon.

She found herself looking at the overrun in-basket on her desk and decided to take a peek around the office. Lionel's office was wide open and his desk too clean for words. Grace prided herself on her organizational skills, but Lionel's desk made her look like a slob.

Adrian was in, so she knocked on his door and asked how his holiday was. She eyed his inbox and asked what he was working on. By the time she went to Evan's office, she was convinced that she'd been given an uneven amount of the pie. Evan was about to walk out when she pushed him back in and closed the door behind her. "I'm on a mission," she said with a beeline to his desk. "Is this your current case load?" she asked, fingering the folders in his inbox.

"Yeah, why?"

"Because mine is twice as thick. Richard keeps piling it on, and I keep saying fine."

"Are you sure?"

Grace started rambling off the projects she was a part of or lead on.

Evan stopped her halfway through. "Did you ever think the reason Richard gives you all the work is because you don't complain?"

"I don't complain because I want to keep my job."

"C'mon, Grace. He isn't going to fire you if you tell him you're too busy for more."

"Can you promise me that?" she asked.

Evan shrugged, leaned a hip on his desk. "I understand why you think the way you do, but if you're ever going to break this pattern between the two of you, you're the one to do it."

She didn't like the fact that Evan was right. Grace never had problems with confrontation when it came to her personal life. But with Richard, she didn't have it in her. "Okay . . . the next time he tries to give me more, I'm going to say something."

"Good. Tell him to give it to Lionel. He's always taking time off."

She opened the office door. "Thanks, Evan."

"Don't think I've forgotten about the Christmas party and a certain someone . . ."

"I don't know what you're talking about."

"Yeah, sure."

She stepped out and didn't elaborate.

An hour later she was walking back into her office to hear her phone ringing. She scrambled to pick it up. "Grace Hudson."

"You're working today?"

Dameon. Why did she feel like a high school senior talking to the football hero?

"I'm guessing that means you're not."

"No. I give my staff the week off. If there's anything that needs to get done, they can do it from home."

She set her coffee down and found her seat. "Lucky them."

"I tried calling your cell first. I wanted to stop by your place and give you your Christmas present."

Grace paused. "My what?"

"It's late, but . . ."

"Dameon, that's not necessary."

"That doesn't mean I didn't get you something."

161

Now she felt bad. "I didn't . . . I mean—"

"I wouldn't expect you to get me anything. If that's what you were about to say."

She sighed. "I guess that means you're in town."

"Yup. Just did a Home Depot run and was about to get dirty."

"Doing what?"

"Scraping off the popcorn ceilings."

"You're serious?"

"Yup," he said. "They're nasty and stained. I think the owner smoked."

She hadn't noticed. "Seems like a lot of effort for a place you're going to eventually tear down."

"It's honest work and I could use the exercise."

"You don't appear unfit."

"Checking me out, are you?"

She grinned. "Maybe."

"I like that. So, what do you say? I can stop by later?"

"Tell ya what. I'll come to you. Five thirty?"

"I'll be here."

They said their goodbyes, and Grace smiled at the phone.

A noise outside her door had her looking up.

Richard walked by and stared as he did.

Her breath caught. How much had he heard?

She ignored the pounding in her chest and ducked back to the work in front of her.

The last task of her day was finishing up her expense report for the month. She sent the file through the office e-mail system to Richard's desk. They were always due before the first, and he preferred them early.

Grace shut down her computer and tucked her files away with the next morning's workload on top.

Most of the staff that had shown up had left early or were walking out as she closed her office door behind her.

Three steps later she heard her name.

"Hudson."

She paused, gritted her teeth, and turned toward her boss. "Yes?"

"A word?" He stood in his office doorway and motioned for her to come in.

What now?

"Close the door," he said as she walked in.

"Is there a problem?" she asked.

He sat behind his desk and motioned to the chair.

"Can this wait for tomorrow? I have somewhere to be." And as she saw it, he had all day to ask for a meeting instead of 5:01 in the afternoon.

"This won't take long."

She sat with her purse in her lap.

"I received your expense report for December." He looked at her like he had a problem.

"Okay."

"It's a bit extravagant, don't you think?"

"Extravagant? What do you mean?"

"Your mileage is up fifteen percent from last month. You logged in overtime that wasn't approved."

Was he really bitching about the mileage on her car? "Every mile is accounted for. You added to my caseload twice this month, and field meetings were necessary. And if you're talking about the late request for me to meet Mr. Sokolov—"

"You're on salary. Overtime needs approval."

"You sent me at the end of the day."

"Then you should have come in late the next day, not request overtime compensation."

She bit her lip to keep the profanity she wanted to spew inside her head. Grace glanced at the clock in the room. "So you'd like me to come in ten minutes late tomorrow to make up for today?"

He handed her the expense report. "I expect a revised version of this tomorrow."

It took all her willpower to gently take the report from him and stand without storming off.

In her car, Grace gripped the steering wheel and called Richard every name in the book. It took five minutes for her to calm down enough to pull out of the parking lot.

Halfway home, she remembered that she had an impromptu date with Dameon. She cussed Richard again and pulled a U-turn.

She stopped at the home improvement store on her way and picked up a welcome mat as a last-minute gift before texting Dameon to tell him she'd be a little late.

By the time she pulled into the dark driveway and parked behind his truck, it was almost six.

The porch light brightened her path, and Dameon stood in the open doorway wearing jeans, a sweater, and a smile.

Just looking at him pushed away the anger that simmered in her blood. "Sorry I'm late."

"You don't need to apologize," he said as she walked up. Their eyes met and his smile fell. "Someone is stressed."

She didn't bother denying it. "My boss is a dick."

"I have vodka."

She wanted to weep. "God, I love you. Yes and please." The words were out of her mouth before she realized what they were.

Dameon, on the other hand, took them in. "I could get used to that."

Grace brushed it off. "Don't let it go to your head, Locke . . . that's the vodka I'm talking to."

He laughed, and Grace sighed in relief that he bought her excuse as they walked in the house.

The first thing she noticed was the warmth.

The fireplace crackled and popped and a three-foot Christmas tree sat in one corner of the room. Tiny lights illuminated the branches, and glass bulbs dangled from its limbs.

"When did you have time to do this?"

"Last week." Dameon closed the door behind her. "I thought about what you said about fireplaces and Christmas trees and felt inspired."

The grandma couch had been moved to the center of the room, and from the looks of it, cleaned. A tablecloth covered something that worked as a coffee table in front of it. The out-of-date track lighting brightened the corners of the room that the fire and tree didn't reach.

"I'm not sure how you managed to make a room cozy with one couch, but you did." She placed the bag in her hand down by the tree and turned to find Dameon looking at her.

"I'm glad you like it."

She dropped her purse on the sofa and shrugged to remove her coat.

Dameon was there to help.

"About that—" Grace swallowed the word *drink* when Dameon turned her around and lowered his lips to hers.

He was as warm as the fire and tasted faintly like whiskey. Maybe it was the scent of pine and firewood, but Dameon felt one hundred percent man. She'd kissed enough boys to know the difference.

She closed her eyes and settled into the moment.

His arms closed her in and she grasped his sweater, enjoyed the feeling of his chest under her hands. His tongue swept briefly at her lips before playing with hers.

She was pretty sure she moaned.

Like before, he broke it off before she forgot where she was.

The more he did that, the more she wanted to forget. "Hello to you, too," she said.

Dameon wiped his thumb over her bottom lip. "I hope you're hungry."

Oh, she was hungry all right. That's when she smelled it.

"I'm warming up. I wouldn't call it cooking."

It smelled familiar. "Roast?"

He led her into the kitchen. He'd brought in two barstools and a small dinette set. "Sit. Tell me about your day."

Grace followed his advice and watched as he moved around the out-of-date kitchen. "My boss is a dick."

He laughed. "You already mentioned that."

She explained her encounter before leaving the office while Dameon poured vodka, ice, and a dash of something else into a shaker. He poured the drink into a proper martini glass and plopped in an olive.

Grace accepted the drink with a question. "How much time have you been spending here?"

"More than I expected." He lifted her glass to hers. "To martinis at home."

She couldn't help but smile. "Cheers."

They both drank and put the glasses down. "So, your boss pulled the permission card."

"There's a card?" she asked.

Dameon shrugged. "It's an asshole move, but yes. My guess is somewhere it's written that he has to approve overtime for every salaried employee. I have the same clause, but can't say I've ever had to use it."

"It's bullshit."

"I agree. It's assumed when you run to do a last-minute request from your boss, that the overtime is good."

"Exactly."

"Did you say that before you left the office?"

"No."

"There's the loophole. Next time clarify. If he says no, skip his request."

Grace sighed. "And give him a reason to fire me."

Dameon leaned against the back counter facing her. "Are you really worried he will?"

Instead of answering his question point-blank, she asked, "Do I look like I'm insecure?"

He laughed. "No."

"Right. I'm not. But with Richard, I feel like I'm on eggshells. This last year has been awful."

"Was there anything that prompted it?"

"No." She took another drink. "In the beginning, I was new. Thought everything was normal for a new employee. Six months in, I realized that I was the only woman there and it meant I needed to prove I was as capable as the men." She paused and looked Dameon in the eye. "It's been five years and I'm tired of proving myself."

"And when did your feelings change?"

"I don't know . . . six months ago, maybe a year."

Dameon waved two fingers in the air. "And that, hon, is the shift. You got fed up and Richard noticed. Now he's flexing to show his power."

"By being an ass?"

"Maybe. Your boss felt a crack in his control, so he's fighting back."

She knew Dameon was right. "So, what do I do?"

"Are you good at your job?"

Grace looked at him like he was crazy. "I'm fabulous at my job! I run the track twice before the second employee under Richard runs it once."

Dameon folded his arms across his chest, his cheeks pulled up in a grin. "Then man up. Stick to your guns and follow his rules. If he fires you, get another job and hire a lawyer. I know a few."

"You make it sound easy."

"Know your worth. It's what separates workers from bosses. From what I've seen of you, you're a leader. Richard probably sees that and is either intimidated or pushing you to realize it."

Dameon's words rolled around in her head. "Richard doesn't like me. I doubt this is about him wanting the best for me."

"Then he's the one who's insecure."

Grace stopped talking and looked at the man. Suddenly, the whole Richard ordeal felt less. Less of a concern, less important, less needing to take up her time.

She smiled. "So, what are we eating?"

CHAPTER TWENTY

He'd ordered dinner from The Backwoods and kept it warm in the oven.

Grace sat beside Dameon eating prime rib and listening to his run-down of the details of Christmas day with his brother and mom.

She couldn't stop laughing. "So dinner was popcorn and mashed potatoes?"

"And pie. Don't forget the pie."

Apparently, his mom made pie the day before, so that was prepared and in the fridge.

"No wonder there's enough food here for a week."

Dameon asked for the whole rib roast and not just a slice. "Probably not a good idea to go to the store hungry," he said.

She looked at the remainder of the slab of beef. "You think?"

"She had to know she was high. I kept asking her if she was okay and all she did was giggle."

"Did you ask your brother what he gave her?"

"No. I haven't seen my mom that happy since before my dad passed. I wasn't about to put my brother in the hot seat."

"Aw . . . that's sweet."

"He's staying through tomorrow. Then going back to Seth and Barney."

Grace found herself laughing again.

"It's not funny."

She tried to keep a straight face and failed. "It's a little funny."

Dameon finally cracked a smile and she helped him find the humor. "We need to introduce my aunt Beth to your mom."

Grace pushed aside her plate.

"Thank you," he said.

"For what?"

"For coming over. For making me laugh at what normally frustrates me."

"I unloaded my baggage about my boss. The least I can do is listen to yours about Tristan."

Outside, the cry of a coyote stopped their conversation.

"I don't know if I will ever get used to that." Dameon stood and looked out the back window.

"I would rather hear a coyote than the siren of a police car or ambulance." Grace gathered both their plates and walked into the kitchen.

"I'll do that," he said.

She looked around for a garbage can, found it under the sink. "In my world, the one who cooks doesn't clean."

Dameon moved to stand beside her over the sink. "Since I didn't cook, that doesn't count."

"I'll wash, you dry and put away."

Dameon spun around. "I don't have dish towels."

"Oh. Does the dishwasher work?"

His face lit up. "Yes. But I don't have the right soap."

"You need help," Grace teased.

The two of them loaded the dishwasher and put the remainder of the food in the refrigerator.

With the chores out of the way, Dameon put another log on the fire and encouraged her to sit.

When she did, Grace realized quickly that the couch was as worn down as it was old. No matter where you sat, the missing springs in the middle forced you to roll toward the center.

"It's pretty bad," Dameon said. "I had the people that cleaned the carpet clean the couch before I sat on it."

Dameon tried to sit a foot away, but they both ended up in the middle.

"That was a waste of money." She scooted forward and started to lift the cloth covering the coffee table.

Dameon's hand reached out to stop her. "Home Depot boxes."

She laughed. "This reminds me of the days right after college when I was broke."

He sat back and lifted his arm behind her shoulders and pulled her close. Not that he needed to do much of the work since the couch had already made it impossible to sit far away. "I keep going back and forth between hiring someone to do the shopping for me or doing it myself."

"You hire someone to shop? How do I get that job?" She found the comfort of his arm and the crackle of the fire hypnotic.

"You're overqualified."

"Find me a woman who doesn't like to shop with other people's money."

"I doubt that exists," Dameon said.

She certainly didn't know any. "So the house is lacking essentials, but I'm guessing the garage is already well equipped."

"Of course. I know my way around the home improvement stores. Dish towels and coffee tables are a different story."

"That's a man for you. Buy a hammer you *might* need before a towel you use every day."

Dameon took her hand in his and traced her fingers. His simple touch pulled a flutter from deep within her belly.

She gazed up to find him watching their hands. He stopped and looked at her. "I should probably be encouraging you to leave."

"Probably." Grace lifted her chin a fraction of an inch, and Dameon accepted her invitation.

The way the man kissed . . . slow and sexy. His arm around her shoulders pulled her in tighter as she opened her lips in acceptance. Her eyes closed, and the space between them did as well. This wasn't a kiss good night in the front seat of a truck, or at her front door. No, this was hello. An awakening of sensations brought on by more than just the act. More than the feel of Dameon's arms roaming down her back and up into her hair to tilt her head. This was more, somehow.

Grace didn't want to question the butterflies in her stomach and the excitement of his touch.

She just wanted to feel.

Her hands reached for him, his chest . . . his arms.

The small brush of his thumb on her breast caught her breath in her throat.

Dameon moved his hand away and kept kissing her.

Grace reached for his retreating hand and put it more firmly on her chest.

He sighed and took what she was offering.

She started to squirm. The desire for more and closer and without clothes slowly became a need. Her fingertips pulled at the edges of Dameon's sweater until she felt skin.

His lips broke away and his hand reached for her face.

Grace opened her eyes to find him staring. "This isn't why I invited you over," he whispered.

"I know that"—and she did—"but it's what we both want."

The firelight swirled in his eyes and he lowered his lips again.

Feeling free to touch, Grace let her hands roam. The strong muscles of his chest and the tapered waist to the belt he wore with his jeans . . . everything excited her more.

Dameon's lips moved to her jaw with a playful scrape of his teeth.

Grace crawled on top of him, straddling his legs with hers. She felt his heat through their clothes and reveled in his hands as they moved down her back and squeezed her backside. She tugged at his sweater. "This needs to go."

He helped her pull it over his head and relaxed against the couch as she explored his bare chest with her hands.

She looked him in the eye as her fingernails ran over his nipples.

When his hands squeezed her hips and he lifted his pelvis toward hers, she knew she'd found one of his sweet spots. He was certainly pressing against all of hers.

She kissed him this time, leading his tongue into a dance with hers. More urgent with need. It had been a long time since she'd been intimate with anyone, and even longer since she felt this kind of buildup inside of her.

Her shirt met his on the floor, and Dameon filled both his hands with her breasts through her bra. "Is there any part of you that isn't gorgeous?" he asked before he leaned forward to press his lips on her flesh and push her bra aside. Her nipples were already tiny nubs of desire, and Dameon captured them with his teeth.

She rocked against him, enjoying the friction between her legs. "Please tell me you have a proper bed in this house," she said with a sigh.

His chest rumbled with laughter. "Hold on."

Before she could move, Dameon was on his feet, and his hands held her against him so she couldn't escape.

With her legs wrapped around his waist and her arms holding on to his neck, Dameon walked them down the hall and into his bedroom. "I can walk," she told him.

He shook his head. "I like this better."

~

Dameon set her down on his mattress and helped her scoot up the bed. For a moment he simply looked at her, the rise and fall of her chest, her swollen lips from their make-out session on the couch. The couch he hated but had to give props to for keeping her so close to him while they sat there. Grace was sexy and beautiful and staring at him with her hair sprawled all over his pillows. There were so many things he wanted to say to her in that moment, but there was something he wanted to do to her more.

He spread out over her, his knee resting between her legs, and pressed his skin to hers. Their lips met, and Dameon melted into her kiss. He matched her nibble for nibble, sigh for sigh. He could kiss the woman forever and bask in the heat from her body.

Her fingernails clawed into his back and teased the edge of his jeans. His cock twitched in his tight clothes. Pulling away, he moved his kiss to her neck. "You taste like honey and smell like flowers."

His words had her hips lifting around his leg.

Dameon smiled and gave her the friction her body asked for.

"I want more than your knee," she told him.

"Patience . . ."

But Grace wasn't. That beautiful hand he liked to play with while they sat next to each other eating, or talking . . . or anything slid down his waist and covered his erection through his clothing.

Not to be outdone, Dameon slowly unzipped her slacks and ran one finger over the edge of her panties.

Their eyes caught again.

Grace was smiling and stroking him as he let his fingers reach the folds of her sex.

She bit her lower lip with a moan. "I'll show you mine if you show me yours."

Dameon smiled and cupped her completely. He wanted this to last all night.

"I need . . ."

He didn't let her finish. His teasing needed more room.

She lifted her hips to aid in him tugging off her pants. He pulled at hers and she worked frantically to get him just as naked. And they kissed. Hot open-mouth kisses mad with desire.

With their clothes lying wherever they were thrown, Dameon teased her sex again. This time she pushed against him and opened to give him better access. "So beautiful," he whispered above her breasts before taking his time bringing them into his mouth.

"Dameon, please," she called out as her hand circled the length of his erection.

All thoughts of making this first time last forever vanished. He rested his head on her chest and savored the feeling of her touching him.

She called his name again, and he pulled away long enough to remove a condom from the nightstand by the bed.

Grace touched his hand as he put the condom on. "I'm on the pill," she told him.

Her words felt like permission to continue without his layer of protection. Her trust didn't pass him by. But right then, with both of them setting off fire alarms with desire, was not the time for clarification. "I'll remember that for the future."

"Okay."

Grace wrapped her legs around him as he covered her body.

Dameon placed his hands in hers and stretched them over her head. Their eyes never lost contact as he moved into her for the first time.

The sheer look of wonder on her face was something he would never forget.

Her breath caught and her entire body contracted around him.

"God, Grace . . . if you keep doing that I won't last long."

Her body did it again. "I can't help it," she sighed. Her hips reached for him.

He was going to lose it. He closed his eyes and pushed the desire to release far away where the cold lived and Inuit had sex with their clothes on.

"Please . . ."

C'mon, Dameon, he silently chided himself.

Finding control, he slowly moved, inched deeper, and touched more of her.

Grace pulled his head down to hers and possessed his lips. "Yes," she whispered, her hips setting the pace. Then, without warning, her sex tightened and her breath caught. His name on her lips as she found release was music to his soul.

He watched her come apart and stopped moving while her body sent pulses through his.

"Damn, Grace."

Her eyes closed and her breath shuddered. "Your fault," she said, accusingly with a tiny laugh.

Once she was lax and her eyes opened, he brushed her hair with his fingers.

This was good . . . all of it.

"You look pleased with yourself," she said.

"Not yet."

"Oh?"

He pushed into her again. "I want another one from you," he told her.

She started to laugh, and Dameon started to move.

~

Grace had fallen asleep.

Her body tucked so close to his, it was as if she were a human blanket. Dameon hadn't doubted for a second that sex with Grace would be amazing, but he hadn't expected magical. They fit like pieces of a puzzle, which, as cliché as it sounded in his head, was exactly what it felt like. She matched his energy, his pace, and his appetite.

Dameon lay there stroking her hair as she slept. He knew he was falling. Felt it the moment they properly met. Wasn't that why he was making a home out of a property he planned on tearing down? To be closer to her. To have an excuse to ask her to come over after work so he could hear about her day, and tell her about his. He liked that part, too.

He'd lived alone since he graduated from college. Never once did he invite a girlfriend to move in with him. He didn't want the hassle and commitment. But lying next to Grace, and feeling her breath on his chest, he didn't want her to leave.

Dameon closed his eyes and willed his brain to settle.

CHAPTER TWENTY-ONE

Grace hadn't meant to stay, and certainly didn't think she'd wake up to the sun peeking in Dameon's bedroom window.

But that was exactly how she woke up.

Dameon had offered breakfast and a leisurely morning, but that would have to wait for a weekend. She hated to scramble off, but she would have been late to work if she hadn't rushed out the door.

But not before Dameon kissed her senseless and whispered promising words of what he wanted to do with her the next time they were together.

Morning fog accompanied her on her way home, and the streets were relatively bare with so many people off for the holiday week.

She took stock of how she felt after a night with Dameon.

Blissfully sore in areas of her body that hadn't moved that way in some time, and emotionally charged. He was a patient and giving lover, and she'd responded in a way she never had before. Most of her lovers needed to spend more than a night to figure out what worked for her.

Not Dameon.

Right before Grace started to walk out her door, she checked the time.

Remembering her meeting with Richard the day before and him denying her overtime, instead of rushing, she drove first to the coffee shop and took her time.

The office bustled with activity when she walked in exactly forty minutes late. She dropped her purse on her desk and went straight to Richard's office with a revised expense sheet in her hands.

She didn't knock. Didn't say hi.

"I'll be sure and clarify overtime in the future. But the mileage is accurate. If you want someone to audit my time, by all means. I have nothing to hide." She placed the paper on his desk and turned to leave.

Richard didn't utter a syllable as she walked away.

It was the closest thing to standing up for herself she'd ever done with her boss, and her adrenaline was pumping when she went back to her office.

She sat motionless and waited for her nerves to calm. When they did, she smiled.

This was who she was. Strong, centered, and in control.

Somehow she'd stopped being that since summer.

She tackled her inbox with purpose. It was time to spread the workload. And by the time they had their early monthly meeting in January, she'd be prepared.

~

Grace called an emergency girls' night.

If there was one thing consistent with a new man in your life, it was the need to talk about it with your girlfriends.

Parker brought a cheese plate, Erin brought wine, and Grace pulled out an array of fruit and cold smoked salmon. They met at Grace's condo since both her brothers were home, and the last thing she wanted to do was clue them in on her love life.

Erin and Parker arrived together.

179

The minute Grace opened the door, the two other women paused. Parker spoke first. "Someone is getting laid."

Grace knew she was blushing. "Is it that obvious?"

Parker squealed and walked through the door. Erin handed her not one but two bottles of wine.

"I knew it!" Erin said. "You sounded way too excited in your message for tonight to be bad news."

"Oh my God, you guys . . . I can't tell you how great it was."

They shuffled around her small kitchen while Grace found a wine opener.

"I thought you were going to wait. At least that's what you said the last time we talked, which was what, Christmas?" Erin grabbed three glasses out of the cupboard and placed them on the counter.

"I was. We were," Grace corrected herself. "And then we didn't."

Parker made rolling motions with her hands. "Details."

Grace pulled the cork free and filled their glasses. "I had a shitty day at work. Richard was being his typical asshole self, went a little further than normal, and Dameon invited me over to his place."

"In LA?"

"No. The house in the canyon." She sipped her wine. "I get there and he has a fire going and a cute little Christmas tree in the corner. He bought dinner from The Backwoods and was keeping it warm in the oven."

"Sounds like he's working it."

"We talked and laughed. He gave me pointers on how to deal with Richard. We ended up sitting on this god-awful sofa the previous owners left behind. Did I mention the fire?"

Parker was ear-to-ear smiles.

"Next thing I know, we're making out on the couch like teenagers trying to get to the next base." She stopped and closed her eyes at the memories. "It was so amazing. Like the best sex I've ever had amazing. Do you know what I mean?" Grace opened her eyes to find both women staring at her and nodding.

"I thought I knew what good sex was . . . and then I met Colin and realized I didn't know jack shit," Parker said.

Erin shook her head. "I forgot what an orgasm felt like without a battery-operated toy before Matt."

Much as Grace never wanted to hear about her brothers' sex lives, she couldn't exactly deny Parker and Erin their time to talk.

"It's more than sex, though. It was everything. I find myself wanting to talk to him at the end of my day to tell him about work. I want to hear about his mom and know if he made it to Target to buy kitchen towels and dishwasher detergent."

Each of them grabbed a plate of food and moved into the living room.

"It sounds like you really like him," Parker said.

"I do."

Erin kicked off her shoes and tucked her legs under her on the sofa. "What about your work? Aren't you concerned Richard is going to find this relationship a conflict of interest?"

"I've been so mad at my boss, I don't know if I care what he thinks. The worst he can do is pull the project away from me. Which is fine."

"You're not worried about getting fired?"

"He'd have to find some kind of foul play, and that isn't happening. I'm an honest employee and I do my job well. Dameon's project is barely off the ground. And I certainly haven't used city time or money to see him privately."

Parker lifted a piece of cheese to her mouth. "You might consider telling your boss before he finds out. Tell him if he doesn't approve, he needs to pull you now."

Grace saw the wisdom in Parker's words. "Maybe."

"So, when are you going to bring him around? Matt is dying to meet him."

"I don't know."

"Have you met any of his friends?" Parker asked.

"No. We're going out for New Year's Eve. Something fancy downtown. My guess is he knows someone we're going to see."

"Friends always shed light on a man's personality that he doesn't always want to share when you're first going out," Erin said. "At least that's what my therapist says. Everyone loves Matt, and most of the people who knew Desmond only tolerated him."

Grace sighed. "How is therapy going?"

Erin lost her smile briefly. "I have good days and bad. I still see him when I close my eyes. Have nightmares. Matt is so patient with me. Careful."

Grace placed a hand on Erin's knee. "Matt loves you."

"I know."

"Have you guys talked about marriage?" Parker asked.

She nodded. "A little here and there. It's what we both want, but we don't want any clouds of this last year anywhere around us."

"Take your time getting married, but that shouldn't stop him from putting a ring on your finger," Grace said.

Erin smiled. "I don't need a ring to be committed to your brother. He has my heart and he knows that."

Yeah, but Grace didn't see Matt waiting too long to stake his claim. Her brothers were territorial like that.

"I already consider you my sister-in-law. Matt just needs to make it official."

"Yes, please. And get your aunt off my empty uterus," Parker said.

"Isn't it crazy how life is constantly changing?" Grace asked. "I didn't even know you guys two years ago and now we're all family."

"Everything changes," Erin said. "And then you meet the right guy who changes everything."

Grace smiled into the thought. Dameon was doing exactly that for her.

She unfolded from the sofa. "Time for a fashion show. I need help picking out what to wear for New Year's."

～

Dameon walked into his condo for the first time in five days.

The place felt cold, partially because the heater had been turned down, but more because it was starting to lose its appeal.

When had that happened? He liked living in the city. Enjoyed the closeness of restaurants and bars, nightlife, and energy the city afforded him.

But there weren't as many stars in the sky and certainly a lack of yipping coyotes and rabbits avoiding his truck as he drove away.

He'd always looked at his home in the city as temporary. Having grown up in the suburbs in a traditional home with a yard and neighbors who shared a fence instead of a wall and hallway, he knew he'd one day return to a more rural lifestyle.

Granted, the house he was in now was pretty far off his spectrum. His closest neighbor was half a mile away, and he could throw a small Woodstock and not bother anyone. But that, too, would change once his development went in and the homes started going up.

He had spent quite a bit of time reflecting on the neighborhood, just as he intended. But he found himself thinking about it like a man with a family. Not a single developer turning raw land into a money-making machine.

And that was entirely Grace's fault. Or caused by her entering Dameon's life. He told his head to slow down, but his heart wasn't listening.

He liked her . . . a lot.

He cranked his heater up and turned on his sound system. The simple comforts of his home that he was living without when he was in Santa Clarita. He opened his refrigerator and cracked open a beer. He tossed several items in the trash that had spoiled or otherwise wouldn't be eaten. He moved a bottle of good champagne from a storage rack to the fridge so he had some on hand when he brought Grace back after the New Year's Eve party. Here, she couldn't giggle about an outdated couch or lack of a coffee table. He appointed his home with only his tastes in mind. He wasn't one for clutter, so the tables and walls were minimally decorated. Contemporary furnishings in dark colors. His TV and sound system were state of the art and lacked nothing. He paid a housekeeper to come in twice a month to keep the dust down.

He looked out the large bay window at the city below. It was late, and the lights glistened against the small droplets of rain that fell from the sky.

This might be where he lived, but it no longer felt like home. And that reality was a little unsettling.

He set about doing laundry and gathering several items he wanted to take with him the next time he went to the canyon house.

When his phone rang, he saw Grace's name pop up on his screen. He turned his music down and answered. "Good evening."

"Hi."

"How is ladies' night?"

"Already over," she said. "But it was fun. Were your ears burning?"

He grinned. "I guess that means you were talking about me."

"That's okay, isn't it?"

He walked away from the window and sat on his leather sofa. "I would be more concerned if you weren't."

"Really?"

"Yes, really."

Grace was silent for a second. "Dameon, I need to ask you something. A favor."

"Consider it done."

She laughed. "I'm serious."

His brain buzzed with questions. "I'm listening."

"I've been dating since I was fifteen. Well, my parents thought I was sixteen, but in all reality, I was fifteen."

He laughed.

"Anyway, I've found the more interested I was in someone, the less interested they were in me. I've been stood up, ghosted, and even left in a restaurant halfway through a meal. I've had more than my share of catfishers when I subscribed to the online dating racket. And the last guy I was on a date with . . ." Her words trailed off.

"The last guy what?" He knew what she was about to say because Colin had filled him in. But since she hadn't shared the information willingly, he tried to pull it out of her.

"Never mind."

"No, Grace . . . the last guy what?"

"I don't want you to think I'm being overdramatic or looking for sympathy. Or want you to feel sorry for me enough to pretend that we're on the same page here."

"The only thing I feel sorry for is the guys who didn't see you for how amazing you are. But I'm glad they didn't so I have a chance."

"Do you always say the right things?" she asked with a nervous laugh.

"Talk to me, Grace."

"The last guy . . . was Erin's late husband. He pretended to be someone he wasn't online and asked me to meet him at a bar. When I got there, the guy, or the picture of the guy I thought I'd been talking to, never showed up. But Erin's ex did. I didn't know anything about him. I'd never seen a picture, had no way of knowing who he was. I thought it was organic. That I'd met someone not through friends or a stupid dating app."

Dameon felt his hand gripping his phone too tight as he waited for her to tell him the whole story.

"He said his wife was dead. That he hadn't dated. I believed every lie he told me. I almost went back to the hotel with him, Dameon. I remember him putting his hands on my neck and squeezing just a little too hard when he kissed me." Her voice cracked.

He closed his eyes. "God, Grace."

"I don't know what he planned to do that night. We were by the mall and one of my dad's friends from the sheriff's department saw us. Desmond was noticeably shook."

"His name was Desmond?" *Oh, damn . . . that's not good.*

"Yeah. But that wasn't the name he was using. Anyway . . . he backed off. Told me he was still married and his wife was trying to leave him. I was pissed. It wasn't until later that I realized who he was. He was completely crazy. Tried to kill Erin instead of letting her leave him. I was lucky. You hear about things on the news, disappearing people, and I realized I was one bad choice away from being that woman."

"I can't imagine what you were feeling."

"You don't have to, I'll tell you. I felt stupid. Like how the hell did I fall for his lines and believe him when there were red flags? I stopped trusting my instincts. Stopped trusting myself."

"I'm sorry." And he was.

"I don't want your sympathy, Dameon. I want your word."

"On what?"

"That if this isn't working for you, or you get bored, or anything . . . that you'll be honest with me. You won't just stop talking to me, or pretend you're happy when you're not."

The words he'd used describing his relationship with Lena flew back at him. He wished he could take them back. "You have my word."

"Even if it's painful."

"Even if it's painful, Grace. I respect you too much to consider any of those things."

The line was silent.

"Thank you," she finally said.

"No . . . thank you. For trusting me with that story."

"It feels good to say all of that out loud."

"Is this the first time you did?"

"My family knows what happened, but yeah. I don't talk about it with them. Erin could have died. She was in the ICU for days. Seemed my brush with her ex was nothing in comparison."

Dameon rubbed the tension settling in his shoulders. He wished he was there, holding Grace as she told her story. "I'm not a therapist, but I'm guessing they might point out that watching someone *get* shot and being the one who *is* shot can have long-lasting effects on both people."

"I-I never thought about it like that."

"I do." And since Dameon had an insane desire to lift Grace's mood, he told her something he thought she'd want to hear. "I told my mother about you."

"You what?"

"Yeah. Right after we met. You hadn't agreed to date me, but I told my mom that we already were."

"You were that sure I'd cave?"

"I was that sure I wasn't going to let you slip away without trying everything I could to give me a shot."

"Really?"

"Really. Now that we have that out of the way . . . What the hell is a catfisher?"

CHAPTER
TWENTY-TWO

New Year's Eve was meant for sequins and sparkle and dresses that hugged your curves and high heels that made a man take you in from the tip of your head to the bottom of your toes.

So when Dameon showed up at her condo to pick her up, she opened the door to a bouquet of white roses and a man who couldn't find his tongue.

He blew out a slow whistle. "Whoa."

"Is that approval?" She knew it was, but asked anyway.

Dameon held the flowers to the side and walked through her door. "We can pretend we went and just stay home instead." He slid a hand around her waist and wiggled his eyebrows.

"It took me forever to get ready."

"It will take me less than ten minutes to mess it all up," he teased.

She ran her hands up his suit and fiddled with his perfect tie. "Hi," she whispered before reaching up for a kiss.

He kissed her thoroughly and moaned when she moved away.

Grace wiped the red lipstick off his mouth. "This isn't your color."

He licked his lips and smiled.

She glanced at the flowers in his hand while he stared at her. "Are those for me?"

Dameon lifted the roses toward her. "You make me forget my own name."

"They're beautiful."

"You're stunning."

Yeah, that didn't suck to hear.

He walked behind her while she gathered a vase to put the flowers in. Dameon's strong hands held on to her waist and his lips kissed the side of her neck.

"You're making this hard," she said.

"I'll stop." Only he kissed her neck a second time before placing his lips to her ear. "I want to show you off."

Because Dameon had told her they were going into the city, she'd packed an overnight bag to stay at his place. So with that in his hand, and a coat on her shoulders, they headed out for their first official date.

He led her to a Cadillac sedan and opened the door. "When did you get this?" she asked. She thought she'd be hiking it up in his truck instead of sliding into luxury.

"I have more than one car," he told her.

"Of course you do."

He closed the door, rounded the car, and got in on the driver's side.

"Are you going to tell me where we're going now?" she asked.

He pulled away from her complex and onto the main road. "Since my dad died, I've helped sponsor a Heart Association New Year's Eve event."

"Sounds fancy."

"Don't be too impressed. I'm one of many sponsors. I buy a table, invite some of my senior staff to join in. It works for charity and employee morale."

Which meant she was going to meet people he worked with. That made her nervous. "I'm glad I dressed up."

He reached over, grabbed her hand in his. "They're a relaxed group. Down to earth."

"I won't dance on a table, don't worry."

His eyes traveled to hers. "Now that I'd like to see."

~

Dameon had seen Grace in her life, her world. Now it was time to see what she looked like in his.

He drove up to the hotel where the event was taking place and pulled in line for the parking valet.

"There are a lot of limos." Grace stared out the windshield.

"It's flashier than the Prius the Uber driver uses."

As they rounded the corner, Grace found something else to comment on. "Are those reporters?"

He laughed. "My guess is they call themselves that, but I'm guessing *paparazzi* is a better description. But don't worry, they won't take pictures of us. Not on purpose, anyway."

"There are famous people going to this party?"

He shrugged. "I think so. Those kinds of things don't impress me."

"I haven't met anyone famous. Don't let me make a fool of myself."

"I'll let you know if you're drooling."

When their turn came, the valet opened the doors for them. The flashing bulbs and loud clicks of the camera went crazy. By the time Dameon rounded the car and took Grace's hand in his, the paparazzi had aimed their cameras somewhere else. In his experience, only the new photographers bothered to take his picture, unsure of who he was. And that was how he liked it.

But Grace was smiling, and it was worth it for him to see the look on her face.

They were greeted at the door first by the hotel staff, and then by a woman in a black evening dress with a small microphone hanging from an earpiece.

He approached her and gave both his name and Grace's.

Grace squeezed her fingers on the crook of his arm as they walked toward the bank of elevators that would take them to the party.

"This is a first," Grace said as they walked through the hotel.

"If you get enough of that and want to leave . . ."

"I'll let you know."

Once they were in the main room on the top floor of the hotel, Dameon checked their coats and walked her through the sea of people. The men wore suits, some without ties, some in full-blown tuxedos. The women were a combination of flashy to classy. But it was Grace who managed both. The room was decorated in silver, white, and gold with tons of twinkling lights. A dance floor was set up, and a band filled the space with music. Each table was numbered for dinner seating.

"Champagne or martini?" Dameon asked.

Grace looked at the lights above their heads. "This screams champagne."

When a waiter walked by with a tray of flute glasses, Dameon snagged two. Before Grace took a sip, he offered a toast. "To new beginnings," he said.

She smiled and tapped her glass to his. "I like that."

Her eyes glistened as she looked up at him. "Have you ever been to New York?" he asked.

"No."

"I want to see the lights of that city shine in your eyes." He wanted to see the lights of every city in her eyes. Or maybe even the flickering stars in a moonless desert sky.

"Either I'm out of practice, or that's a new pickup line," she teased.

Dameon leaned down and whispered in her ear, "I've already picked you up, so it isn't a line." He kissed the side of her face before settling back on his heels.

He saw the warmth on her face and the ease of her smile.

"Excuse me, is this man bothering you?"

Dameon heard Omar's voice before he turned to greet his friend. They shook hands and went in for a half hug. "Happy New Year," Dameon said.

"Happy New Year to you, too. This must be Grace."

Dameon set his glass down and introduced them. "Omar is my CFO and longtime friend."

"Friends long before he was my boss," Omar said as he shook Grace's hand. "I've heard a lot about you."

"Is that right?" Grace glanced at Dameon. "I've heard nothing about you."

Omar reached for his chest and winced. "I'm wounded."

Dameon laughed. "If I talked about you, she would never have come tonight."

The chest Omar was pretending pain with now puffed out like a peacock. "I'm a lady magnet, Grace. He's just afraid you'll find me more attractive."

Grace visibly relaxed. "The one who struts the most has the least to brag about," she told him.

Dameon pointed at his friend. "She's got ya there."

Omar narrowed his eyes. "I like this one."

"How many of *us* are there?" Grace asked, her eyes shifting to Dameon.

"Let's see, there's Ally, Brandy, Connie, Darlene—"

Dameon nudged Omar away. "Don't listen to him. He's reading off his little black book, not mine."

"I did like Darlene . . . she did this thing with her ton—"

"Enough with the details," Dameon cut him off.

Grace was laughing, thank God.

"Have you met the rest of the staff?" Omar asked Grace.

"Not yet." Dameon looked around the room, saw a few familiar faces at the silent auction table. "Let's see what we can spend some money on." He slid his hand along Grace's waist and led her away.

"I see someone I want to say hello to," Omar said before walking in the opposite direction.

"Omar doesn't have an off button," Dameon told Grace.

"You two are obviously good friends or he would have kept things polite," she said.

"I'm glad you saw that. Because there isn't a Brandy or Darla."

"Darlene," Grace corrected him.

"Her either. I date one woman at a time."

Grace looked at him. "Really?"

"I have to juggle work. I refuse to do the same with women."

For a minute, he wasn't sure Grace believed him. But the slow smile that washed over her face told him his words hit home. "Okay, then."

They approached the auction table, and Dameon placed both his hands on Grace's waist while looking over her shoulder at the items being sold.

"A trip to someone's summer home in Italy? Who does that?" Grace asked.

"Someone who doesn't visit their second home and needs the write-off."

"That's nuts."

They moved down the table filled with pricey trips and jewelry. There were studio audience tickets for talk shows based in LA. Spa baskets for her and eighteen holes on exclusive golf courses for him. Each item she looked at and passed over.

"See anything you like?" he asked.

She giggled and whispered, "It's all out of my price range, but it's fun to look at."

"It's not out of my price range," he told her. Although he was fairly certain Grace knew that.

"Then what do you want? Do you play golf?" She pointed to the golf package.

"Only when I have to."

"The spa? I know you like a good foot pampering," she teased.

He lowered his voice and whispered in her ear, "I thought we agreed never to talk about that again."

"We did? I don't remember that conversation."

He quickly shifted her gaze to a sapphire necklace displayed on a black cushion. "What about this?"

"I didn't know you liked women's jewelry," she said. "I never see you wearing any."

He squeezed her waist and she squirmed away. "Someone is ticklish."

She held his hand to her hip. "Stop," she giggled.

Dameon filed away her funny bone for another, more private, time. "Seriously, the necklace would look fabulous on you."

"You're crazy," she said.

He kissed her ear before whispering, "Wearing *only* the necklace."

Dameon loved making her blush.

And to prove a point, he grabbed a pen and wrote his name, table number, and price he was willing to pay to make his fantasy come true.

Grace placed her hand over his. "What are you doing?"

He kept writing. "It's for charity."

"You're nuts."

He winked and pulled her along.

Halfway up the other side, Omar returned. Some of the playfulness from before was gone. "Max is here," he said while nodding to the opposite side of the room.

Dameon felt the blissfulness of the night try to sour. Resisting the urge to turn to look at his onetime friend, he kept pace with the people moving through the silent auction line. "It's an open venue."

"He's sitting at your table."

Now that, Dameon wasn't expecting. Although he probably should have. In years past, Max had been welcome and in fact would often fight to pay for the table.

"How did that happen?"

Omar shrugged.

"Is something wrong?" Grace asked.

This wasn't the place to go into details.

"Dameon's ex–business partner managed a slot at our table," Omar said for him.

Grace's eyes opened wide and her jaw dropped. "Banks . . . Maxwell Banks?" Grace asked.

Dameon focused on her. "You know about him?"

She made a strange face. "I may have looked you up when we first met."

This woman never ceased to amaze him. "Is that right?"

"I only found what the papers talked about."

"The details will have to wait," Dameon told her.

"Do you want to leave?"

The fact she even asked made his night. "Do I look like a quitter?"

Omar laughed.

"Okay, then. Let the show begin."

Dameon wrapped an arm over her shoulders and pulled her close. He was falling fast for this woman.

CHAPTER
TWENTY-THREE

To say she was blown away by the entire experience of walking into a red-carpet, star-studded New Year's Eve event, having Dameon place an obscene bid down for a necklace he wanted to see her naked in, and finally landing in a full-blown soap opera drama with an ex–business partner was an understatement . . . Grace was on a rocket shooting to the moon.

Dameon walked her around the room, introduced her to more people than she would ever remember.

A few stuck out.

Chelsea, who worked with him . . . Omar, of course, and Tyler, who she had met before.

Everyone else was a blur.

At one point, someone took a microphone and told everyone the silent auction was closing and dinner was about to be served. She felt tension roll off Dameon in waves. Instead of pointing it out, she squeezed his hand and smiled anytime he looked at her.

They took their seats for dinner. Half the people there were all smiles, the others were reserved.

And when the cause of those half smiles walked up, Dameon's hand reached for her knee under the table and squeezed.

She heard more than one person suck in a breath.

For the first time, Grace watched Dameon put on a political face. The kind one had to use when dealing with adversity while remaining polite. "Max? This is a surprise." Dameon stood and reached out a hand.

Maxwell Banks had a very distinct look.

Privileged.

His skin was tan, his hair blond, and his suit screamed money.

He shook Dameon's hand before looking around the table. "I see the team's all here," he said before unbuttoning his jacket and taking his seat.

"How have you been?" Dameon asked in an obvious attempt at small talk.

"Never better." Maxwell's eyes moved to Grace.

Instinctively, she smiled.

"And who is this?"

Dameon looked at her. "Grace Hudson, this is Max."

Max reached across the table. She had no choice but to shake the man's hand. "Max Banks," the man corrected. And when he did, he squeezed Grace's hand . . . twice.

She held in every possible comment on that move.

"Nice to meet you," she said.

Grace settled next to Dameon, making sure it was clear she wasn't available.

Max's eyes flared.

"What brings you here tonight?" Dameon asked.

"Same as you. A little entertainment, a good cause. A happy New Year . . ."

Omar shook his head with a laugh.

Max turned his eyes on him. "Have something to say?"

"Nothing that wouldn't make everyone at the table uncomfortable, so I'll keep it to myself." Omar lifted his glass filled with amber liquid and drank.

"I see *nothing* has changed."

Chelsea leaned forward. "How's your father, Max? I heard he isn't well."

For a brief moment, Grace saw Max's armor crack. "He's doing better than the news would lead you to believe."

"I'm happy to hear that."

The staff at the hotel took that moment to arrive with their first course. Some kind of morsel on a plate that looked more like art than food.

The tables around them were idly chatting while theirs was filled with tension and silence.

"You're a new addition, Miss Hudson. What do you do for Dameon?" Max asked.

"I'm not sure I understand your question."

Dameon glared at Max. "Grace doesn't work for me."

"Is that right?" Max kept staring at her.

"What do you do for a living, Mr. Banks?" Grace asked, changing the subject.

Before Max could answer, Omar spoke up. "Max spends his father's money."

Max shifted his gaze. "It's called managing the family empire, Omar. Something you know nothing about."

Two of the guests at the table were purposely looking away.

"I've seen firsthand how you manage Daddy's cash—"

"Okay, guys. Let's not do this here," Dameon interrupted Omar.

Grace placed a hand on Dameon's knee.

Omar leaned back, ignoring the food on his plate.

"Do you work, Grace?" Max continued.

"I'm a civil engineer."

Max actually laughed.

"How is that funny?" Dameon asked.

"That's not exactly your type."

Before Dameon could say something, Grace leaned in. "When you were a child, did your report card tell your parents that you didn't get along well with others?"

Max lost his grin.

Omar laughed.

Dameon kept his voice low. "I'm not sure what your point is by being here, Max. It's obviously not to bury any hard feelings. And it certainly isn't for the entertainment or charity work. But I would appreciate it if you left my date out of whatever bone you're trying to pick."

The waiters swooped in and removed the untouched appetizer plates.

"Must be a serious relationship," Max said.

"Why do you care?" Grace found herself asking.

"Dameon, Omar, and I go way back. We used to pass our dates around, didn't we?"

"That's enough," Dameon warned him.

But Grace had heard enough to realize what Max was doing.

"Too close to the truth for you, old friend?"

It was Grace's turn to laugh. "So this is a penis-measuring contest, right?"

All eyes turned her way.

"I have two older brothers who always had friends around when I was growing up. And whenever they had a falling-out with someone in their friend group, it always ended with some kind of chest-bumping *I'm a bigger man* thing." Grace glanced at Chelsea. "Classic *mine is bigger than yours*." Grace shifted her gaze to Max. "Only my brothers both grew out of that behavior in college."

Dameon grasped her hand.

"Grace is right, Max. This is beneath you. If you came here to say something, do it. But leave Grace and everyone else out of it."

Max pushed his chair back. "You're right, Dameon. This is beneath me. I honestly thought half your employees would have realized they were on a sinking ship and not be here tonight. But you must be keeping up the facade since the gang is all here. I'll be sure and check back in six months when you claim bankruptcy." He stood to leave.

"Don't hold your breath," Omar said.

Max played with the cuff of his jacket, his eyes glued to Dameon's, and then walked away.

There was a collective sigh at the table when he left.

"That was entertaining," Grace joked.

"What an ass," Chelsea said.

Dameon brought Grace's hand off his lap and kissed her fingers.

Omar cleared his throat. "So, did anyone taste the appetizer?"

~

Grace ran her foot down Dameon's leg as she stretched beside him on his bed. She played with the sapphire necklace he had put on her before they left the hotel.

"Jewelry is meant to be worn, not sit in a box waiting for a special occasion," he'd told her.

And when the clock counted down, Dameon kissed her long and hard, and she vowed to wear his gift so the small fortune he'd spent wasn't in vain.

The evening had been nearly perfect. They wished everyone a happy New Year and left after pouring Omar into a cab.

When Dameon walked her into his condo, she'd barely managed a glimpse before he whisked her off to his bedroom.

But now, in the afterglow of their lovemaking, Grace felt strangely awake as her fingers played with the stupidly expensive sapphire dangling from her neck.

Her thoughts shifted around to earlier in the evening when Max had flexed in front of Dameon's staff and friends.

"You're awfully quiet for not being asleep," Dameon said.

"Don't count on it lasting long. I'm exhausted."

He sighed. "I'm happy Max didn't ruin it for us."

"You're thinking about that, too?" She rested her head on the pillow so she could look at Dameon while they talked.

"I'm sorry you met him like that. There was a day I called him a close friend."

"He's obviously bitter. What do you think he was trying to gain by showing up tonight?"

"I'm not entirely sure. Undermine my team? Gloat?"

"Gloat about what?"

Dameon rolled on his side, took her hand in his. "He was a silent partner from the day I started Locke Enterprises. Last year we had a falling-out. He took his capital and walked away."

"But you're still in business."

"I am. Without Max's help, it is harder. He knows that. It's why he cut his finances out of the business. He wants to see me fail."

"Why?"

For a second, she wasn't sure he was going to answer. "Remember the woman I told you about . . . Lena?"

"The Greek girlfriend?"

"Yeah, her. When I broke it off, Lena met up with Max."

"Met up or hooked up?"

"Both. I honestly didn't care, but I think she thought she was going to hurt me. When I found out, I gave Max my blessing. I thought they were a better fit. She didn't work, liked the lifestyle Max could give her. A few months went by. Max didn't come into the office very often. We'd meet casually and I'd let him know how his investments were going. He told me he was going to ask Lena to marry him."

"I'm guessing that didn't happen."

Dameon shook his head. "He threw a party, asked me to come. Lena was there, wearing his ring . . ."

She had a feeling she knew where this story was going. "And then?"

"Lena drank too much and came on to me. I pushed her away. She kept trying. I told her she was acting like a child, and how could she tell Max yes when it was obvious she wasn't ready to settle down."

"Did Max walk in?"

"No. But the next day I told him what had happened."

"Good for you."

Dameon shook his head. "Max didn't believe me. Or took her side. Either way, our friendship ended and so did our business relationship."

"What happened to Lena?"

"Last I heard they were still engaged."

"That explains his comments about sharing women."

"Which was all crap. Even in college. He said that to get a rise out of you."

Grace yawned. "It takes more than that. I know someone who's grandstanding and know to ignore what they're saying when they are."

"I really hope he wakes up before he actually marries her. But I can't say any more than I already have. Besides, he isn't listening to me any longer."

"It's kind of sad."

"I agree."

Grace felt her eyelids getting heavy. "What about all the bankruptcy talk?"

"I'll find another investor before I let that happen."

"Then you are having trouble."

"Nothing more than any other growing business out there."

She wanted to ask him more questions, but she was having a hard time staying awake. "You don't have to pretend with me."

"Shhh. Go to sleep."

She snuggled closer. "I mean it."

"Good night, Grace."

"Happy New Year."

The last thing she heard before falling asleep was him whispering *happy New Year* in her ear.

CHAPTER TWENTY-FOUR

A new year and a new beginning.

That's what Grace kept saying to herself as she geared up for the bimonthly meeting with her colleagues. She was bound and determined to set a new course with her job, starting with calling Richard out on his passive-aggressive way of dumping work on her by implying she wasn't holding up her end. She needed everyone to collaborate on Dameon's project. It was simply too much for one person to do. And on a personal level, she knew it was important for things to move swiftly to meet his goals. Besides, it was smart to bring others in. If her relationship became public knowledge, she didn't want Richard accusing her of playing favorites. Which would be hard for her not to do, if she was honest with herself.

It was afternoon nearly a week into the new year when Grace sat in the conference room with Evan, Lionel, and Adrian. The interns had switched out, and two new college kids took their places.

Richard walked in a few minutes late. He was followed by Vivian Jewel, who was the head of their human resources department.

Her presence wasn't a normal occurrence, and everyone in the room seemed surprised to see her there.

"I asked Vivian to join us," Richard said before he took his seat.

Evan looked at Grace and shrugged.

The interns eagerly sat up with their notepads opened.

Adrian started passing around a folder.

Richard stopped him. "I thought we'd start with Grace today."

Grace felt her breath catch. Since when was she first . . . and when had he realized she had a first name?

Adrian pulled his folders back, and Grace told her heart rate to slow down.

She found her gaze collide with Vivian's.

The woman's smile felt off.

"Uhm . . . okay." Grace cringed. When did she ever stutter? "I have a lot to go over." She started with her most pressing files before moving on to Dameon's project. "I've spent quite a bit of time on the early side of the Locke Enterprises project to help save time later. Richard, you told me when you handed me this last month that it was something new for me to tackle. When I took a good look, I realized there isn't anything new here, just more of it. I need more hands if we're going to expedite this project."

"What's the hurry?" Richard asked.

"Dameon . . . Mr. Locke," she corrected herself, "told us both he wanted to break ground by spring. Get through the rainy season and acquire the necessary permits and zoning changes."

"We won't rush anything if it isn't right."

"I don't believe I said we should do that. I'm saying I need more manpower to accommodate the land developer's request. It seems reasonable—"

"If you're unable to do the—"

"I didn't say I was unable." Why was he throwing words in her mouth? "I'm suggesting if anyone is leaving early or has a half a day to throw toward this, I could use them." She looked around the room.

No one said a thing. Even Evan looked too scared to come to her defense.

"I'll take that into consideration," Richard said.

Grace moved away from Dameon's project. "I've put into motion a crew to begin work on the Sokolov project next week." She slid over the necessary paperwork that needed Richard's signature.

Richard looked at it, looked at her, and slid it back across the table. "We've decided to work with the landowner."

"Excuse me?"

"I met with Mr. Sokolov myself. Leave his file on my desk. That should free up a few hours for you."

"Did he hire—"

"I have it handled, Grace. Is that all?"

Why did she feel like she was in quicksand?

"Yes."

Richard turned his attention away. "Lionel . . . where are we on the wash?"

And the subject was changed. For the next forty-five minutes, reports were given and ideas were exchanged. For the most part, Grace fell silent.

When the meeting was over, Richard and Vivian stayed behind while everyone else left the room and headed straight to the water cooler room.

"Do you know what's going on?" Adrian asked once they were out of earshot of their boss.

"That was strange, right?" Grace asked.

"Did someone file a complaint against Richard?" Evan asked.

"Do you think that's why Vivian was in there?" Grace asked.

"Why else would HR be in our meeting?" Adrian poured a cup of coffee.

Grace knew she didn't file a complaint, not that she wasn't willing to. And if Evan had, he would have told her.

"I suppose we'll find out sooner or later." Lionel walked out of the room, Adrian followed.

"Why did he start with me?" Grace asked Evan. "And he even used my first name."

"Maybe he wanted to impress Vivian."

Something didn't smell right. Her hand reached for the necklace Dameon had given her and she heard his voice in her head. *"Know your worth."*

Thirty minutes before the workday was over, her olfactory senses were confirmed.

Richard requested a meeting with her in a conference room.

When she arrived, Vivian was there sitting to Richard's left. A man she didn't know was on Richard's right. One chair sat on the opposite side of the table making it painfully clear she was sitting in the hot seat.

"What's going on?" Grace asked before she sat down.

"Please have a seat, Miss Hudson," the man she didn't know said.

Her palms started to sweat. This wasn't good.

She sat as calmly as she could and folded her hands in her lap.

"Grace," Vivian started. "This is Mr. Simons. He's one of the city's attorneys."

"Okay."

"Do you know why I'm here?" Mr. Simons asked.

"I have no idea what's going on."

The attorney kept a stoic expression while Vivian smiled.

Richard was something in the middle. "The city received a formal complaint where you were named."

"What kind of complaint?"

"The city has been accused of asking for money in order to approve permits."

"All permits cost money," Grace told them.

"Not a fee, Miss Hudson. A bribe."

Grace closed her eyes and sighed. *Sokolov.* "This is about Mr. Sokolov on the Sierra Highway project, isn't it, Richard?"

"So you know about this," Mr. Simons said.

"A bribe was offered. But not requested by me. I informed Richard the day after it happened." Only Richard was looking everywhere but at her.

"Why not immediately?" Mr. Simons asked.

"It was late. After hours."

Richard sat shaking his head and saying nothing.

"You explained to them what happened, right, Richard?" He finally made eye contact with her.

"I told them what you told me," Richard started. "And that you didn't want to press charges."

"I didn't think it was necessary." Only now she was kicking herself for that decision.

"When the city is faced with pending legal action of this nature, we have very strict protocols that have to be put in place," Vivian said.

"Sokolov waved his wallet at me. Not the other way around," she explained.

"You don't have to get defensive, Grace. No one here is accusing you of anything," Richard said.

"Except Sokolov. And you are all listening to him." Fury swelled inside of her.

"We have to, Miss Hudson. He filed the complaint. Now, with your cooperation we can clear this up quickly and quietly."

Grace looked the attorney in the eye. "I have nothing to hide."

"Good."

She sat back, knowing they wouldn't find anything.

"In the meantime, we need to place you on paid leave."

Grace felt like someone punched her in the stomach. "What?"

"It's protocol. You're not to contact any of your clients while this investigation is taking place."

She immediately thought of Dameon. "Why?"

Instead of answering her direct question, the attorney kept talking. "Nothing can be removed from your office with the exception of your personal belongings. An audit needs to take place. When we have questions, we expect your cooperation."

"This is unbelievable. Not only was Sokolov the one who offered the bribe, he took it further to scare the living hell out of me before I left."

"And you didn't report it."

"I've dealt with bullies before, Mr. Simons. They thrive when they know they've gotten to you. Ignoring them is the only way to make them stop."

She was physically shaking.

"I know this is hard, Grace. But I assure you that we're on your side here." Vivian's soft voice tried to reason.

"So what, I don't come to work tomorrow?"

"No. You need to fill out an incident report and tell us in your words exactly what happened the night Mr. Sokolov accused you of this. And any subsequent meetings with the man. Anything you can think of. We have investigators with risk management who are skilled in discovering the guilty party. If Mr. Sokolov's accusations are found fraudulent—"

"They are," Grace interrupted.

"Then you can return to your job without any disciplinary action."

"And how long will that take?"

"It depends on many factors." That was lawyer-speak if she ever heard it.

"I'll accompany you to your office so you can get your things," Vivian told her.

"Because you don't trust me."

"It's to protect you, believe it or not. The day you are notified of this serious of a complaint you have no way of removing any files. We will be interviewing your colleagues as well. It's best you don't discuss this with any of them. Or they may be implicated."

Even though she didn't like it, the excuse sounded reasonable.

Richard finally spoke. "That's a beautiful necklace, Grace. Is it real?"

Her hand reached for Dameon's gift. "Excuse me?"

The smug look on his face made her want to scream.

"Richard." Vivian said his name as if it were a warning.

"What are you suggesting, Richard?" Grace was finding it hard to breathe.

"Take the night and write down everything," Vivian interrupted her. "Incident reports are brought up in court if it ever goes that far."

The whole thing was making Grace nauseated. "Can I leave now?" She looked directly at Vivian, ignoring Richard and Mr. Simons.

"Of course." Vivian stood and walked with her out of the meeting room. Her eyes started to well. The last thing she wanted to do was be seen leaving the office—no, being escorted out of the office—in tears.

Some of the staff had left for the day, and that was a blessing.

But Evan stood outside of his office when she and Vivian walked by. "Is everything okay?" he asked.

She shook her head and tried hard not to cry.

"There will be a staff meeting in the morning," Grace heard Vivian tell Evan. "Grace has been asked not to talk to anyone right now."

"What the hell?"

Grace sat behind her desk and looked around. She removed her purse from the bottom drawer and shoved in the few pictures of her family. There were other things, but since she knew she was guilty of nothing, she didn't bother packing them up. Besides, if she left things behind, people would know she'd be back. She stood and grabbed her coat from a peg on her wall.

Vivian smiled.

"You need to leave the cell phone the city issued."

Grace dropped her purse on her desk, dug the cell phone out, and placed it in Vivian's hands. Without so much as a backward glance, Grace walked out of her office, past the gawking employees who stared, and out the door.

Vivian watched her leave.

~

Dameon had the music turned up and all the lights on while he painted the living room. Grace said she'd call him when she got off work, so he hadn't bothered checking the time. The color on the walls did a great job of hiding the sins of the house. And the more he did, the more he wanted to.

His back yelled at him, told him he hadn't worked with his arms over his head for a long time.

Rubbing the back of his neck, Dameon placed the roller in the pan and looked at his handiwork.

The satellite radio station called out the time as six thirty.

Dameon picked up his cell phone to check if he'd missed a call while he was working.

He sent a text to Grace. Are you working late?

When she didn't respond, he assumed she was.

Even though it was cold outside once the sun set, he opened a few windows to air the place out.

He heard gravel kicking up in his driveway and saw lights flash into the house.

Grace. He could hardly wait to see her.

He set the paintbrush down and used a shop towel to wipe his hands.

He made it to the door before Grace had the time to knock.

Only when he opened the door, it wasn't Grace standing there. A man he'd never seen before stood staring. Broad shoulders that looked as if he spent a fair amount of time either at a gym or in a field of heavy labor.

"Hello," Dameon greeted him.

"Are you Dameon?"

"I am. Are you one of the neighbors?"

He shook his head. "I'm Matt, Grace's brother."

Dameon's first thought was that Grace was right. She said Matt would find an excuse to come over and here he was, unannounced.

Only the expression on Matt's face was concern and not curiosity. Dameon reached out his hand for Matt to shake. "Is Grace okay?"

"Can I come in?"

Dameon stood aside. "Please."

"Grace sent me over here."

Dameon walked over to the speaker blasting music and turned it off. "What's going on?"

Matt stopped looking at the space and turned to him. "Grace is fine. Well, physically. Someone accused her of taking a bribe, or offering a bribe, and she was told to leave work."

What? "That's ridiculous."

"We know. She wasn't fired, but she was told she can't contact any of her clients. And since you're a client—"

Bullshit on that. "Where is she?"

"Our parents'. Grace asked me to come over and tell you what's going on so you wouldn't worry or think she's ignoring you."

No wonder she wasn't answering his texts. "What is your parents' address?"

Matt started to smile. He held up a hand. "She's worried your project will come under scrutiny if you two make contact."

"Grace worries too much." Dameon held up three fingers. "Give me three minutes to change and I'll follow you over."

Matt nodded. "I'll drive. Two people that work in the city office with her live on our parents' street."

"You're serious."

"Grace is—"

"Worried," Dameon finished for him.

Three minutes later, Dameon sat in Matt's truck as it rolled down the road.

"Grace would never take a bribe."

"We all know that. But it sounds like the city is gearing up for a lawsuit. Which is why she's been put on leave. She said you knew about the guy who is spearheading this. Something about a mobile home park."

Dameon felt his blood starting to boil. "The guy who scared her the night she lost her phone?"

Matt glanced his way. "Yeah, that guy."

"She told me he offered her money."

"That's what she keeps saying. She's blaming herself for not officially reporting him."

"Sounds like the guy is trying to get out of paving the driveway by pointing fingers at other people. The city has to see that."

Matt turned into a neighborhood and started weaving through the streets. "I'm sure they will, but in the meantime, she has to play by their rules."

Dameon shook his head. "It would be a lot quicker to just kick the guy's ass."

Matt chuckled. "Much as I agree, it would cause more problems than it would solve."

A short time later, Dameon followed Grace's brother up the walkway to the parents' house.

All the lights were on inside and cars were parked in the driveway and on the street.

Matt walked in without knocking.

Dameon skipped over the faces of those he knew and those he didn't while looking for Grace.

She wasn't there.

Colin walked up to him, stuck out his hand. "She told Matt not to bring you here."

Dameon shook his hand. "Where is she?"

"Lying down."

Parker walked up and gave Dameon a hug. "She's really upset."

Colin turned around. "This is our dad, Emmitt, and mom, Nora."

Dameon shook Emmitt's hand. "Sir. A pleasure to meet you."

Emmitt looked at Dameon's hand speckled with dry paint. "Sorry," Dameon added. "I was painting."

For whatever reason, that made Emmitt smile. "Nice to meet you, son. Gracie is gonna be pissed you're here."

Yeah, he'd considered that.

Nora was all smiles. "Can I get you something to drink?"

"I'm fine."

Matt then introduced the only other person in the room he didn't know. "This is Erin."

"A pleasure."

"Dameon?"

He turned to the sound of Grace's voice calling his name.

She stood in a hallway, her eyes swollen and bloodshot. An overly large sweatshirt swallowed her whole.

"What are you—"

He didn't give her time to ask her question. He walked up to her and pulled her into his arms.

Her head fell on his chest and her arms wrapped around him. "I told him not to bring you."

"I know. But I'm not good at following directions."

That had her chuckling through her cries.

She squeezed harder.

"Shhh. It's going to be okay."

CHAPTER
TWENTY-FIVE

Grace sat on the sofa, Dameon at her side, while the others put together a late dinner for everyone. She explained exactly what had happened for the third time since she arrived at her parents' house. She'd gone directly there after being told to leave the office. One by one, everyone in the family showed up.

"Richard just sat there shaking his head. It's like he believed Sokolov and not me."

Dameon squeezed her hand. "It sounds like everyone is protecting their own butts."

"Which is how business runs," Erin said from the kitchen.

"An audit will come up empty, and in the end, this will be his word against yours," Dameon told her. "I bet if we look into this Sokolov guy, we'd find something dirty on him."

"This is all such a joke," Grace said. "I can't believe one accusation and I'm out of a job."

"Paid leave isn't the same as being fired," Matt told her.

"Might as well be. By this time tomorrow, everyone in the office will know what's going on. Who knows how many people are going to believe it? It was mortifying walking out of there."

"Well, you can't quit. That makes you look guilty," her dad said.

"He can't prove what didn't happen," Grace said.

"He may not have to. If there is any doubt, at all, the city will settle before going to court. Which is something this guy probably knows," Colin said. "It's why he is saying the city is responsible, not you."

"He's going after the deeper pockets," Dameon added.

"If you get hit by the city bus, you sue the city, not the driver."

"I have done nothing wrong." Grace started to feel some of the hurt going away and the anger set in.

"We know that, Gracie," her dad told her.

"It wouldn't be a bad idea to consult your own attorney."

Grace turned to Dameon. "Why?"

"You said you felt like you were on the witness stand when they called you into the office. The city lawyers have to protect the city. A part of that is you, but you're dispensable."

Grace hated to hear her fears vocalized by someone else.

"He has a point," Erin said. "If you have your own lawyer only fighting for you . . ."

"I don't have that kind of money."

Erin and Dameon both spoke at the same time. "I do."

Grace looked between both of them. "I can't ask that of either of you. And besides, how would it look if my client with the city pays for legal counsel on my behalf? Next thing you know they'll be investigating you."

"Eventually someone is going to realize that you two are a thing," Parker said while she set the table.

"You're going to have to explain the necklace," Erin chimed in.

"And that's going to look bad," Grace said.

"Last time I looked, we're both adults who can date whoever we want. And since there hasn't been one permit signed or approval for anything, no one can claim special treatment," Dameon told her.

"This whole thing is going to set you back." And after spending time with him, she had come to realize how important the project was to his overall success.

"The last thing you need to do is worry about me. Construction always has delays. And on a project of this scale, they are months and years, not days and weeks."

Her mom pulled the last dish out of the oven. "Okay, guys. Let's eat."

Grace wasn't hungry, but she took her place at the table anyway.

The food was passed around, and slowly the conversation started to shift.

Her dad asked Dameon what he was painting, and he went on to talk about the house and project up in the canyon.

Parker chimed in about how the area felt like an outpost when she drove through it.

With her family chatting about other things, Grace's mind took a break from the problem at hand. Her mom's chicken casserole and buttermilk biscuits always cheered her up. She found herself eating, despite her lack of appetite.

She loved her family.

The minute she'd shown up at her parents' door, her mom called everyone in for support. It was as if her getting put on leave was some kind of tragedy. It wasn't. Not really. But having them there offering advice when she couldn't think for herself was uplifting.

By the time dinner was done, and the dishes were cleared, Grace felt her backbone start to return. She'd found paper and a pen and started to work on describing what had happened the night Sokolov claimed she suggested a bribe.

"When did they say they wanted this?" Dameon sat by her side, watching her work.

"Tomorrow."

"I'll have my attorney come over in the morning to go over it with you before you deliver it."

"Dameon, that isn't necessary."

"Gracie?" her dad called to her from the living room where he sat with her brothers. "You listen to him. What did I tell you to do if you ever got in trouble with the law?"

"This isn't the same, Dad."

"Taking a bribe, offering a bribe . . . both are a crime."

"No one is pressing charges."

"Yet," her dad said with a stare.

Dameon placed a hand on her back and idly rubbed against it.

"Fine," she said.

Dameon smiled and pulled out his cell phone. He dialed a number and silently walked out to the backyard, closing the door behind him.

Erin reached across the table and tapped her arm. "I really like him," she said quietly.

"Does he have a lawyer on speed dial?" Grace asked.

"I don't know too many people in big business who don't," Erin said.

"He's a lot less of a suit than you described," her dad added from his perch on the sofa.

"He can probably hear you," Grace said.

"Nothing I won't say to his face."

"He seems like a very nice man." Her mom gave her two cents.

～

Carson Phillips looked completely out of place standing on Dameon's doorstep first thing in the morning. He was one of three partners in the law firm Dameon had in his court from the minute he'd started Locke Enterprises. In his midfifties, Carson still had a full head of hair with just enough salt sprinkled in the pepper to help him look his age.

"Thank you for coming on such short notice," Dameon said while he opened the door wider to let the man inside.

"That's what retainers are for."

"I'll have you follow me over to the Hudsons' to talk with Grace, but I wanted to meet with you first," Dameon told him.

Carson walked in the house and looked around. "So this is the location of your next venture."

"It is."

"I can't say I've been out this far in a long time."

"It grows on you after a while."

Dameon offered him coffee, which he refused, and they both took a seat at the table.

"So, tell me about this woman I'm going to represent," Carson started.

"Grace Hudson is a friend."

Carson cleared his throat.

"More than a friend. Like I told you last night, she works for the city. That's how we officially met." Dameon recapped what he'd told him the night before. "She's mentioned to me on several occasions that she felt her boss had a grudge against her."

"Why?"

"No idea. Grace might be able to answer that. What I do know is these allegations are bogus. She called me the night she met with this man, and she was a mess. Once you get to know Grace, you know that doesn't come easy for her. She's in control, like every engineer I've ever met. Strong, independent. But this guy rattled her cage."

"Why do you think this man is making these claims?"

"The way she described him, he's a macho type who doesn't take direction from women very well. When he didn't get what he wanted by pushing her around, he took another route. You couple that with a boss that has a grudge, and she feels alone in this."

"Which is why you called me."

"Right. Grace is the kind of person that believes if she just tells the truth, all of this will go away."

Carson laughed.

"Right. Naive of her, I know."

"No one has filed charges, right?"

"No. Not that we know of."

Carson nodded. "I've already talked with a PI I like to use in these kinds of cases. She'll look into this Sokolov person. And take a good look at Miss Hudson's life and these accusations so we can better defend her when and if the time comes."

Dameon sighed. "I'd appreciate it."

Finished with their conversation, Dameon grabbed his suit jacket and truck keys.

By the time they pulled into the street the Hudsons lived on, it was after nine in the morning.

Grace's father opened the door. He hesitated a moment. "So you really do wear a suit," he said instead of hello.

"Good morning, Mr. Hudson. This is Carson Phillips, the attorney I hired to help Grace out."

Emmitt looked a little uncomfortable but stepped aside all the same.

The men shook hands, and Nora emerged from the back of the house. "Good morning, Dameon." Unlike Emmitt, Nora hugged him with a smile.

Grace walked out wearing a smart dress suit with a pencil skirt and matching jacket. She looked worlds better than she had the night before. She either slept really well, or understood the finer tricks of wearing makeup to hide a night of crying.

Her high heels brought her all the closer to his height when she walked up.

Her lips lifted and Dameon took the liberty of a quick hello kiss. "You look like you slept," he told her.

"I did. And when I woke up, I was pissed."

"Good." He turned to the side and introduced Carson.

In no time, they were seated around the table drinking coffee and listening to Grace repeat her story again. It took a good half an hour to tell the whole of it and ended with her pushing the written version over for Carson to read.

"We can fix this," Carson said when he finished.

"Is there something wrong with it?"

"No. But it can be better. You don't say anything about you being sent out late in the day to a hostile client by yourself. You didn't point out that Richard sent you after you had repeatedly explained that this particular landowner had wasted your time in the past. Is Mr. Sokolov a big man?" Carson asked.

"I'm pretty short. Most men are big compared to me."

"That needs to be pointed out."

Grace glanced at Dameon, unsure. "Okay."

"Have you ever had a lawyer before, Miss Hudson?"

"You can call me Grace. And no. I've never had the need."

"We don't trust men in suits very often," Emmitt said.

Nora shushed her husband and Carson laughed. "That's probably smart, Mr. Hudson. Grace, you need to understand that the attorneys working with the city are there to minimize the damage."

"I didn't do anything."

"They don't care about that. They're not interested in the truth. I'm sorry. If you sat right here and told me that you did take a bribe and had a history of doing so, I'd have to go into any meetings or courtroom with that information in my head and never tell anyone."

"Attorney-client privilege," Nora said.

"Exactly. As it stands, I believe you did nothing wrong. But someone out there accused you of doing this. For what reason, we don't know. Could be the guy is just an asshole and wants to throw his weight around. Could be he saw the opportunity to stick it to the person he views as getting in his way. Maybe he received some barroom advice and thinks he's going to walk away with settlement money instead of having to fix his property. We don't know his motivation. We just know you're at the center of it. And that's where I come in." Carson looked around the room and then asked, "You're a Dodgers fan?" he asked.

"Uhm, yeah." Grace looked confused.

"Think of this like a baseball game. The team at bat isn't guaranteed to win the game unless there isn't anyone on the field stopping them. Right now, you're playing defense, but sooner or later you're going to be at bat. That could happen if they terminate you without evidence or harass you to the point of quitting. Mr. Sokolov may slander your name, and arguably already has. Any of us who have a workplace know how soon gossip is spread and believed. Me being in your dugout is going to make a difference."

Dameon saw the moment Grace really understood what Carson was telling her.

"So when I walk into the office with an attorney, I don't look guilty, I look smart."

"Exactly. Michelle Overland is a private investigator who is going to be in contact with you later today. She's going to ask you a lot of questions, want to see your finances, ask you about your relationships at work. Be honest with her."

"Why a private investigator?"

"Good question," Carson said. "If you were on the take, where's the money? Have you bought any fancy cars, taken an elaborate trip lately?"

"Dameon bought me a necklace," she pointed out.

Carson looked between the two of them. "Did you tell anyone that?"

"No. But Richard asked me about it."

He shrugged. "Your boyfriend is allowed to buy you gifts."

Dameon reached for her hand and squeezed it. "Our relationship isn't public. Grace was worried her work would find it a conflict of interest."

"Somewhat irrelevant at this point. But for now, just keep things under the radar."

Grace turned to Dameon. "I knew you shouldn't have come over last night."

"No, that's not what I'm saying," Carson said.

"I was told to stay away from my clients."

"So they don't have to investigate those clients," Carson explained. "Unless you two are willing to end your relationship—"

"Not gonna happen." Dameon's voice was stern enough to make everyone stare.

"Then be prepared to answer questions. For now, go about your normal routines. Just don't waltz into city hall holding hands until we have a handle on this. But don't sneak around like you're doing something wrong either." Carson offered a kind smile.

Dameon kissed her cheek.

Carson picked up her statement. "Okay, let's get to work on this. But before we do, call the office and tell them you're requesting that the same three people that were in the room yesterday are there today when you come in."

"What if they can't?"

"Doesn't matter. It's a power move. If they all show up, it's a bonus. I guarantee you they will all be there the next time when word that you've hired an attorney gets around."

Grace was smiling. "This feels good."

～

Grace really wanted Dameon by her side, but Carson made it clear that this first meeting wasn't the time or place.

The other thing she wanted but wasn't going to get . . . was the ability to say anything to anyone.

They arrived together in Carson's car. It was eleven thirty, the requested time to meet Richard, Vivian, and Mr. Simons.

"You ready?" Carson asked.

"More than I was yesterday."

"Let me do the talking. This should be brief."

Grace lifted her chin and led the way into the office. They walked into the lobby, and already she felt the stares.

Good gossip never takes long to spread.

They walked past the front lobby and into her corner of the city offices. Because there wasn't a general secretary greeting people, Grace walked through the hall to see if anyone was around.

Evan saw her first. "Holy shit, Grace. What's going on?"

She accepted Evan's hug, but didn't answer his question. "Where is Richard?"

"They're in the conference room. Are you okay?" Evan looked over her shoulder.

"I'm fine. I can't talk now."

Grace walked around her friend, past her office, and into the conference room.

Like the day before, Richard and Vivian sat on one side of the table.

At first glance, Richard stayed in his seat.

When Carson walked in behind her, Richard and Vivian both stood.

"Hello, Grace," Vivian said first.

Grace smiled and said nothing.

Carson moved forward and removed two business cards from his pocket. "I'm Carson Phillips, of Franklin, Phillips, and Bowers."

"Oh." Vivian looked at Grace and back to Carson.

It took everything in Grace to not gloat.

Vivian introduced herself, and so did Richard.

"Please have a seat," Vivian said while taking hers.

"Are we waiting for Mr. Simons?" Carson asked.

"No, he had a prior commitment."

"I see." Carson turned to look at Grace, then back to the others.

"I'm confused as to why you're here," Vivian said.

Richard looked past Carson and straight to Grace. "You didn't have to hire a lawyer, Hudson."

Grace bit her tongue. The polite *Grace this* and *Grace that* from the day before was gone, and *Hudson* was back.

"My client has been put on leave, isn't that right?" Carson asked.

"Yes, pending an investigation."

"Was there paperwork that went along with this request, because it seems that was neglected."

"Of course. Things were hectic yesterday," Vivian said as she shifted through a folder that sat in front of her.

"You need to sign that," Richard said to Grace.

Carson took the paperwork, glanced at it, and put it in his briefcase. "We'll get this back to you."

Richard opened his mouth, but Vivian placed a hand on his arm, stopping him. "Do you have the incident report we requested?" she asked.

Carson removed three copies and handed them over. He gave them very little time to read through it before scooting his chair back. "If you have any questions or requests from my client, you will need to go through me until this matter is settled."

"Really, Hudson?" Richard started.

Grace kept a polite smile on her face.

"Thank you for your time," Carson said before opening the conference room door.

Grace walked in front of him, her heart beating a little too fast.

Evan, Adrian, and Lionel all stood outside of the kitchenette doorway watching as she walked by.

CHAPTER TWENTY-SIX

Grace jumped into Dameon's arms when she returned to her parents' house. It had taken less than ten minutes to go to the office and make a stand for herself.

"I take it things went well," Dameon said when he set Grace back down to her feet.

"It was awesome."

Carson smiled. "Well, now that they know what they're dealing with, things will get very professional and very quiet."

Dameon shook Carson's hand and patted his shoulder. "Thanks for jumping on this."

"No problem. I'll be in touch. Grace, remember, if anyone from the office calls or asks anything, they come through me. Even what seem like innocent questions from your friends may not be."

Evan was the only one she truly thought cared enough to ask. But she didn't want him getting caught in the crossfire of all this.

"Thank you."

Carson got back into his car and pulled out of the driveway.

Her mom and dad, who had been standing outside, walked back in the house.

"Did they talk your ear off while we were gone?" Grace asked.

Dameon looked over his shoulder. "I think I won your mom over, but your dad had fifty questions. He really doesn't like suits."

She laughed. "He hates 'em. But if he didn't like you, he wouldn't have bothered asking questions."

"He all but asked the name of the girl I lost my virginity to."

Now Grace was laughing. "Awww, he loves you."

Dameon shook his head. "I told your mom I'd stay through lunch, but as long as you're going to be okay, I have to get back to the city."

"I am now. Thank you, Dameon. I wasn't thinking yesterday."

"You're obviously not alone. I'm glad Carson can help."

She sighed. "He's expensive, isn't he?"

"I don't want you thinking about that."

"I'll pay you back."

Dameon placed a finger on her lips. "Stop."

She would figure out a way to make it up to him.

"It's good to see that smile again," Dameon said.

She lifted her lips, asking for his kiss.

Dameon dipped his head to oblige.

Her dad's voice yelled from the front door. "Are you going to molest my daughter on the front lawn or come inside for lunch?"

She broke away and giggled.

"I think he hates me."

"He's an ex-cop. If he hated you, he'd tell you to leave at gunpoint."

～

Grace had never met a private investigator, and she certainly didn't picture Michelle Overland when she thought of one.

In her midfifties, Michelle looked more like a PTA mom than someone who investigated anyone or knew anything about what Grace was going through.

Grace welcomed Michelle into her condo and played hostess before they sat down at her dining room table to talk.

"I've already spoken to Carson in depth. He e-mailed me your statement and a copy of what the city gave you when they sent you home. I'm going to ask a lot of personal questions, and I'm sorry about that. I need financial information, your banks, loans, debt. Absolutely anything you can tell me about your accuser. I need phone numbers and any online social media you use."

"Wow. It really sounds like I'm the bad guy."

Michelle smiled. "I'm looking for anything to prove you did do it so I can prove you didn't."

"Sounds backward."

"Your employer has your work records. They have to audit to obtain anything not work related. So we'll get a jump on that first. If they want your personal stuff, they have to make a move on the chessboard first."

"Officially accuse me of taking a bribe."

"Exactly. If and when that happens, they have to give your lawyer any evidence they found at the office."

Grace rolled her eyes. "All they are going to find is that I was over-worked and did the job of two people."

"Tell me about Richard. I get the feeling he doesn't like you."

Grace shook her head. "Richard may not like me, but he's not the kind of guy to plant something in my office to prove I did something I didn't do."

Michelle looked at Grace as if she was five. "You really never know what someone is capable of. I can tell you plenty of stories."

"I have only been with this job for five years. For the first two, almost everything I did had to have a second signature on the plans. There are a lot of eyes on nearly everything I do. We work independently on some things, but for a lot of stuff, we work as a team. So if someone put my signature on something I didn't approve, chances are there had to be a second one there somewhere."

"Is there anyone in the office who might be taking bribes?"

Grace shook her head. "There are five of us. Richard, who took the senior position six months after I was hired. Before then, he was like the rest of us. Yeah, he'd been there the longest, but he had his own caseload and had to report to the boss. Adrian has been there the longest after Richard. If he's guilty of anything, it's overlooking an issue and signing off on it because he wanted to get out of work on time. Lionel is recently divorced, spends his free time watching the games during happy hour for the two-dollar beer. Evan is the next in line as far as seniority. I consider him my friend. We get along the best. He has my back."

"How so?"

"He just does. He worked the Sokolov property with me. Knew the guy was an ass. He mentioned to Richard more than once that the guy was stalling and wasting our time."

"So you're closest to Evan at the office?"

"Yes. We don't keep secrets from each other."

"So he knows about your relationship with Dameon Locke?"

Grace paused. "He knows I'm interested in Dameon. We might have both talked about how good-looking he is."

"Oh?"

"Evan is gay. But not open about it. I'm pretty sure the others know, but he hasn't talked about it at work. He doesn't want to deal with Richard's censure."

Michelle wrote something down on her notepad. Grace hadn't noticed when the woman pulled it out. "Can you think of anything else about Richard's character?"

"You know what I think it is with him . . . he's an unhappy man. He's old-fashioned and doesn't see women as equal. He's on his fourth marriage, and I'm guessing he hasn't had sex in years."

Michelle laughed.

"My parents both knew him in school. They said he was as uptight then as he is now. And probably bitter that he can't afford to retire when all his friends are spending their days on the golf course."

Michelle stopped laughing. "Your parents knew him in high school?"

"Don't be surprised. There are a lot of people who live in this community going back three generations."

"I had no idea."

"I know it's not a small town now, but it was for a long time."

"Is there any bad blood between your parents and your boss?"

Grace shook her head. "What? No."

"Your dad was a local police officer?"

"Yeah. He retired about the time I was graduating from college."

"He never gave Richard a ticket or anything?"

Grace had to laugh. "I don't know, but I'd think my dad would have told me if he remembered doing so. I've been complaining about Richard for years."

Michelle scribbled a note.

"You really don't think a traffic ticket could prompt this?"

"People run people down for cutting them off in line at the drive-through at McDonald's. So yes, I do. You might ask your dad if he remembers anything of this nature."

Grace thought it was stupid, but she would do it.

"Who knows about you and Dameon?"

"My family," Grace said. "We've gone out a few times in town, so we could have been seen. But no one at work has said anything. And they're not a shy group."

"No one else?"

"We went out on New Year's Eve. There was a function with some of the people he works with. It was obvious we were together. Dameon bid on this during a silent auction and gave it to me." Grace pulled the necklace from under her shirt.

"It's beautiful," Michelle said, looking at it. "Expensive?"

"Yeah."

Michelle put her head down to her notes.

"Is dating Dameon a problem? Carson seemed to think it wasn't."

She shrugged. "The question of ethics comes up. Have you single-handedly approved of anything?"

"No. The project is new for the city. We barely got started on it. I was considering telling Richard about our relationship when all of this happened. I was pushing hard for more hands on Dameon's project."

"Why?"

"Because it's too much work for one person. There are a lot of pieces to the project that would take me months doing alone. Dameon wants to break ground in the spring."

"That seems fast."

"It is. I'm guilty of wanting to help him do it. But I knew eventually our relationship would come out and someone, likely Richard, would try and find fault. That's why I asked for more help from the team."

"And did you get it?"

"No. Not yet. This all happened yesterday before I was put on leave."

For the next half hour, Michelle asked about Grace's finances. She wrote down bank names and account numbers. She said she wanted to see statements.

"Let's talk about Sokolov."

Grace told her everything. The early meetings when he ignored her to the last one when he wasted her time and tried to bribe her. ". . . so as I was walking to get into my car, he did this jump thing and startled me. I know I jumped and he knew he got to me. Even said something about me being on edge. I drove off. Halfway home I realized I'd left my cell phone on the hood of his car."

"Did you go back to get it?"

"Later. With Dameon. It didn't feel safe by myself."

"But you didn't find your phone?"

"No."

"Do you think Mr. Sokolov took it?"

"Not sure why he would. It was password protected and I replaced it the next day. The old one would have been turned off."

That's all Michelle seemed to need. She put away her pen and stood. "It's going to take me a few days to go over everything." After giving Grace a to-do list, the woman told her she'd be in touch and left.

CHAPTER
TWENTY-SEVEN

"It's been three days and I'm bored stiff."

Grace sat on Parker's front porch with the two of them taking turns tossing the ball for Scout to chase. The Labrador loved his tennis balls almost as much as he loved running after them.

"I would think you'd be catching up on all the things you can't do when you're at work."

"I did that. My bills are paid, my place is clean. I even organized my closets and sock drawer. Who does that?"

"Someone who was told not to show up at the office," Parker said.

Grace rolled her eyes. "I still can't believe I'm in the middle of this bull."

Scout placed his slobbery snout on Grace's lap with ball clenched in mouth. His tail thumped on the wooden planks of the porch, and his eyes shifted back and forth. "Aren't you getting tired?" Grace asked as she took the ball from his mouth and tossed it over the railing of the porch. Since Parker's ranch house sat on top of a hill, the ball rolled down the driveway and into a large grassy portion of the property. Scout ran down the steps of the home in search of the ball that had already stopped moving.

"When I was let go last year, I realized I was in the wrong job. Not that I ever thought assisting in an elementary school was the end all, be all, but it helped push me to figure out the next phase."

Parker's next phase was to get married and go back to school. Which she had decided to do online.

"I've been unhappy at work for a while," Grace confessed. "I like the work, but the long hours and lack of kudos make it hard to go in."

"So maybe this is a sign to move on."

"Perhaps. But if I'm fired under the cloud of fraud, who is going to hire me?" As much as she started to feel like she had the right team to help her get through the allegations against her, she worried this would follow her wherever she went next.

"If I were you, I'd think about what's next. Get through all this, get your job back, and then leave."

"Seems a waste of time to fight for a job I don't want to keep."

"It's not the job, it's your integrity you're fighting for."

"You're not kidding."

Scout had returned with the ball and a dirt-filled nose.

"How is Dameon doing with all this?"

Grace couldn't help but smile when she heard Dameon's name. "He's a breath of fresh air. All the duds I've dated over the years . . . after Dameon, the others don't compare. Like, why did I ever waste my time?"

"Because you were searching for Mr. Perfect. And that guy isn't out there."

Grace repeated the ball-throwing process for the dog. "I wasn't looking at all when Dameon came along. I even tried hard not to date him. And he's about as perfect as they come."

"But he's complicated by the fact that you work with him . . . or did. So he isn't someone you would instantly try and date. You had to look past all that to start dating him."

"Now that I don't really have the job, it seems like a stupid reason to not date him. Jobs come and go, ya know?"

"Exactly."

"How often are you guys able to see each other?" Parker asked.

"Every week is different. Weekends are a given so far. He flew to New York last night to meet with a potential investor today. But when he comes back, I'll either meet him in LA or he'll come here."

"You can always look for a job in the city."

Grace sighed. "I might not have a choice. But I don't want to change my employment to accommodate my boyfriend. If I can even call him that."

"I think that's a safe bet."

Grace looked over the railing to see Scout rolling around on the grass at the bottom of the driveway.

"I really don't know how he labels me."

"Future Mrs.?"

"It's a little soon to be talking like that."

"Don't tell me you haven't thought about it."

"I really haven't." But she was now that Parker had planted the seed.

"Mrs. Locke has a nice ring to it."

"Stop, you'll jinx it."

Scout bounded up the steps and somehow had completely covered himself in mud. He ran straight to Grace and looked like he was going to jump in her lap.

"No way, dog."

Scout thought it was a game and started to bark, and as he did, he placed one paw on her leg.

"Ewwww!"

She and Parker both laughed.

"I haven't had a dog since I was a kid," Grace said. "I wonder if Dameon likes pets?"

Parker laughed harder. "Yeah, right . . . you're not thinking about being a wife."

Grace found a clean spot on the dog to pet. "Maybe just a little."

∼

"I think that went well." Tyler sat across from Dameon at a crowded coffee shop in Manhattan's financial district.

"It's always easier to win over investors when you meet with them in person."

Dameon had come to the conclusion that pushing through the next two years without the financial help he went into it with was reckless on his part. Too many people in his company were depending on his corporation to pay their bills. And even though the profits would help him reach all his financial goals without an investor, the risks could bankrupt him if it all fell apart. Watching what Grace was going through helped him take the plunge to start looking for the right fit.

"I have the feeling that their concern about all the wildfires in California is the only thing holding them back."

"The photographs didn't help. If they pass, we might try and focus on West Coast firms."

"It's a different life here."

There was a half a foot of snow lining the streets, and people were bundled up from the top of their heads to their booted feet.

Dameon's phone buzzed in his pocket. He saw an image of his mom light up the screen. She didn't usually call him in the middle of a workday.

"I should get this."

Dameon accepted the call and lifted the phone to his ear. "Hi, Mom."

"Hi, honey. Am I disturbing you?"

"You never disturb me, Mom." Dameon glanced at Tyler, who was smiling at him. "What's up?"

"I won't keep you long. I just called to ask if you sent the clown."

"Did I send the what?"

"The clown?"

Yep, she said *clown*. "What clown?"

His mom started to giggle. "You should get your money back because only half of it came."

"You're not making any sense."

"Maybe Tristan sent it."

"Mom, can you start over? Is this clown a person or a doll or what?" All he could picture was some kind of stuffed animal.

"No, it's not alive. But it looks like it could be. Only it's sliced in half. It's the darndest thing."

If his mom wasn't giggling as she talked, he would swear she was having some kind of a stroke.

"Mom, what were you doing before the clown showed up?"

"I was sleeping. Tristan gave me these cookies that help me sleep. You know I've had trouble since your dad passed. These cookies really help."

Dameon rubbed his temples. "Tristan gave you cookies?"

"Yup."

Damn his brother. "Any chance these cookies make you hungry?" Dameon found Tyler listening intently to one half of the conversation and quietly laughing.

"Of course they do. There's a little bit of *pot* in them." His mom whispered the word *pot* and started to laugh.

"For fuck's sake."

"Oh, honey. Don't cuss like that. Just come over and make the clown leave."

"I'm a little far away." And it was obvious that his mom was hallucinating. Dameon's thoughts turned to Grace. "I'll see if Grace can come over and help."

"I hope it doesn't scare her."

Dameon shook his head. "I'm sure she can handle it. Just stay in the house and please don't eat any more cookies."

Tyler quietly laughed.

"Okay, honey."

Dameon hung up the phone and shook his head.

Tyler busted up. "Tristan is the one who works in a marijuana dispensary, right?"

Dameon dialed Grace's number. "I can't make this shit up."

"Hello?"

He tuned out Tyler's laughing to talk to Grace. "I have a huge favor to ask."

~

Grace pulled into Dameon's mom's driveway thirty minutes later. The house sat in the hills of Glendale in a subdivision that looked like it had been built somewhere in the fifties.

The front yard was minimally landscaped with a single maple tree and an evergreen hedge that separated the yard from the sidewalk. She double-checked the house number with what she'd written down and knocked on the door. She stood waiting for several seconds and started knocking again.

Still nothing.

Grace looked under the planter by the front door and found the house key Dameon said she'd find. Feeling a little awkward letting herself into a home she'd never been to before, Grace called out Lois's name as she opened the front door. "Lois?"

"Back here."

Grace sighed in relief and let herself in.

"Did you bring the pizza?"

She followed the woman's voice to a back room behind the kitchen. Lois sat on a sofa with a pile of laundry and a bag of potato chips. She glanced up and smiled at Grace. "Oh, aren't you a pretty little thing."

Grace smiled. "Hello, Mrs. Locke. I hope you don't mind that I let myself in."

"No, no, of course not. I'm sure Dameon said it was okay."

"He did."

Lois patted the pile of laundry beside her. "Come sit down. Let me get a good look at you."

Grace moved around the table holding the partially folded laundry and scooted the clothes aside so she didn't sit on them. "Dameon was a little worried. Said something about a clown?"

Lois waved toward the front of the house. "Oh, he's in the other room. I just left him in there since he wasn't hurting anything."

Grace bounced back to her feet. "Can you show me this clown?"

"Sure." Lois knocked the towel she was folding off her lap as she stood. Backtracking the route Grace had taken to find Lois, they stopped in the living room, and Lois pointed to a recliner in the corner of the room. "He's right there."

Grace looked at the empty chair.

"Can you show me the cookies you were eating?"

Lois scowled. "Did Dameon tell you about the cookies?"

Grace nodded.

In the kitchen, Lois pulled out a cookie jar and a plastic bag inside. There wasn't a label, just a handwritten note: *Eat ¼ to sleep.* Grace sniffed the bag. Oh yeah, it had been a while, but she knew that smell. A tiny sticker on the bottom of the bag said 120 mg each.

"Mrs. Locke. How much of this did you eat?"

"I had one of the four, just like it says."

Grace turned the note to her. "It says take one quarter."

"Oh. That's dumb. Who eats only a quarter of a cookie?"

Grace tried hard not to laugh.

The doorbell rang and Lois rubbed her hands together. "*That* must be the pizza."

The cab dropped Dameon off in front of his mom's house at ten thirty that night. The porch light was on, and the flashing of light inside the front room suggested someone was watching TV.

He let himself in and walked around the corner.

Grace was curled up asleep on the couch under an afghan his mother had crocheted sometime in the seventies.

He took off his jacket and set his suitcase on the floor.

After a quick check in his mom's bedroom to confirm she was there and asleep, Dameon went back in the living room and sat at Grace's feet.

The motion on the couch woke her. "Hey."

"Hi."

She sat up, looked around. "I must have dozed off."

He leaned over and kissed her. "How is she?"

Grace started to chuckle. "Your mom is a riot."

Dameon ran his hand through his hair, surprised there was any left. "She was higher than a kite."

"You have no idea. She took a hundred and twenty milligrams before Bozo showed up." Grace pointed to his father's recliner that had a sheet thrown over it. "She had to hide the clown."

"You're kidding."

Grace rubbed her eyes and crossed her legs under her. "For a tiny woman, she sure can eat. Pizza, chips, popcorn, ice cream . . . it was like a twelve-year-old's slumber party. She finally went to bed a couple of hours ago."

"I'm going to kill my brother."

Grace clasped on to his hands. "It's okay. She didn't read the instructions right."

"Still gonna kill him."

"Outside of a sliced-up clown sleeping in the chair, there wasn't any real harm done."

Dameon kissed her fingers. "Thanks for rushing over."

"You don't have to thank me. Your mom is adorable. She showed me every single picture she has of you growing up. Even the naked ones."

He was too old to be embarrassed about naked baby pictures. "I owe you."

Grace shook her head. "What are girlfriends for if not to rescue parents who ate too many edibles?"

Dameon laughed for the first time since the phone call. "It's like Christmas all over again."

"Only no raw turkey."

He laughed at that.

"How did the meeting go?"

Dameon settled on the couch, toed off his shoes. "Good. I'm not sure if it's the right fit, but they seemed interested."

"What wasn't right about them?"

"It's not that it isn't right. Just different locations. I can't help but think a West Coast company would be best."

"So you keep looking until you find the right partners."

"I think I'm pressing my luck," he said as he pulled her into the crook of his arm.

"Oh, why is that?"

"Finding the perfect business partner and the perfect woman in the same year seems impossible."

"Ahh." Grace looked at him with a smile. "We met last year."

Dameon laughed again, then lowered his lips right above hers. "Yes, we did."

CHAPTER
TWENTY-EIGHT

Grace found herself spending a lot of time at Dameon's project house in the canyon.

He'd given her a key so she could be there even when he was stuck in the city. Not that she stayed the night without him, but she did use the house as a workstation. Even if the city wasn't sanctioning her efforts, she didn't think they would be in vain if she jump-started the project. If she left the city, the work she did could be used by whoever took over for her. And even if they didn't, she knew what the city needed. Besides, it was the only way she knew to pay Dameon back for everything he was doing for her.

She coordinated the work with Tyler, and learned that Dameon had purposely pushed himself into the driver's seat solely to get to know Grace better. According to Tyler, Dameon was determined to win her over from the moment they met.

As the project coordinator, Tyler really was the person to talk to.

A good week after the clown cookies came and went, Carson asked for her to come into his office. The city was requesting a meeting, but Grace needed to be prepared.

The law office was in Sherman Oaks, and Carson had already coordinated with Dameon's schedule to be there.

She met Dameon in the lobby and kissed him hello. "You didn't have to break out of your day to be here."

"Carson asked me to come. Besides, if it affects you, it affects me." They walked to the elevator together.

"And when did that happen?"

"What?" he asked.

"When did our individual lives become *ours*?"

In the elevator he turned and kissed her again. "I don't know, but I like it."

Considering the richness of the suit Carson had worn on their first and only meeting, Grace expected the office to be one of opulence and stature. But holy *wow* was this over the top. Sleek lines and rich woods. The kind that made the perfectionist in her sing. Whoever had designed the interior had spectacular taste.

Dameon told the receptionist who they were after they walked into the lobby. She didn't delay as she led the two of them to Carson's office.

"Thank you both for coming," Carson said as he walked around his oversized desk to greet them.

The men shook hands before Carson turned to her to do the same. "You look good, more relaxed."

"I've had some time to come to terms with what's happening."

"Good. It's better to approach this stuff rationally."

Grace took the seat Carson offered. "Easy for you to say when you're on that end."

He laughed. "Very true."

With all of them seated, Carson opened a file on his desk. "The city contacted me yesterday. They said that Mr. Sokolov has officially filed a lawsuit against the city."

"What ambulance-chasing lawyer agreed to that?" Dameon asked as he squeezed Grace's hand.

"No one we know, so yes, it's probably exactly that. But, since the suit has been filed and you're named as the witness and representative of the city, you now have the obligation to answer the complaint."

"In English," Grace said.

Carson picked up a packet of papers and handed one stack to each of them. "In short. Sokolov had to tell the courts why he feels he has a case. We'll go over this line by line, but he is trying to paint a theme that you've taken bribes in the past, and he says he has proof that you did."

Grace glanced at the legal papers without reading them. "What proof?" She looked up to find Carson staring at Dameon.

Dameon had his nose down reading the papers. He paused and looked up. "My name is in here."

Carson nodded once. "It is."

"What?" Grace skimmed the papers again. On the second page she found Dameon's name. "Acquired private texting conversations between Mr. Dameon Locke and Miss Grace Hudson." Grace read the next part to herself.

DL: What can I do to convince you to keep today a secret?

GH: My price is steep.

DL: Name it!

GH: Never mind. I'll hold onto the information to lord over you.

DL: I see how this works. Blackmail.

GH: We all have our ways and means.

Grace turned to look at Dameon. "That bastard stole my phone."

"So this conversation did take place?" Carson asked.

"As damaging as this sounds, there's a simple explanation for it."

"I'm listening."

She smiled at Dameon. "This was before Dameon and I started dating. He followed me into a nail salon, and I wouldn't talk to him unless he was sitting in a chair."

Dameon looked at Carson, and put a hand in the air. "I swear I didn't like it."

Grace laughed. "He got a pedicure and I was giving him a hard time." She looked at the piece of paper and started to paraphrase the text . . . "'What can I do to keep today a secret?' He's talking about the pedicure. 'My price is steep.' That's me poking at him. This is all a joke."

Carson was biting his lip. "Did you pay cash?"

Grace shook her head. "No, Dameon paid with a credit card."

Now Carson laughed. "Okay, good. I need a copy of that statement."

Dameon was smiling. "I'm never going to live that day down."

Carson pushed those papers aside and pulled up another one. "My first thought was to throw the evidence out. Sokolov didn't obtain it legally and the message wasn't sent to him. Pretty cut and dry. But it might explain this." He handed over a statement from her bank.

She and Dameon looked at it together. "What am I supposed to be seeing here?"

"Look at your savings account. I'm guessing you have online banking you access through your phone."

"I do."

"Then Sokolov has access to your account numbers," Carson said.

At first glance, she saw the number. "That's not right."

"What?" Dameon asked.

"The amount. I don't have twenty thousand in my savings, I only have five and some change."

She turned the page to find three deposits of five thousand dollars each added to the account. "What is this?"

"Good question. I was hoping you had an explanation for it. The first thing that stands out is the even amount. Five thousand. The other thing is when they were deposited. These were cash deposits through a mail drop during the Christmas holiday."

"My Secret Santa gave me fifteen grand?" Grace asked.

"Or someone is going out of their way to make it look like you had extra money you can't explain going into your account. And since your December statement just came out, you didn't notice it until now."

"I would have said something if I saw it," Grace said.

Dameon put the paper back on Carson's desk. "So this idiot steals Grace's phone, screenshots a private conversation, and makes up a story about me bribing Grace. And then money falls into her account."

"Bingo."

"Don't banks have cameras on deposit boxes?"

Carson nodded. "Which we will subpoena if we need to."

"Who knows about the money in the account?" Grace asked.

"Right now, just us. Michelle found it. But if this ends up in front of a judge . . ."

"So we have Michelle dig up who put it there," Dameon said.

"Exactly."

"In the meantime, we need to answer the complaint and at the same time toss in a lawsuit of our own."

"Against the city?"

"No, against Sokolov. Libel, slander, theft, assault."

"He didn't touch me," Grace said.

"Assault is verbal and intent, not physical. And considering how far he's taking this . . ."

"Oh, I'm game. You don't have to say it twice," Grace said.

Carson sat back in his chair and folded his hands on his desk. "Now would be a good time for your relationship to become public."

"It's not like we're keeping it a secret," Dameon said.

"Nothing flashy, just a simple something in the local newspaper. Santa Clarita is a small enough town that the rich new land developer falling for a hometown girl could make the fourth page. That makes pedicures and flirty texting completely believable and might even lead Sokolov to drop his case. It can't hurt."

~

Grace stood in her mom's kitchen chopping up the makings of a salad. It was family dinner night, something they did twice a month on average. "I've known Dameon less than two months. How is it possible I feel like I've known him for years?" she asked her mother.

Right now it was just the two of them in the kitchen. Dameon was on his way from picking up his mother so she could get to know Grace's family.

"That's what happened with your father and I. We dated for three months before we were walking down the aisle." Nora offered a wistful sigh.

"You were pregnant," Grace said, deadpan.

"Colin was early," Nora said with a wink. "I knew your dad was the one."

Grace dumped the cut-up carrots into the bowl and moved on to the tomatoes. "How do you know? Is there some kind of divine sign? A flashing light with arrows pointing?"

"You're watching too much television."

She laughed. "Seriously, Mom."

Nora went to the fridge and removed a bottle of wine.

"What's this?" Grace asked when she took a glass from her mother.

"Truth serum."

They both sipped.

"Do you love him?"

That had Grace taking another sip. "I've never felt so connected to anyone the way I do to Dameon."

Her mom smiled and quietly drank her wine.

"He's smart and funny. He treats me like an equal and values my opinion."

"He's good-looking," her mom said.

"Right! Like how did I land that?"

"You're beautiful."

"You're biased," she told her mom.

"How is the sex?" Nora asked.

Grace wanted to pretend shock, but that wasn't how their family rolled. "It's off the charts, Mom. I never have to fake anything. Even if I'm tired he makes it happen for me."

"I knew I liked that boy."

Grace went back to cutting tomatoes. "Does Dad like him?"

"Your dad's a hard sell. As long as Dameon asks him for your hand first, your dad will ignore the fact he wears a suit."

She shook her head. "Oh, we're not there. No one is getting on one knee anytime soon."

"I wouldn't bet on that. I know a man in love when I see one, and your Dameon is all of that and more."

"Mom, don't start the marriage talk or you'll scare him away."

Nora laughed. "You don't have to worry about me. It's your dad that will take that too far."

"He should get on Matt. What's taking him so long?" Grace asked.

Nora just smiled.

"What do you know?"

"You know Matt and Erin were just in Chicago visiting her sister."

"Yeah?"

"I'm pretty sure he asked Erin's father for his blessing."

Grace stopped slicing. "You're kidding. Erin isn't close with her dad."

Her mom shook her head. "That isn't going to stop Matt from doing the right thing. And since everything that happened with Erin, I think her father is really trying."

"It's going to take some time to make up for being a bad parent all those years."

Erin's father had money to give, but not love, to his daughters. But as the man grew older, he started to realize what he missed out on.

"People make mistakes, honey."

"I guess."

Noise from the front room drifted in as the house began to fill. "We're here," Colin's voice called out.

~

Dameon hadn't seen his mom laugh this much since before his father died. Well, except when she was high on Christmas.

Here in the Hudson home, she sat beside Grace's parents, and they all chatted as if they'd known each other for years.

Every once in a while, Grace would look at him silently and just smile.

In those moments, he smiled back and reached for her.

A hand on his thigh, a whisper in his ear of some private thought . . . he wasn't sure how this had happened, but somehow she'd wedged herself into his world and he never wanted her to leave.

Sometime after dinner, Dameon was on the back porch with Matt and Colin. Matt had dragged them out there saying he needed help with something. Once they were out there, he stood on the side of the house and pulled out a cigar. "I'm going to ask Erin to marry me on Sunday."

Colin pulled his brother in for a hug. "That's huge. I'm so happy for you."

Dameon felt honored to be a part of the conversation. "Congrats," he said with a handshake.

Matt lifted the cigar to his brother with a laugh. "This is a new tradition," Matt explained to Dameon. "Colin lit up a cigar when he told me he was asking Parker."

Dameon didn't smoke, but he had no problem taking a puff or two for brotherhood.

"Does she know?" Colin asked.

"I don't think so."

They both looked at Dameon. "Grace hasn't said anything."

"Good."

"So, did you ask her dad?" Colin said.

"Of course. Dad would be pissed if I didn't."

Dameon took the stogie when it was offered. "You asked her dad if you could marry her?"

Matt nodded. "Our dad lives by the man code. If she's pregnant . . ."

"You marry her," Colin finished for him.

"If you want to marry her . . ."

"You ask her father first." Colin gave his brother a fist bump.

Dameon laughed. "My dad would have liked your dad."

Colin cupped Dameon's shoulder. "That's tough."

"Thanks."

Colin twisted quickly to Matt. "Wait, is Erin pregnant?"

Matt missed one beat.

One!

Colin tossed his hands in the air and pulled them both in for a hug. "Holy shit."

"Shhh. You don't know this yet." But Matt was all smiles.

Colin raised both his hands. "We need whiskey."

"Hello, Captain Obvious." Matt looked around the corner, then back.

Their smiles were contagious. Dameon felt himself laughing right along with them.

"We talked about kids, a lot." Matt looked to Dameon. "Erin didn't care about getting married again. She's so excited."

"Why hasn't she said anything?"

"I asked her to hold off. Told her you and Parker needed the spotlight for a little while after the wedding." Matt tapped Dameon's shoulder. "Then you come along and suddenly Grace is the center of attention."

"You're welcome?" Dameon said with a laugh.

"Thanks." Matt took a puff of the cigar. "So, Sunday . . ."

Colin just kept shaking his head. "Damn . . ."

"I need your help . . ."

Ten minutes later, straight faces in place, the three of them walked back in the house.

Dameon's mom was talking about something and laughing while Nora and Emmitt laughed with her. Grace was sitting beside Erin.

Parker slid up next to Colin.

She sniffed a few times and asked, "Have you guys been smoking?"

Dameon couldn't help but laugh.

Colin looked guilty, and Matt shrugged.

"Smoking?" Emmitt asked as his eyes narrowed to all three of them.

"Oh, you don't have to smoke that stuff anymore," Dameon's mom said. "It comes in cookies."

CHAPTER TWENTY-NINE

Dameon found the way to get Grace and him into the local paper.

All he had to do was sweet-talk a reporter to show up at a certain fire station on a certain Sunday when a certain someone might be popping the question to his girlfriend. And with Valentine's Day but a couple of weeks away, who could resist?

"Where are you taking me?" Grace sat in the passenger seat wearing a classic little black dress and high heels.

"It's a surprise."

He'd told her they were going to catch the sunset somewhere special and they needed to get an early start.

Dameon had the easy job. Get Grace to the fire station by five.

Colin had to manage Parker and Erin.

"Have I told you I don't like surprises?"

He glanced at her. "Everyone likes a surprise."

"Are we going to the beach? Sunset over the ocean?"

Dameon drove east on a back road. "I'm not telling."

"Fine."

He laughed.

She moaned. "Whatever."

He stopped at a light, looked at the time. They were cutting it a little close.

"Isn't he cute?" Grace was peering out the window at a black and white husky that had its head sticking out the window.

"Adorable."

"Have you ever had a dog?"

What was up with the traffic light? They had five minutes.

"Dameon?"

"What?" Oh, the dog. "Yeah. My dad was partial to German shepherds."

Finally the light turned green.

Dameon tapped the steering wheel with his thumbs.

"I love dogs. But I never thought it was right for a dog to be cooped up in a condo."

He made it through the light on the yellow. Only a few more blocks.

". . . don't you think?"

"What?" Something about dogs.

"You haven't heard a thing I've said."

He glanced over, smiled. "We were talking about dogs."

Grace shook her head.

He sighed when the fire station was in sight. "Isn't that the station your brother works in?"

"Yeah."

"Would you mind if we took a little side trip? I've never been in an actual fire station before." He moved into the turn lane.

"I don't know if Matt is even working today."

"Isn't that his truck?"

Grace leaned forward. "Okay, what's going on?" She pointed out the window. "That's my parents' car."

"Huh . . ."

"Dameon?"

He pulled in and put the truck in park. He cut the engine and unbuckled his belt. "C'mon."

They both got out, and he rounded the truck to take Grace's hand.

On the side of the station, Nora and Emmitt stood next to three firefighters and a woman with a camera.

"Oh my God." Grace squeezed his hand. "Matt's going to pop the question."

Dameon smiled and placed a finger over his lips. "Shhh."

Grace kept squeezing his hand. "Eeekkk!"

When they stopped in front of Grace's parents, Dameon shook Emmitt's hand. "Fancy meeting you here," Emmitt said with a grin.

Grace and her mom hugged. "This is awesome."

"Where is Matt?"

"He's inside sweating," one of the firefighters said.

The woman Dameon assumed was the reporter walked up to them and introduced herself. She barely finished her introduction when Colin's car pulled into the driveway.

One of the firefighters spoke into a radio. "She's here."

Colin, Parker, and Erin piled out of the car right as the garage doors of the station started to open.

Dameon stood behind Grace and wrapped his arms around her as they watched.

The photographer snapped pictures as Erin's eyes took it all in.

Matt stood in full uniform holding at least two dozen red roses. Draped across the fire engines was a massive banner in red and white and dozens of heart-shaped balloons with the question *Erin, will you marry me?*

Grace shivered in Dameon's arms.

He looked at her and saw a single tear fall off her cheek.

Dameon kissed the side of her head.

Matt walked straight up to Erin, who stood with her hands over her face. He dropped to one knee and opened a small box.

"Erin. I have loved you from the minute I set eyes on you. I want to wake up to you every day for the rest of my life. I want all the good times and the bad times with you by my side. I want to dance in the kitchen with you until we're both using walkers and remembering when we were both young and crazy."

Dameon felt a lump forming in his throat when Matt choked on his words.

"Erin, my love, my life, my everything . . . will you please do me the honor of becoming my wife?"

Erin was a mess of tears as she nodded and reached for him.

Matt set the roses on the ground, got to his feet, and pulled her in for a kiss.

Dameon looked around to see Grace's family all smiling and crying. One of the firefighters had a cell phone camera pointed at the happy couple.

When Matt let Erin up for air, everyone started clapping. Matt whispered something in Erin's ear as he slid a ring onto her finger.

Dameon never considered himself much of a romantic, but he had to admit he was pretty impressed with how Matt handled the whole thing.

There were hugs and cheers. When it was Dameon's turn to congratulate the happy couple, he hugged them both. "Way to set the bar high, Matt," Dameon said with a laugh.

"Let's see you beat that," Matt challenged.

Dameon looked over to Grace and saw her blushing.

The reporter snapped pictures and then interviewed Matt and Erin. She took down everyone's names in the family, including Dameon's. He was fairly certain a picture with him and Grace in it would make its way into the paper.

The bell inside the fire station went off, and Matt's colleagues moved into action.

Colin and Matt scrambled to take the sign down.

"Do you have to go?" Erin asked over the noise.

"Nope. I'm not on today."

They backed out of the way when the engine pulled out of the garage.

With the noise of the siren fading as it left the station, Dameon turned to the crowd. "If it's okay with you, I booked the private room at The Backwoods to celebrate."

Matt shook his hand. "Let me change real quick, and Erin and I will meet you there."

The two of them slipped into the station while everyone else watched them go.

"Anyone wanna lay bets on how late they'll be?" Colin asked.

"Leave the lovebirds alone," Grace scolded.

Emmitt walked up to Dameon and patted him on the back. "I hope you took notes, son."

"Dad!" Grace yelled.

Instead of feeling the pressure, Dameon smiled.

~

They made the second page, not the fourth.

Grace woke at Dameon's canyon home the next morning to text messages from both family and friends.

"Your phone is buzzing off the hook," Dameon said as he brought her a cup of coffee in bed.

She pushed into a seated position and accepted the coffee with a kiss. "Good morning."

Dameon was already showered and dressed. "Good morning." He sat on the edge of the bed and placed a hand on her leg over the blankets covering her.

"What time is it?"

"Almost seven. I have to get out of here if I'm going to beat traffic."

"You're not beating anything if it's seven," she told him.

He kissed her again. "Maybe I'll just stay."

"Someone has to work." Grace sipped the coffee before setting it aside. "Thank you."

He brushed the hair out of her face. "This is a great look."

She knew she was a mess. They'd gotten back relatively early but spent the evening exploring each other's bodies in very satisfying ways.

Her phone buzzed again. "What's going on?"

Dameon pulled his phone out of the breast pocket of his suit. "The local paper."

Grace rubbed the sleep from her eyes and took his phone. She expanded the pictures and the memories of the previous day came back.

Erin was emotional, Matt was teary-eyed.

Then there was a picture of Dameon holding her from behind and saying something in her ear. The caption was "Love is in the air."

"Slow news day," Grace said.

"This should do the trick." Dameon took his phone back and put it away. "I hate to run."

She started to get out of bed. "I'll be right behind you."

"No. Don't rush. Stay as long as you like."

She relaxed. "I'm starting to get lazy."

Dameon shook his head. "I've seen the drawings and site plans. There isn't a lazy bone in your body."

"There are a couple of sore ones after last night."

Dameon flashed a knowing grin. "I have early meetings tomorrow in Long Beach. I'm aiming to be back here Wednesday night."

"I remember."

He kissed her again and stood. He made it as far as the door before turning around. "Do you want a big family?" he asked out of the blue.

"What?"

"You know, kids? Are you thinking one or two? Or half a dozen?"

Grace felt her jaw dropping at the unexpectedness of his question.

"I, ahh . . ." How did she answer that? "More than one, less than six."

Dameon kept nodding as he walked away.

Grace pulled her knees into her chest and hugged them tight. Holy shit, Dameon had just asked her how many kids she wanted. In all her years of dating, never once had someone asked her about having a family.

She couldn't stop smiling.

Dameon poked his head back around the corner. "What about five?"

She was starting to hyperventilate. "You're going to be late for work."

He marched back into the room, kissed her again, this time with a little more something to talk about, and then abruptly walked away.

Only when she heard the front door shut did she let out a squeal and kick the covers back.

CHAPTER THIRTY

"What are the chances of getting Dameon to bowl with us?"

Grace was on the phone over her car speaker talking to Parker.

"Considering he asked me how many kids I wanted to have this morning, I'd say the chances are pretty high."

"He did not."

Grace was still giddy. "He did."

"Oh my God . . . why didn't you call me?"

She pulled the car to a stop at a traffic light. "My phone has been going crazy. Seems the paper made the rounds at work."

"The pictures are pretty telling."

The light turned green. "I'm having a hard time believing this is all happening. I'm not even upset about work anymore."

"How can you care about something you were beginning to hate?"

"I love the job, can't stand the politics. Even more now."

"I bet." Parker paused. "So how did the conversation about kids come up?"

"It didn't. He literally just asked out of the blue."

"Have you talked about getting married?"

"Parker, we haven't been dating long."

"Yet he's talking kids."

They were both silent for a while.

Grace merged into the turn lane and checked her rearview mirror. "Wait . . . was Erin drinking last night?"

"We went through two bottles of champagne."

"Yeah, but how much did Erin drink?"

"I didn't measure," Parker said.

Grace's mind started to calculate. "She said she was driving on our family dinner night."

"Oh . . ."

"Are you thinking what I'm thinking?" *Erin's pregnant.*

"No. She would tell us."

Grace switched lanes once the light turned green. "I'm going over there."

"To Matt and Erin's?"

"Matt's at work," Grace reminded her.

"I'll meet you there."

Grace disconnected the call and buzzed the car around traffic to get in the correct lane. She didn't see any cops, thank goodness. Because she was driving a little crazy even for her. Although the dark sedan behind her could be an unmarked police car.

She slowed down and paid a little more attention to the road.

With one eye on her rearview mirror and the other on her speedometer, Grace started to feel like maybe the car behind her *was* a cop.

The cars opened up on the road and Grace moved into the slower lane.

The sedan stuck right behind her.

"C'mon, pull me over if you're going to."

Only that didn't happen.

At the next red light, Grace stared through her rearview mirror. The expression on the man's face was only partially hidden by sunglasses. He looked vaguely familiar, but she couldn't place him. Was it someone she knew who was just messing with her?

When she pulled into Erin's neighborhood the car kept pace.

"Okay, this is bullshit." Grace pulled over to the side of the road suddenly and slammed on the brakes.

The car behind her buzzed around at that point.

She looked at the license plate to find a dark covering over the numbers. The kind of thing people use to get away with driving on a toll road without getting charged.

"What the hell?"

Maybe she'd just imagined the car following her.

She shook out her nerves and continued to Erin and Matt's place. But being the cautious person her dad taught her to be, Grace parked a house beyond Erin's.

Parker pulled into the driveway and watched Grace walking across the street. "Afraid I was going to hit your car?" she teased.

Grace shook her head. "No, it's just . . ." Yeah, an overactive imagination. "Nothing. Let's go ask Erin if she has a dead rabbit on her hands."

She and Parker stood in the doorway and rang the doorbell.

Erin opened the door. "Hi."

Parker hit Grace with her elbow.

She elbowed Parker back.

"What?" Erin asked.

Grace looked at Parker. "Chicken."

Parker acted shocked.

"Fine." Grace looked Erin in the eye. "Is it a boy or a girl?"

Erin's face went stone white. "Who told you?"

Parker and Erin both screamed at the same time, and then it was nothing but hugs and tears.

$\sim$

Dameon had the phone on speaker. A week's worth of paperwork spread out in front of him.

"I just got off the phone with Carson," Grace told him. "The dirt-bag was served with papers yesterday, and my response was given to the city this morning."

Dameon stopped looking at the numbers on his spreadsheet. "What happens now?"

"Carson seems to think the city is going to lift my furlough and ask me to come back to work."

"That's a change in tune."

"Yeah, he spoke with Simons, the city attorney, and offered a little information about Sokolov. The guy has a less than clean record. Spent a few nights in jail for a DUI and a few domestic calls to his mobile home park when he tried to strong-arm a tenant to leave."

Dameon cringed. "When I think of you out there alone with that man . . ."

"I hear ya. Carson said the same thing to Simons. Suggested that Richard had been informed of this man's hostility and still sent me there alone. That precautions needed to be in place."

"Sounds like the city is going to be doing some backtracking."

"I hate playing the fragile woman card. It's not who I am."

Dameon closed his eyes. "Honey, you're what, five three? And I'm gonna guess a hundred and fifteen pounds on any given day."

"You're sweet. A hundred and twenty."

God, he loved her sass. "You're missing my point."

"I hear ya."

"Do you? Because I've seen you hold your own with your brother but he would just as soon cut off his own hand before hitting back. Those tricks won't work with a man twice your size with a grudge."

It took Grace a second to respond.

"Hon?"

"I'm here. And I know you're right. I need to be smart and trust my instincts. I knew Sokolov was a shitty man the first time I met him. But I ignored it."

Dameon pulled his copy of the paper that had her picture in it and smiled. "Well, don't ignore it anymore, okay? I just found you and I'm not ready to lose you."

He heard her sniffle over the line. "Grace?"

"Yeah?"

Okay, she was choked up.

"Are you crying?"

"No." Another sniff. "Okay, yes."

"What's wrong?"

"Oh my god. Nothing. You say the sweetest things to me, and I don't know how to handle it."

That turned his worry into a smile. "Well, get used to it."

She sighed.

"Better?" he asked.

"Yeah."

"Are you home?"

"I am. But if it's okay with you I'm going to stay at the canyon house tomorrow night. We're supposed to get some significant rain and I want to see how the runoff behaves. We don't want surprises when you start building."

He couldn't stop smiling. "You're something else."

"I know," she teased. "Just remember that when I ask you to join our bowling league."

"What? Bowling?" Did she just say *bowling*?

"You heard me. It's a smallish town. We take our kicks when and however we can get them."

"You're serious? This isn't like the pedicure man-card stealing thing, is it?"

"Call Colin or Matt if you think I'm kidding. Our first game is Thursday night."

"You're not kidding."

She laughed and laughed.

CHAPTER
THIRTY-ONE

Grace sat beside Carson and across the table from stoic Richard, apologetic Vivian, and matter-of-fact Simons.

In front of her was her reinstatement paperwork.

"We sincerely hope you understand the position we were in when these accusations were brought to us," Vivian said, speaking for the team.

Grace looked to Carson for direction. He lifted his hand as if telling her to feel free to say her piece.

She placed her folded hands on top of the table and spoke up for herself for the first time since everything had blown up.

"While I understand there are precautions and protocols in place to protect the city, I fail to see why there was never once a time where my character was upheld by anyone at this table." She looked directly at her boss. "I have worked under your direction for five years. Have I ever once not performed in my job? Have I ever given you reason to consider these allegations had any merit whatsoever?"

Richard stared without expression. "Your performance evaluations have always been satisfactory."

"That's it?" It was clear Richard wasn't going to budge on this.

"We value you as an employee," Vivian said in an effort to ease the tension.

There is power in silence, and Grace did her best to channel that.

Carson took her silence as his cue to speak. "As everyone at this table is aware of, Miss Hudson has filed a civil suit against Mr. Sokolov. In the many points in this suit, the man's assaultive behavior is the one thing that stands out as a serious safety concern. If Miss Hudson chooses to continue her employment with the city, this suit and her safety have to be considered."

"Of course. It goes without saying that Grace wouldn't be expected to work on anything in regard to this property." Vivian was doing all the talking.

"And in light of the romantic relationship Miss Hudson and Mr. Locke have developed, Grace feels it would be in her best interest to relinquish the charge of this project to one of her coworkers to avoid any possible questioning of her character."

Vivian and Richard exchanged glances. "That seems reasonable."

"What do you say, Grace? Are we able to move past this?" Simons asked.

Carson looked at her, then back at the others. "Can you give us a few minutes?"

Richard looked annoyed, while the other two attempted to smile. "Of course."

Once Grace and Carson were alone, she finally released the breath she felt she'd been holding. "He is such an asshole."

"I don't think that is going to change."

She was completely torn. "I need some time to think on this."

Carson nodded. "That's reasonable."

A few minutes later, Carson asked the others to return. When they did, he told them she was going to take the rest of the week and weekend to make her decision.

"Thank you, Carson," she said as they walked out to the parking lot.

"We're not done yet. Unless you've changed your mind about the countersuit."

"Oh, no. I hate bullies, and that's what this person is."

"Couldn't agree more."

She stopped at her car. "Listen . . . something is bothering me. I want to run it past you."

"Okay." Carson turned to look at her.

"The other day I was driving to my brother's. This sedan pulled in behind me. At first, I thought maybe it was an unmarked police car because he was right on my butt. I slowed down, he slowed down. I turned, he turned."

"You were being followed?"

"That's what it felt like."

"Was it Sokolov?"

She shook her head. "No. The guy looked familiar, but I didn't get a good look at him. When I turned into my brother's neighborhood, I pulled over to the side of the road and the guy pulled past me."

"When was this?"

"Yesterday."

"Nothing since?"

"No."

"You wouldn't be the first person to get harassed after filing a lawsuit. It does take a special layer of stupidity to do so once things are already in the courts. Unfortunately, there are a lot of unintelligent people out there. The problem is we can't do anything about it until Sokolov makes contact, directly or indirectly. If the man contacts you at all, you need to call me immediately. I'll file an emergency restraining order."

Grace instantly thought of Erin. "Like that will work."

"I know. But it's all we have. You need to keep your eyes open. Be cautious. This guy had your cell phone. There's a lot of personal information in there."

Grace nodded. "It might have just been my imagination."

Carson stared her down. "Is that what your gut is saying?"

"No."

"Okay, then. Did you tell Dameon?"

Grace wavered. "No."

"Tell him. And your family. The sooner we nip this, the better our chances of nailing this guy if he's behind it."

The sky started to open up, and small droplets of rain fell.

"Thanks for your advice," she said.

"I'll be in touch."

~

Grace went straight to her condo after the city meeting and changed. She packed her mud boots and parka for her drive to Dameon's canyon home. She had started to pack an overnight bag and decided against it. As a rule, she wasn't a woman afraid of the dark, or being in a house alone. But the canyon house was isolated without a lot of traffic going by. Heeding Carson's advice, she didn't think it was in her best interest to be there alone once the sun went down.

As she drove through town, Grace paid close attention to the cars behind her.

Nothing out of the norm stuck out. Outside of the slapping of her windshield wipers, the drive was uneventful.

Grace waited until she was inside the house before calling Dameon using his landline.

His phone went to voice mail after the third ring. "It's me. I wanted to tell you how everything went today. And bring you up-to-date on a few things. I'm at the house, so call the landline. You know how bad the service is out here. I'm going back to my condo in a couple of hours. Before dark. I don't want you to worry. Oh, and if I don't answer right away, it's because I'm outside. Now I sound paranoid." She laughed and then had to stifle the urge to tell him she loved him.

When she hung up the phone, she realized how easy the thought rolled through her head.

She'd fallen in love with Dameon Locke. He'd somehow become the person she wanted to talk to every morning and every night. There wasn't a single red flag warning her that loving him was wrong. She smiled into the thought.

She walked over to the thermostat to turn up the heat and decided against it. She wouldn't be in there long enough to need it. And that disappointed her. She'd actually looked forward to staying the night, even if Dameon couldn't be there with her. Being in his space and seeing the few memories she'd shared with him made her feel more connected. Like she belonged.

But Carson's advice sounded in her head. *"You wouldn't be the first person to get harassed after filing a lawsuit . . . Tell Dameon. Tell your family."*

Grace stared at her phone and thought of who she should call. It was the middle of the day, so she knew Colin was working. She was pretty sure Matt was home, but telling him about the car thing would go straight to Erin. And yeah, Grace didn't need the pregnant woman worrying. So Grace called Parker.

"How did it go?" Parker asked the second she picked up the phone.

"They want to give me my job back."

"That's great."

Grace sighed. "I don't know if I want it."

"That's fair."

"Listen, I'm at Dameon's. I have about an hour of work to do here, two at the most, and I'm headed back to my place."

"I thought you were going to stay through the storm."

"I was, but I don't think it's wise to be out here by myself right now." She took a few minutes to tell Parker about the car that followed her and was quick to say that it hadn't happened twice.

"That's scary," Parker said.

"I don't want to be paranoid, but I really don't want to be stupid."

"I think you're smart to get out of there long before dark," Parker told her.

"Yeah. I'm still sensitive after Erin." Although Grace had to admit, if only to herself . . . Erin's ex and all the insecurities he'd created were fading into her past. She had to credit Dameon for that. For showing her that there were good men out there.

"We all are. I have you on Friend Finder. Call before you leave the house."

"I will. And I'll call when I get home," Grace said.

"I'll keep my phone handy."

Grace hung up and bundled into her rain gear.

She took a good look around once she stepped outside. There weren't any strange cars parked on the road or driving by. In fact, there weren't any cars on the road directly in front of the drive.

She walked through the mud and the rain off Dameon's fenced-in property and onto the larger part of land he would be developing. It was raining enough to run down the hillsides and into the uncontrolled wash. She kept her distance to avoid being swept away. Unlike other places in the valley where rain funneled into flash-flood danger zones, this particular area wasn't that dramatic. But that didn't mean it didn't come with its own set of challenges. Grace took pictures from every angle she could manage. She used voice-to-text to write notes for herself. Controlling what Mother Nature brings would have to be a high priority for Dameon's project. More than once she really wished he was there to see firsthand what the property looked like during a storm.

In addition to pictures, she let a video run for quite a while.

It had been a little over an hour before she traversed the route back to the house.

By now the rain was pounding the already soggy roads, and she'd taken on enough water to resemble a duck.

She shook off her rain gear and hung it on a hook by the front door. Her mud boots stayed on the tile.

A message from Dameon was waiting for her on his answering machine.

"Hey, hon. I just spoke with Carson. Why didn't you tell me about someone following you?"

"Oops."

"I get it, you're my fiercely independent, take-no-prisoners woman . . . it's one of the many things I love about you. But please don't keep these things from me. I'm leaving the office now. Traffic report says I will be there in an hour and a half. Call me if you leave the canyon and I'll go straight to your condo. Okay?"

Grace double-checked the time stamp on the message and looked at her watch. He was less than thirty minutes out.

She lifted the receiver and dialed his cell.

"Hello, Wonder Woman" is how he answered.

"I know. I'm sorry. I should have told you."

She could tell he had her on a speaker through his car. The muffled sound of the rain and swish of the windshield wipers had her straining to hear everything Dameon said. "Yes. You should have. When Carson told me . . . it scared me, Grace."

She leaned against the kitchen counter. "This sharing of my life isn't something I'm used to," she said in her defense.

"I've met your family. And the whole lot of you overshare everything."

Grace laughed. "If I told them about this, they'd have me locked in a room somewhere."

"Maybe that's wise."

She couldn't argue. "How far out are you?"

"Traffic sucks, but it's moving. I've got another thirty minutes."

She walked over to the thermostat and turned it up. "It would take me at least twenty minutes to drive to my place, so I'll just stay here."

"All right. Lock the doors."

"I already did."

He chuckled. "Good. I, ah . . . yeah, I'll see you soon."

"Drive carefully."

CHAPTER
THIRTY-TWO

Using a towel from one of the bathrooms, Grace patted down her soaked pants and attempted to dry her hair. She pulled back the shades on the front window and peered outside. The rain was really coming down and the sky was dark with clouds. But it was still a couple of hours until sunset, so even though she knew Dameon was on his way, it was a relief to know he'd be there before dark.

She made herself busy by rummaging through Dameon's freezer. She removed two individually wrapped chicken breasts and put them on the counter to thaw. Then to chase the silence away, she turned on the TV and found a music station to listen to. At one point she wanted to toss her wet pants into a dryer, but realized there wasn't one in the house. Instead, she stacked small pieces of wood in the fireplace and turned on the gas to get it going.

It took a good five minutes while the flames built up enough to push out heat. Once it was hot enough, she tossed on a couple of bigger logs and turned down the gas.

In the time she'd known Dameon, Grace hadn't spent more than a few hours alone in his house. And even though he'd been working to improve the space, he was adamant that the house would be removed in the future. She had to admit, the place was growing on her. From the awful carpet to the window coverings that had been left behind. Maybe Dameon wouldn't mind if she spent a little time making the place more livable. And damn if the chill from the single-pane windows wasn't the worst. Even heavier curtains would help with that.

With nothing left to do but stare at the fire and listen to music, Grace moved into the dining area and rolled out the plans she'd been working on.

No matter who Richard assigned Dameon's project to, they'd happily take any plans Grace mapped out, which would cut their work hours in half if not more.

She opened up her phone, listened to the notes, and transcribed them to paper.

Whenever she found herself in the zone of work, she lost track of time. In her head she asked herself if she could still work under Richard. If only the man would retire, and she'd be able to go back to her job without the politics. Her thoughts drifted to the office and all the things that had been said about her.

When Dameon got home, she'd talk it out with him. And that was a nice change. Yeah, she could discuss things with her family, but they had so many other concerns in their lives right now.

Three sudden, sharp knocks on the front door made her jump and drop her pencil.

She glanced at her watch. It had been close to thirty minutes.

"Did you forget your key?" she called out as she walked to the door.

Her hand hesitated over the doorknob.

She pushed open the window covering she'd closed to keep the heat in.

Next to her car, in the driveway, was a high-end SUV.

Her smile dropped and she peered through the peephole in the door.

Max? Her heart rate double-timed.

What was Maxwell Banks doing knocking on Dameon's front door?

He stood far enough away that Grace felt comfortable opening it a crack.

She spoke through a three-inch opening. "What are you doing here?"

"Oh, hi . . . ah, is Dameon here? I tried calling him, but the cell service sucks."

"He'll be here any minute."

Max stayed where he was and shoved his hands in his jacket pockets. "I really need to talk to him. Any chance I could wait inside?"

Grace shook her head. "No. Last I looked, you and Dameon had a falling-out."

Max blew out a breath. "I know. I get it. I'll go into town. Can you tell him I was here? He doesn't owe me anything, but I'd really like to talk with him."

"I can do that."

"Thanks. I appreciate it." With that, Max pulled up the collar of his jacket and ran back out in the rain.

Grace closed the door and secured the lock and watched Max through the window as he jumped in his car. *What the actual hell?*

As he backed out of the driveway, she sighed in relief.

~

Dameon was halfway up the canyon road to the house when the paved roadway became a mess of mud and rock. He understood what Grace had originally told him about the area and the road conditions after a big rain. She wasn't kidding when she said it could become impassable.

Driving through the area in the rain brought home his need for an investor. This was going to take twice the amount of roadwork and infrastructure to make it work. Not everyone buying a home in his development was going to want to drive a truck . . . or a massive SUV like the one headed toward him.

Driving slow enough to avoid the larger rocks that were being knocked into the road by the rain, Dameon passed the SUV. He made it less than two yards before he recognized the car and the driver and slammed on his brakes.

In the rearview mirror, he saw Max do the same.

What the hell are you doing out here?

The red backup lights went on, and Max slowly pulled his car alongside Dameon's truck.

They both rolled down their windows.

"What are you doing out here?" Dameon asked over the noise of the drumming rain and the vehicle engines.

For a minute it didn't seem like Max was going to talk. Then he did. "Lena left me."

Ah, shit. Much as he wanted to pretend Max's words meant nothing to him, they had too much history to ignore. But he wasn't about to say he was sorry. Lena was wrong for Max. All wrong. "That's hard."

Max looked out his windshield and then leaned out the window and yelled, "I'm sorry, Dameon. I've been a shitty friend."

Damn. What was he supposed to do with that?

"My dad's sick. Really sick. It had me thinking."

The girlfriend card Dameon could pass on, but the dad card? No way. He remembered how Max had been there for him when his own dad died.

Max turned his gaze out his windshield. "I feel like my world is falling apart. Lena called it quits right after Christmas, and I thought she hooked back up with you."

"That isn't who I am, Max."

He closed his eyes and shook his head. "I know. I went to the charity dinner thinking maybe she'd be there. And when I saw you and your girlfriend and the team . . . it's like I reverted back to a cocky high school kid again." Max turned his gaze to Dameon. "I just want to talk. I know you don't owe that to me, but I want to make this right."

Dameon watched the rain running down his windshield and the ticktock of the wipers.

~

Grace walked back to her drawings and picked up her pencil. She stared at the plans for two solid minutes and knew her concentration was off.

She moved to the fireplace and stoked the logs. There was some serious cold coming from the back bedrooms. After checking the vents in the main room and feeling heat blowing out, she walked through the hallway to make sure all the windows were closed. Sure enough, in an empty room at the very back of the house, a window was open, and the old curtains from the previous owner were blowing in.

Grace walked in the room and attempted to slide the window closed.

She tugged twice and then put some muscle behind it on the third.

The window slid closed with a loud click.

Grace shook off the rain that had blown in on her as she turned.

Her stocking feet then stepped in a soaked carpet. Only when she looked down, it wasn't rainwater she noticed. It was mud.

Muddy footprints.

~

"I'm sorry about your dad. Damn, Max."

Max kept shaking his head. "I fucked up, Dameon. I let my dick get in the way of a solid friendship."

Dameon motioned out the windshield. "The house I'm using is just up the way."

"Yeah, I know. I was just there. Your girlfriend wouldn't let me in."

That made Dameon smile. "She's a smart woman."

Max grinned briefly.

"Follow me up."

They made eye contact. With a single nod, Max rolled up his window and pulled forward. It took a four-point turn, but he pulled in behind Dameon and they both drove back toward the house.

~

Oh shit.

Oh shit.

Oh shit.

Grace's hands shook, her heart rate took off like a racehorse, and her breathing became erratic.

Someone was in the house.

Her first thought was Max. But she'd seen him drive away.

She spun in a circle. There was absolutely nothing in the empty room to grab. Her hand grasped the curtain and she looked up.

Without a second thought, she ripped the cheap rod from the wall and quickly pushed the curtains off and onto the floor.

Her eyes traveled to the closed closet doors.

On the carpet, the footprints stopped in front of them.

The door to the room was in the opposite direction so she ran for it.

She made it down the hall before a man stepped in front of her and pushed her against the wall.

She screamed and swung the cheap metal curtain rod with every ounce of power she had.

The rod made contact and the man spoke.

"Fucking bitch."

She looked up and kept swinging.

It was Sokolov. He tried to disguise his face with nylons pulled over his head, but she could tell it was him.

The third time she swung the rod, he grabbed it and wrestled it out of her hands.

She turned to run back the way she came when a second man, this one bigger, grabbed her by her shoulders.

"Now where do you think you're going?"

The man holding her also wore nylons over his face, squishing it in a way that made his features unrecognizable.

He turned her to face Sokolov.

"You're not going to get away with this," she yelled.

Sokolov lifted his hands to the room. "Who is going to stop me?"

She tried to wiggle free to no avail. "I know it's you, Sokolov."

He took a step closer. Almost in kicking range.

Her mind scrambled.

"Oh yeah?" He pulled the nylons off his face. "That's too bad. But that look on your face right now is worth it."

"Dameon will be here any second."

Sokolov started to laugh.

The man holding her did as well.

"Did you hear that? The cavalry is coming."

Another step closer.

"I got to thinking. If I'm going to be accused of assault and battery, I might as well do the crime, right?" Sokolov ran his tongue over his lips, his eyes moving slowly from her face to her chest.

Oh shit.

Another step closer . . .

"Besides, you owe me fifteen grand. You didn't think I'd let that go, did you?" He stopped too far away to kick and looked back at her face. "So this is what we're going to do. I'm going to give you a little taste of what I'm going to do to your friends. I know where they all live and when they're alone. So even if you're stupid enough to call the police, I have friends like my buddy here, who will make sure to take care of them one at a time."

She thought of Erin and Parker. Her mom and dad. His words were screwing with her head.

"I have a rock-solid alibi as to where I am right now, and it's not here, little lady."

She struggled against her hold again.

Nothing.

The music played in the living room with an upbeat song, mocking what was happening at that moment.

"I'll get your money back," she told him.

She noticed a lift in his lips.

Her arms started to scream in pain from the man holding her.

"Just don't hurt me."

Sokolov liked that. His shoulders relaxed and he looked to the man behind her. "Did you hear that? She's singing a different tune now." He took another step, then two.

Grace moved as fast as she could.

She shifted her hips to the side and, with her fist, aimed right for the man's balls behind her.

He lost his grip while Sokolov lunged for her.

Her knee came up and Sokolov doubled over.

She made it three feet and one of them grabbed at her legs, and she fell to the ground with a scream.

~

Dameon pulled alongside Grace's car, and Max pulled in behind him.

He waited until Max joined him before walking up to the house.

Max extended his hand. "Thanks, Dameon."

He smiled. "Don't thank me yet," he said.

They turned to the house, and Max patted him on the back.

Under the cover of the porch, Dameon stomped his feet on the welcome mat Grace had bought him for Christmas.

He was fishing the keys out of his pocket when he heard Grace cry out.

"Grace?" he yelled.

"Dameon! Help!" She was screaming.

He grabbed the doorknob, said the hell with the keys, and kicked the flimsy lock open.

Grace was sprawled on the floor, on her back, and kicking at the man who was scrambling to get out of the way.

Dameon saw red, and he charged in with a full football-style tackle. The man over Grace went down under him.

Grace screamed again and yelled, "Watch out."

Dameon didn't look up. His fist struck out at the man he'd just shoved to the ground.

His knuckles hit flesh.

The man on the ground swung back.

Dameon's lip split and he struck out again.

This time the man under him slumped.

Dameon turned his head enough to see that there was a second man in the house. This one was bigger and he'd just slammed his fist into Max's face.

Grace was scrambling out of the way.

Dameon pushed to his feet and charged the man beating on Max.

He felt a punch to his ribs before landing one himself.

"Help!" Grace yelled to his side.

When he looked, she had the cordless phone in one hand and a fireplace poker in the other. Her yell for help was over the phone.

Her distraction was enough to give the bigger man a clean shot at Dameon's kidney.

He went to a knee, and Grace screamed as she charged with the swinging fireplace poker she used like a sword.

Dameon heard a yelp and saw the steel make contact. As it caught the nylon-faced man, it ripped the fabric.

Dameon pulled himself up and charged right as Max did the same.

The stranger was on the ground with Max's booted foot pressed against the back of his head.

A moan came from the other man, who was trying to stand.

Grace stumbled toward him with the poker and swung. "You son of a bitch!" She lifted the poker to hit again.

Dameon grabbed it after the third hit. "He's down."

And he was. Face-first.

Grace turned her wild eyes to him.

"It's okay." Dameon reached for her.

She stumbled into him and went limp in his arms. "I didn't see them."

"It's okay, baby. I'm here."

And she cried.

CHAPTER
THIRTY-THREE

By the time the police arrived, Dameon and Max had found zip ties in the garage at Grace's suggestion and bound the two men together.

Within twenty minutes, the house was swarming with police, paramedics, and one fire engine with a crew.

Grace sat inside one of the ambulances while the medics cleaned up a cut on her arm and poked around to determine if she needed to go to the hospital.

Dameon and Max both stood beside the officer who had arrived first and was writing everything down.

Sokolov and his thug were both en route to the local hospital, in handcuffs.

The rain had slowed to a drizzle, and a little bit of fading sunlight started to peek through.

"Hey." Miah, one of the police officers that she knew, looked inside the ambulance. "How are you feeling?"

She lifted her bandaged arm. "Not bad, considering."

The paramedic frowned. "She doesn't want to go to the ER. That ankle looks nasty."

Grace wiggled her toes, pretended it didn't hurt. "It's fine."

Miah laughed. "The zip ties were a nice touch."

She found herself smiling. "I did learn a few things being a cop's daughter."

"Your pop is on his way."

"Along with everyone else, I'm sure."

Miah looked at the medic. "You don't have to push her to go to the hospital. Her family will do it for you."

Grace frowned. "Isn't there some work for you to do out there?" she teased, shocked she had it in her to give him a hard time.

Miah lifted his hands and walked away.

She turned to the medic. "I'm really fine. If it gets worse, I'll go in without the lights and sirens."

"I know Matt. He's gonna make my life hell if you're lying."

"Damn right I will."

Grace looked up as Matt swung into the back of the ambulance. He hugged her first, then pulled back to look at her. "Geez, Gracie. Can't stay out of the spotlight for one minute, can you?"

"What can I tell you?"

Matt hugged her tight a second time.

"Is Dad here yet?" she asked next to his ear.

"No, they were five minutes behind me."

"Okay, help me out of here. I don't want them freaking out."

Matt glared.

She pushed him. "Move your butt."

"Just go to the ER."

"Where they just took the guys who did all this? I really don't want to have to bail any of the men in my life out of jail for vigilantism."

Matt blinked . . . twice. "Good point."

"Thank you, now help me down."

Matt made it three steps as she attempted to walk before he gave up and picked her up.

"What the . . ."

"Shut up, Gracie."

Dameon saw them coming and walked toward them. "You need to go to the hospital."

"No, I don't. I need to ice, elevate, and compress . . . and a couple shots of whiskey."

"She's stubborn." Matt nodded toward the house. "Can we go inside?"

"They are swarming in there."

"Prop me up in the garage," Grace told him. "Before Dad gets here."

And on that request, Dameon retrieved a couple of dining chairs that survived the brawl and set them inside the garage so she could elevate her ankle.

Slowly her family started to arrive.

Parker and Colin gushed and hugged and told her she looked like hell.

Erin held her hand and clung to Matt.

But it was when her dad showed up that everything got real.

"Where's my baby girl?" she heard before seeing him.

The crowd that surrounded her separated.

Dameon stood beside her, holding her hand.

Her dad marched in a way dads do, straight to her side.

He knelt down, knees popping as he did. There were unshed tears in her father's eyes. Seeing them broke Grace's armor.

Her dad didn't cry.

It just wasn't in him.

He pulled her in so tight she had a hard time breathing. "I'm okay, Daddy."

"I'm gonna kill him."

"No, you're not."

He hugged harder.

"Oh, baby."

She gave her dad as much time as he needed. Her eyes looked up to Dameon.

"Dameon stopped him, Daddy. I swear I'm okay. Just a few bruises."

Her dad pulled away and looked up.

She knew he noticed what everyone else did. Dameon had a pretty decent bruise on his lip. His knuckles were caked with drying blood, and his clothes looked like he'd been in a barroom brawl. Which he had been . . . minus the liquor.

Max stood across the garage, looking just as banged up.

Emmitt pointed at Dameon. "You and I will talk later."

Grace tried not to smile at the fierceness in her dad's voice.

"Anytime, sir."

He seemed to like the title and stood tall. "Who is the lead on this?" he asked as he walked toward the uniformed police officers standing in the front yard.

Grace turned to hug her mother, who had a much gentler touch. "You okay?"

"My ankle is killing me," she admitted. "I'll have Dameon take me to the urgent care. We can't have dad in the ER with the guys who did this."

Nora nodded several times. "Oh, no . . . we can't have that."

"Thanks."

Her mom reached out a hand and touched her face. "Did you aim for the balls?"

More than one person listening laughed.

"Neither one of them is going to want to pee for a while," Grace happily reported.

Nora winked. "That's my girl."

Her mom stood and reached out and touched Dameon's arm. "Thank you."

$\sim$

Grace's ankle was sprained, not broken.

Dameon left her in her parents' living room with all the women doting on her. Between the painkillers the clinic doctor gave her and the wine she wasn't supposed to be mixing them with, she was fairly relaxed.

The same couldn't be said for the men in the house.

Dameon, Colin, Matt, and Emmitt were all in the Hudson garage where someone had unearthed a punching bag and hung it from a rafter.

Colin, Matt, and Emmitt all took turns punching the thing.

Dameon looked at the state of his fists and sat out on this display of testosterone.

Matt hit the bag hard. "I'm starting to understand why men used to lock their women away in ivory towers."

"There's no way Parker would stand for that," Colin said.

"Grace would burn the room around her to escape," Dameon added.

"It's our job to teach them how to defend themselves. You need to remember that." Emmitt pointed to Matt.

Matt stopped hitting the bag and looked at his dad. "Why are you picking on me?"

"Really, son?"

"What?"

"Do I need to spell it out for you?" Emmitt patted his spare tire.

Matt's expression sobered. "Oh . . ."

Dameon drank from the longneck bottle in his hand. "You did a good job teaching Grace, Mr. Hudson. Those guys were hurting before Max and I showed up."

Colin smiled at him. "She had to keep up with us growing up."

Dameon didn't share the part about her being on her back on the floor as she kicked around like a rabid dog. The image wouldn't leave his brain anytime soon. The last thing he wanted was those thoughts plaguing anyone else.

Colin must have seen the shift in Dameon's mood. He walked over and sat beside him. "I'm glad you were there."

"Me too."

Matt pushed the punching bag his way. "Want a swing at this thing?"

Dameon looked at his hands. "I had the satisfaction of the real thing."

"Lucky you," Emmitt said. He took the gloves from his son and punched the bag.

Colin lifted his empty bottle. "Anyone want another?"

Dameon looked up, shook his head.

"Dad?"

Emmitt stood from where he was perched. "Why don't you go inside? I want a word with Dameon."

Matt and Colin exchanged glances.

Once they left, Dameon swallowed . . . hard.

Emmitt sat silent for what felt like forever.

Dameon spoke first. "I wanted to kill him." He lifted his hands in front of him as if he was grabbing the bastard by the neck. "I never really understood newscasts that talked about blind rage driving a person to extremes. But I get it now."

Emmitt sighed. "When my sons were born, I realized what loving someone unconditionally meant. I knew I could teach them to defend themselves no matter what. But when Gracie came along . . . I was at a loss. Here's this little tiny girl with all the fragile parts girls have . . ." He lifted his hands as if he were holding an infant. "I was scared. I'd seen a lot of this big bad world and what happens when it chews you up and spits you out. So I did what any cop would. I raised her like I did my sons."

Dameon smiled at the image he found himself seeing through Emmitt's eyes.

"Oh, Nora did the girlie stuff. Makeup and those stupid shoes she insists on wearing. But Gracie was tough. She always fought back. Then last year, after that unfortunate incident with Erin's ex, I watched the fight in Gracie fade."

Emmitt met Dameon's eyes. "Then you came along. And I feel I got my girl back."

"I'd love to take credit, but that's all her."

Emmitt shook his head. "Nope. Not completely. You gave her her confidence back. And I want you to know I appreciate it."

Dameon felt his chest fill with pride. "Thank you, sir."

Emmitt nodded. "Your dad would have been proud."

Oh, damn.

Dameon's eyes swelled with tears. He swallowed the lump in his throat.

Emmitt stood and reached for Dameon's hand. Instead of a handshake, the older man pulled him in for a hug. "Thanks for protecting my little girl."

Don't cry.

Don't cry.

Aww, fuck.

They both pulled away and wiped at their eyes as they attempted to look in the other direction.

"I'll let you, ah . . . have a minute," Emmitt said as he started to walk away.

Dameon stopped him. "Sir?"

Emmitt turned and faced him.

"I have a question for you before you go."

∼

Grace's dad walked in from the garage first, his eyes a little watery, his nose a little red.

Her brothers were both sitting on the edge of the fireplace hearth drinking beer. Parker sat on one side of her, Erin on the other. Her aching ankle was propped up on pillows on the coffee table.

Her mom popped up from her chair and went to her husband.

"Hey, Dad?" Grace called from the couch.

"Yeah, baby?"

"I'm okay."

Emmitt waved a hand in the air. "Don't mind me. There's pollen in the air."

Her dad and mom walked up the stairs together.

"Can someone go check on Dameon?" Grace asked.

Matt started to stand when the door to the garage opened.

Parker moved to the chair Nora had just vacated, leaving room beside Grace for Dameon to sit.

He looked about as choked up as her dad.

"You okay?"

His arms wrapped around her shoulders. "I will be in three or four years." He leaned over and kissed her gently.

Matt slapped his hands on his knees. "Okay, let's talk about something pleasant. Erin and I are going to elope."

Grace stopped staring at Dameon to snap her eyes to her brother.

"No way," Parker said.

"Is this because of the baby?" Grace asked.

Matt elbowed his brother. "Did you tell them?"

Erin laughed.

"Oh, please. Like we couldn't figure it out on our own," Parker said.

"You can't elope. Mom and Dad will kill you."

"Okay, not elope, per se, but we're thinking a long weekend in Maui. Get everyone on a plane sometime in the next month." Erin tapped her stomach. "Before it becomes obvious."

"Nobody is going to care if you get married while you're pregnant."

Matt cleared his throat. "No way. Remember what Dad always says. The first baby comes anytime . . . the second one takes nine months."

Grace laughed until it started to hurt.

An hour later, Dameon had carried her to her parents' guest room, the room that was once hers, and closed the door behind them.

Grace leaned back against the headboard. "I think I could sleep for a week."

"You didn't drink a lot of that wine, did you? The doctor said—"

"One glass, and I'm pretty sure my mom watered it down like I was twelve."

Dameon smiled. "I like your mom."

"Was everything okay with you and my dad?"

He slid one shoe off at a time. "I think I might be growing on him."

"You sure? You were both pretty worked up when you came in."

"Nawh. I think there's some solvents open in the garage."

Grace shook her head. "Yeah, and pollen flies around when it's raining."

Dameon slid back against the headboard with her. "Your dad and I are good. He just wanted to talk a little longer. He's a good man."

She leaned her head on his shoulder. "I'm so glad you came when you did."

He kissed the top of her head. "Oh, honey. I am, too. When I think about what could have happened."

"Yeah, but it didn't. And Max . . . what the heck was up with that?"

"We didn't get much of a chance to talk. He told me his dad is sick and the fiancée ditched him."

"Ouch."

"Yeah. He was out looking at the jobsite and feeling guilty."

She sighed and felt her eyelids get heavy. "Sometimes bad things remind you of the good things."

"You can say that again."

Maybe it was the narcotics, or the watered-down wine . . . "Sometimes bad things remind you of the good things."

Dameon's chest rumbled with laughter under her ear. "God, I love you."

It took a second, but her eyes opened as his words sunk in.

She lifted her head from his chest. "W-what?"

"I. Love. You." He placed his palm on her cheek. "One hundred percent head over heels."

"Dameon . . ."

"Sometimes you just know. And that's where I'm at. If you're not there yet, it's okay—"

She shook her head. "Oh, no . . . I'm there. Which is dumb because we haven't known each other very—"

He didn't let her finish before kissing her.

Grace pulled away. "I love you, too."

"C'mere." And he kissed her again.

EPILOGUE

The soft water of the lagoon lapped in the background of the perfect wedding.

Erin's sister had stood at her side while Colin took his place by Matt.

There were only thirteen people total in the lot of them, two of which were Erin's niece and nephew. Everyone was barefoot and wearing white.

And it was beautiful.

Grace cried when her brother vowed to love, honor, and cherish, and completely lost it when Erin started with the waterworks.

The informal reception was brought together with locals playing simple instruments and singing Hawaiian songs.

"Your aunt Beth is going to throw a fit when she learns that we all ran off without inviting her," Nora reminded them all as they sat around a huge table that was overflowing with food, flowers, and champagne.

Grace turned to Dameon.

The sun had kissed their skin in the few days they'd been on the island. His casual white-on-white silk Hawaiian shirt and casual slacks made him even better looking than when he was dressed in a power suit.

"I haven't met her yet, right?"

Grace shook her head. "No, but in a way, she's responsible for the night we met."

Dameon looked confused.

"She was harping on my state of singlehood at Colin and Parker's wedding when I needed that cold walk in the hotel garden."

Dameon slowly started to nod and smile. "I always liked your Aunt Beth," he teased.

"You say that now," Parker said. "Wait until she starts harping about Grace's empty uterus."

There was laughter all around.

"I'm off the hook there," Erin said.

Matt leaned over and kissed his new wife.

"By my calculations, this baby is coming around Christmas, right?" Emmitt said.

"Sure, Dad. Or Halloween, give or take a few weeks." Matt held Erin's hand as if he was afraid to let go.

Colin stood and picked up his glass. "Okay . . . it's time for the sappy best man speech. Which I've been practicing for at least three hours."

Dameon pulled Grace close.

"I always knew that Matt was going to marry a knockout."

Erin blushed.

"I mean, c'mon. He dated all the pretty girls in school. Women followed him around in the supermarket when he was dressed in his hero uniform . . ."

"Hey now . . . ," Matt called out.

"So you being beautiful was a given. But what wasn't a given was this kind, loving, missing piece of Matt's life . . . all our lives."

Grace sucked in a sniffle.

"I knew when I met Parker, she was it. I remember the day I told Matt I was going to marry her that he already knew I was all in. And the night Matt pulled Dameon and me outside in the freezing cold to tell us he was going to propose . . . I was like, *Hell ya!* I couldn't ask for a better sister-in-law, right, Gracie?"

Grace lifted her glass.

"I know I speak for all of us when I say, welcome to the Hudson family, Erin. And thank you for loving my brother the way you do."

A round of cheers and sips of champagne was followed by hugs and more tears.

A while later, Parker and Grace sat to the side while Dameon, Colin, and Matt had some kind of man huddle that included some sort of Hawaiian shots. Erin was talking with her sister, Helen, and her dad. And Grace's mom and dad were entertaining Helen's kids.

"You really quit your job."

Grace nodded. "Gave them my notice after I used up all my sick time."

"I can't blame you."

"I'll start the great job search when we get back. Dameon wants to put me on his payroll for all the work I'm doing for him. But I'm not going there."

"I don't see why not."

"I don't want him to feel obligated. I help him because I love him and want to, not because it's a job."

"I understand."

Erin's laugh had them both looking over. "She's glowing," Parker said.

Grace smiled. "I know. We're going to have to throw a huge baby shower to make it up to Aunt Beth for not inviting her."

"I can't wait. All the tiny clothes and little shoes and stuffed toys." Parker was gushing.

Grace stared at her sister-in-law. "Look at you, the woman who said she doesn't want kids, getting all mushy over the very idea."

"I didn't say I didn't want kids. I said I didn't want to start right away."

Grace's jaw dropped. "That's a total lie. I've heard you say more than once you weren't interested."

Parker looked across the beach to where the men were talking. "I'm young. I can change my mind."

Grace reached out to hug her. "You're going to make Colin so happy."

"He's ecstatic about being an uncle. He already bought tiny overalls."

"You're kidding."

"I'm not. He said overalls can be worn by a girl or a boy, so it's safe. I know he'll be a wonderful uncle, but I think he'd be an even better dad."

Grace clutched her hands to her chest. "Have you told him yet?"

Parker shook her head. "I have to wait until we have some down time. He's not going to let me out of the bedroom until the plus sign shows up on the stick."

Grace laughed so hard she doubled over.

"Right?" Parker laughed with her.

"What's so funny over here?" Colin and Dameon walked up.

"Nothing," Grace laughed.

Colin reached out a hand and pulled Parker to her feet. "I want to dance with my wife."

"There isn't any music."

"Sure there is . . . it's in my heart."

"Awww."

They started to walk off.

"That was sappy, Colin."

"You're just jealous, Gracie."

Dameon reached for her hand. "C'mon."

"You want to dance without music, too?"

"Nawh. Let's take a walk."

Grace glanced over to see Matt and Erin kissing in the light of the sunset and the wedding photographer snapping pictures.

Grace and Dameon walked on the warm water's edge holding hands. "Today was perfect," Grace said.

"It really was. I think they're going to be happy for a long time."

Dameon lifted her hand to his lips and kissed it.

She stopped and smiled.

"I love you, Dameon."

"Those words never get old."

He leaned over to kiss her right as Erin called her name. "Hey, Grace?"

She didn't get her kiss. "What?"

Erin waved her over.

"The bride calls," Grace muttered.

They started back. Less than five yards away Erin held up her hand. "Hold up."

"What?" Grace asked.

Without warning, Erin tossed her bouquet in the air.

Grace let loose Dameon's hand and caught it.

"What the . . ." Behind Erin, Grace noticed Dameon's mom and a man she didn't recognize standing beside her.

What's going on?

"You're the only eligible woman here," Erin said with a laugh.

"Ha, ha . . . very funny. Dameon, don't let them—" She turned to find Dameon down on one knee.

Grace's hands fell to her sides, the flowers loose in her hand.

"Grace . . ."

"Oh my God." She couldn't breathe.

Dameon smiled with a *cat that ate the canary* grin and reached to take her hand.

"You are the single best thing that has ever happened in my life."

"Oh my God."

"I think about you every day when I wake up, and every night when I close my eyes. I envision a half a dozen little Graces running around a twelve-foot Christmas tree and a huge fireplace. I think about you when I toss a pebble in a lake and see the ripples change the texture of the water. Because that's what you did when you came into my life. You changed everything. And I want you to keep changing everything for as long as we have on this earth."

Grace sniffed and brushed away her tears with the flowers in her hand.

Out of what seemed to be nowhere, Dameon held a tiny white box. Inside was a diamond ring.

"Grace Marie Hudson. Will you marry me?"

She dropped to her knees and kissed him like he was water and she was a fish flopping on the shore.

"I love you."

"Is that a yes?"

He was crying.

"Yes, that's a yes . . . Oh my God."

Their families behind them were clapping.

Dameon slid the ring on her finger and kissed her again. "I'm the happiest man in the world right now. I love you."

"I love you, too."

He brought her to her feet and slowly walked back to their families. She couldn't believe this was really happening.

Grace studied all of them. "You all knew about this?"

There were lots of shrugs and maybes.

Mrs. Locke pulled her into a hug.

"Where did you come from?"

"I've been hiding in the trees like a pervert."

Grace couldn't stop smiling. "So glad you're here."

Dameon motioned to the man beside Lois. "Grace, this is my brother, Tristan."

"I've heard a lot about you." She reached out a hand but Tristan opened both arms for a hug.

"I always wanted a little sister."

Grace was pretty sure she was slightly older than Tristan. "It's a pleasure to meet you."

Dameon's arm wrapped around Grace's shoulders the second Tristan stopped hugging her.

"Maybe you can help my big bro relax a little," Tristan said.

Grace laughed and Lois giggled.

And giggled.

And giggled.

Dameon and Grace exchanged glances.

"You guys haven't been eating Maui cookies, have you?"

Tristan stared at his mom. "Oops."

ACKNOWLEDGMENTS

It's always nice to sit down at the end of a book and write from my own point of view. Setting the Creek Canyon novels in a place I called home for twenty-one years of my life came with its own challenges. I wanted to highlight the small town feel of the Santa Clarita Valley while giving the reader enough drama and conflict to keep you entertained. To that end there has to be a bad guy or two. For the record, I have no knowledge of bad bosses at city hall. I have, however, eaten more prime rib at The Backwoods Inn than most. The close-knit communities—from the bowling alley to the block-long Candy Cane Lane–themed neighborhoods—are staples of the city. To my friends, and friends I consider family, I miss and love you all. I simply couldn't stay for another fire season.

This trilogy has been painful at times and cathartic at others. There is closure after writing these stories that I didn't expect but am grateful for.

Thank you, Montlake and Amazon Publishing, for giving me the creative freedom to write the stories that sit deep in my heart.

Thank you to my editors, Maria Gomez and Holly Ingraham. Maria, you always believe in me, and that never goes unappreciated. Holly, thank you for helping me put the sparkle in the finished product. It's been a pleasure working with you.

To Jane Dystel, your guidance through the maze of this crazy publishing world is always spot-on. Thank you.

And last, I would like to put a spotlight on Whiskey. This crazy rescue black Lab had endless energy and spirit. You were a joy from the moment you showed up in our lives. During the fire you didn't leave our side for even a second, and when it was time to flee you jumped inside the car as if you were going to drive us away.

You were one of the family and are sorely missed.

Until we meet again.

Catherine

ABOUT THE AUTHOR

Photo © 2015 Julianne Gentry

New York Times, Wall Street Journal, and *USA Today* bestselling author Catherine Bybee has written thirty-four books that have collectively sold more than eight million copies and have been translated into more than eighteen languages. Raised in Washington State, Bybee moved to Southern California in the hope of becoming a movie star. After growing bored with waiting tables, she returned to school and became a registered nurse, spending most of her career in urban emergency rooms. She now writes full time and has penned the Not Quite series, the Weekday Brides series, the Most Likely To series, and the First Wives series. For more information on the author, visit www.catherinebybee.com.

Made in the USA
Middletown, DE
31 October 2020